Second Awakening

KRISTEN REED

Paperback ISBN: 978-0-9986836-4-5
eBook ISBN: 978-0-9986836-5-2

Table of Contents

CHAPTER 1
A Vision of Light

Rapid footsteps reverberating through the palace's marble tiled hallway weren't abnormal during King Kadoc's reign. Messengers from battlefields and spies often came to the royal palace, bringing news regarding the royal army's progress against the rebels, who relentlessly plotted his demise. Their persistent acts of sedition were cloaked by increasingly advanced spells and wards, which inspired regular reports that ignited the sovereign's infamously deadly ire. But those reports were rarely so crucial that they required delivery after the guards settled in for the third watch of the night and the palace's residents were in the throes of their deepest sleep.

And a child was rarely the messenger.

With every step, the servant boy prayed to the gods that his intrusion wouldn't enrage the King of Eaiven, remembering how gleefully his hot-tempered sovereign shed blood even for the most minor offenses. Upon reaching the king and queen's suite, he slowed his pace to a walk, struggling to catch his breath and gather his courage as he approached the stony-faced guards.

"Aled just had a vision, and he needs to see the king at once," he gasped.

"This may have escaped your notice, but it's the middle of the night. His Majesty is not to be disturbed once he is asleep unless it's an emergency," the guard on the right sneered.

"Aled convulsed violently from having the most intense vision of his life without taking even a sip of blood from one of the virgins. I don't know what he saw, but it was grave enough that he asked the king to come to him immediately."

The two protectors exchanged a worried glance, weighing the consequences of rousing the slumbering king versus enduring the wrath he would unleash if the seer's vision was as dire as the boy claimed. The guard on the right silently mulled over their dilemma, and an idea formed in his mind. He glanced down at the child again, and his lips curved in a half smile that was anything but friendly as he spoke again.

"You may enter and give His Majesty the seer's message yourself."

The color drained from the boy's once ruddy cheeks as the guards stepped aside and opened the door. Steeling his nerves and praying for mercy, he crept into the room, and the two protectors closed the doors behind him. After a moment, his hesitant voice gave way to a strangled scream, a thud, the smell of burnt flesh, and cursing. The king wrenched the door open, and the guards dropped to their knees. Even with his long white waves tousled from sleep and his statuesque form clad in a relatively plain sleeveless tunic, King Kadoc still inspired immediate trepidation.

"Who allowed that brat into my room?" he seethed, heat and fury radiating from his towering form.

"Aled had an urgent vision and sent the boy to find you, Your Majesty."

Without another word, Kadoc stalked down the hallway, and the two guards exchanged relieved glances as they rose to their feet. Moments later, the slave boy dragged himself out of the king's suite with tears on his flushed cheeks, his shirt singed, and a blistering hand-shaped burn emblazoned around his neck. Casting the guards a baleful stare, he drudged back to his shaken master and his merciless sovereign.

★   ★   ★

"Tell me the prophecy again."

Aled lowered his wine with an unsteady hand before repeating himself for a third time.

"I saw a child's birth and a faceless rebel sitting on the throne. Then light filled my vision until its radiance was all I could see, and a voice said, 'A new light dawns in the east, and its light will cast out the darkness forever.'"

"How confident are you that you're interpreting this vision correctly?"

"I'm absolutely certain. No vision has ever debilitated me so greatly. A child born this year will pull the kingdom from your hands. You must protect yourself by any means necessary."

Kadoc stroked his beard, ruminating over the seer's urgent plea as the cringing child refilled his master's wine.

"What would you have me do?"

"Remove anyone who would be a threat to you and increase your power."

"There's no one in the land whose power would actually benefit me. I need my stewards on the fringes of the kingdom to remain strong, and there is no one here worth drawing magic from."

Aled turned his weary brown eyes to his drink.

"There is *one* person, Your Majesty."

"Yes… there is," Kadoc agreed, his gruff voice growing uncharacteristically quiet for a moment. "Never speak of this vision again, seer."

"As you wish, my king."

Turning on his heel, Kadoc left the room as swiftly as he entered, determined to preserve his position at any cost.

CHAPTER 2
The Awakening

Seren's lips curved into a smile as a sweet, floral aroma tickled her nose. To encounter such a pleasant scent in such a dark place was rare in the land, but the hollow she stood in was no mere cave. The gods had used the luminescent waters within Mount Ceallah to bestow power on her people since the elves' creation. Now, on her twentieth birthday, it was finally Seren's turn to experience the gods' blessing. If her power was humble enough, the king would allow her to remain with her family and use it however she saw fit after her training with the appropriate guild. But if the gift the gods gave her proved useful to King Kadoc, she would be spirited away to his palace in Riamon, where she would serve him until death or relinquish her power—and possibly her life—so he could claim it for himself.

Father of Light, please give me a helpful but common power, she prayed, hoping Millam would grant her simple petition.

While living at court could have its advantages—namely delicious food, beautiful clothing, and the most luxurious bath house in Eaiven—that proximity to the covetous king could prove fatal. After all, a man who would order the slaughter of a year's worth of baby boys to instill fear in his subjects and punish them for their rebellion certainly wouldn't be above killing a young woman who displeased him, even if her power wasn't rare enough to tempt him.

After repeating her quiet entreaty, Seren stepped into the cave with two royal soldiers on her heels. The silent sentries' only duty was to record newly awakened elves' gifts and transport them to the king if their gifts would interest him. If the gods answered Seren's prayer, their days would be incredibly uneventful, and their acquaintance would be blessedly unmemorable. If not, she'd be the next victim of Kadoc's greed or wrath.

Seren's pulse drummed more fiercely as she journeyed farther into the cave, and dawn's burgeoning glow gave way to a space swallowed by utter darkness, where the only sounds she heard were her party's footsteps, the guards' clanking armor, and her own ragged breath. Unnerved by the impenetrable darkness and her present predicament, Seren called to mind the song her people sang during the Festival of Lights, which was little more than a week away. During that joyful occasion, the elves surrounded Millam's temples and held lamps from dusk until dawn in anticipation of the day he'd defeat the cursed God of Darkness forever... and hoping that he would grant them relief from their seemingly endless oppression in the meantime.

Maidens faint in dread and fright
Yearning for day to cast out night
Like watchmen waiting for the dawn,
Like watchmen waiting for the dawn.

We long for darkest night to end
And every elven heart to mend
Eyes turned to the east, waiting for the dawn
When the dark is ever gone.

Recalling the familiar lyrics and humming the melody brought a little comfort to Seren's soul, but her anxiety didn't abate until the sacred pool's distant light brightened the passageway. As the luminescence increased, Seren noticed that the cavern's walls had transformed from jagged gray rock to a scintillating white surface somewhere in the dark depths, and the uneven, rocky ground had given way to shimmering white sand that was finer than the most carefully milled flour. The air vibrated with magic, and a low hum filled her ears as the trio drew closer to the silver arch that their ancestors had erected a few yards from the pool. While the guards could observe the simple ritual, any elf who set foot in the pond after his or her awakening would be struck dead in an instant. Thus, their ancestors fashioned the arch to remind them of that peril and to protect them from incurring the gods' divine wrath.

Taking a deep breath, Seren stepped through the gleaming gate. At the water's edge, she removed her cloak and set it on the powdery sand, feeling exposed as she waded into the water wearing only the two-layered linen tunic her mother had created for that highly anticipated yet dreaded day. The water's texture was silkier and thicker than she expected, and its warmth made some of her tension melt away. While she didn't want to displease the gods or Aire, the guardian inhabiting the waters, by loafing around in such a holy place, she had an inkling that she could float without an ounce of effort if she leaned back into the dense, fragrant water. Instead, she closed her eyes and followed her parents' instructions, walking farther into the sacred pool until the water completely enveloped her.

Once she reached the desired depth, Seren knelt in the sand, extended her arms forward, and turned her palms upward, ready to receive the token that would imbue her with power. After a moment of stillness, the liquid around her thinned to a texture reminiscent of lamp oil as it warmed to a temperature that was just a few degrees shy of uncomfortable. Then, Seren felt the pool's unseen guardian place three weighty objects in her hands. The instant the objects settled, she knelt on the shore exactly as her parents had described, shivering more from her brief brush with the divine than the cave's chilly air caressing her moistened skin.

Fear and excitement dueled for control of her thundering heart as she opened her eyes, but confusion ultimately won the battle for her spirit when she finally beheld her gifts. In her left hand, she held a pendant carved into the likeness of Inneh. The ivory and onyx pendant depicted the rosy-cheeked Goddess of Love sitting on her golden throne with a rose in one hand and a dove in the other, and its delicate golden chain perfectly matched the impressive pendant's gleaming setting. In her right hand, she held two more traditional tokens: a small heart-shaped ruby and a teardrop-shaped sapphire.

Even without understanding what power the necklace symbolized, Seren knew that her life was no longer hers. While empathetic gifts were common enough that the king didn't covet them, he thirsted for elemental gifts more than any… and water was especially valuable considering the droughts and famines some parts of Eaiven had endured for the past year. As Seren considered her increasingly dim future, her gaze traveled from the troublesome droplet to her mysterious accessory, which called to mind the love song often sung at elven weddings. Written from the Goddess of Love's perspective, the ballad told the tale of a prince who fell in love with a common woman because he saw past her sun scorched skin and calloused hands to see the true beauty that radiated from her pure and humble heart.

The farmer's daughter who once gazed at the skies
Found greater delight drowning in his eyes—
Eyes that shone brighter than Millam's three stars,
Eyes that saw beauty in all of her scars.

For he saw in her what no man had seen.
Beauty and grace that were fit for a queen.
A most precious gem once hidden from his sight,
Until he beheld her in the silver moonlight.

The wedding song typically cheered the hearts of common elven maidens, feeding their fantasies that a man of esteem or valor would raise them from their humble stations and cherish them as the prince in the ballad did. Yet on Seren's woeful awakening day, it only reminded her that such a match was now impossible. Whether she would use her power over water for the kingdom or surrender it for the king's use remained a mystery, but her life was no longer her own.

Why would the gods tease me with the possibility of love on such a day as this? Even if I return from the palace with my life and virtue, few honorable men will marry a woman who was alone with the king.

"What gifts did they give you?" one guard called from beyond the arch.

"Power over water, the ability to know people's hearts, and… I'm not sure about the third one."

"Gather your things and come with us."

With a silent nod, she donned her cloak once more, pulling the hood over her dark waves and passing back through the gate. While the guards didn't lay a hand on her on the walk back to the mouth of the cave, Seren noticed that each one had drawn his sword, no doubt prepared to strike her down if she tried to run as many elves did. But Seren had no plans to flee. Her life was in the gods' hands, and if they meant for her to serve the unpredictable, dangerous man who sat on Eaiven's throne, she would be obedient.

Resigned to her grim fate, Seren placed the ruby and sapphire tokens in the pocket of her cloak and donned the expensive necklace, which hummed with power as she clasped it. The moment the necklace was in place, a gust of air encircled her, and a blinding light filled the cave. Just as she thought to close her eyes, the radiance dimmed, but what she beheld was no longer Mount Ceallah's dark depths. Instead, she stood on a white marble floor in the grandest bedroom she'd ever laid eyes on.

Its massive bed was easily three times as large as hers and buried beneath a mountain of blankets and furs. Its four artfully carved posters towered above Seren's head, also drawing her hazel eyes to the fresco on the ceiling, which the artist had embellished with gold and silver accents. As she took in her surroundings, Seren recognized that whoever slumbered there was incredibly wealthy.

If the master of this home is an honorable man and has the king's ear, maybe he can convince him to—

A door slamming shut pulled Seren out of her hopeful reverie, and she whirled around to see who had joined her in the opulent room. The man had his back to her as he removed his cloak, and without the flowing garment, she could see his waist-length white waves and fine ensemble. Upon noticing his toga's deep purple hue, Seren's stomach dropped.

The necklace had brought her into one of the royal family's households.

"You're a bit early, Orla, but I suppose now will have to do. Pour me a glass of wine."

When the man turned around and his eyes met hers, Seren dropped to her knees, placing her hands and forehead on the cool mosaic floor in fear-driven supplication. Only one man in the kingdom had eyes like those… irises the color of polished steel with vibrant, prismatic specks that were usually reserved for diamonds and other gemstones. And that one man had an infamous temper as well as the power to execute her with his bare hands or a half-thought for violating his most sacred space.

"Please forgive me, Your Majesty. I didn't mean to intrude. I finished my awakening moments ago, and a token that Aire gave me brought me here."

Even with her eyes on the floor, Seren could see King Kadoc approach, his shadow drawing nearer as he closed the distance between them.

"Look at me," he commanded.

Oh, Millam, please don't let my life end here, she pled, lifting her head but keeping her eyes downcast instead of locking eyes with her king.

"Please have mercy on me. I didn't mean to trespass, my king. If I'd known that the necklace would bring me here, I—"

Seren braced herself and closed her eyes as the king reached out, but he neither struck nor grasped her in anger. He simply tipped her slightly cleft chin upward, scrutinizing every inch of her face and as skepticism and hope thawed his guarded heart.

"Show me this token you received."

Seren lifted the pendant from where it hung on her neck with clumsy, trembling hands.

"What is your name?"

"Seren of Gridein, daughter of Kalbhac, Your Majesty."

"And your awakening was today?"

She nodded, cursing her anxious heart and begging Millam for deliverance as a tear fell from her eye. The fearsome king surprised her yet again by kneeling so that they were eye to eye and wiping away the tear with unnerving gentleness.

"For twenty years, I've lived in fear that Millam had condemned me, but now… now I see how terribly wrong I was. It wasn't Millam at all… Malok was simply testing me under the guise of judgment, and my deeds have pleased him."

"I'm sorry, Your Majesty. I don't underst—"

Before Seren could finish voicing her confusion, Kadoc's lips were on hers.

The maiden had always pictured sharing her first kiss under a moonlit sky or next to the lake south of Gridein, where young lovers often went for afternoon walks or picnics. The man she embraced would be someone she held dear—someone who knew her heart well enough to know that she'd welcome his affection without seeking to erode her self-control. So having her words swallowed by the terrifying king's unexpectedly ardent kiss stole her breath and filled her mind with dread.

Just as Seren's apprehension peaked, her new power rose within her, and she sensed what was in Kadoc's heart. The purity of his love, desperation, and relief ate away her defenses until a strange sense of familiarity and intimacy welled up in her soul. But as his hands wandered from her shoulders to her hips, fear edged out her fledgling passion before she could fully give in to it.

Kadoc was a violent, unpredictable man, and a stolen kiss could give way to a stolen life if she attempted to preserve her maidenhood at the expense of his desires. Dread won the battle for her wits as she remembered tales of his infamous cruelty—rebels tortured within an inch of their lives, priests beheaded for their scathing rebukes, and cooks burned alive to light The King's Highway for overcooking meat.

She needed to leave.

Summoning her courage, Seren shoved Kadoc away and scrambled backward. Just as he advanced to resume their embrace, she yanked at the necklace and broke the delicate chain. Once again, light bathed her surroundings, and she was immediately transported back to the cave, where two bewildered guards awaited her. Seren placed the damaged necklace in her pocket and raised her hands in surrender.

"Where in the blazes did you go?"

"I put on the necklace the guardian gave me, and it took me to the king. I can't go back to him. Please don't take me there!"

"We have orders to take all elementals to King Kadoc," the older guard said. "Submit to the king's will or suffer the consequences."

"I—"

As Seren groveled, the younger guard brandished his blade and decapitated his comrade with merciless haste. When a scream ripped from the maiden's throat, the young man dashed across the space between them, seized her, and covered her mouth with his hand, silencing her the best that he could as he struggled to keep her from fleeing.

"Stop screaming! I'm going to help you."

Remembering her newfound empathy, Seren reached out with her power to discern the man's motives. When she gleaned his protective intentions, she stopped her exhausting and embarrassingly ineffective flailing. Taking a deep breath, the guard released her, and the shaken maiden turned around to truly look at him for the first time. Thanks to the fine lines sprouting around his eyes and crossing his forehead, she surmised that he was about a decade older than she was. While his hair was the same deep brown shade as hers, his skin was a deeper almond hue—a sign that he had spent plenty of days in the sun, whether for his training as a soldier or working outdoors before his awakening. His honey brown eyes held more wisdom and turmoil than she expected in a man of his age, and the scar running from his hairline through his right eyebrow gave her an idea of where some of his pain came from. As Seren studied her unexpected ally, she also spied a portion of a burn scar encircling his neck just above his fraying scarf.

The years had not been kind to her scarred savior.

"My name is Doran," he said, his brow furrowed as he struggled to maintain eye contact. "I know that I'm a stranger to you, but you must come with me. You won't be free or alive for long if you return to your family or strike out on your own."

"Why are you helping me? The king will kill you for this."

"I'm asking myself the exact same question," he muttered. "You are an exact double of Queen Neassa, and your token is a gift that Kadoc gave her decades ago. I thought my eyes were deceiving me when you arrived at the mountain, but when I saw that pendant…"

"Are you sure it's hers?"

"I would recognize it anywhere. I was beaten by the shrew that wore it so many times that it's haunted my dreams since I was a child." Doran shook his head, as if to dislodge the unpleasant memories from his mind. "We can talk about this later. Follow me."

Sensing his anguish and urgency, Seren silently fell in step behind Doran, who kept his sword drawn as they crept closer to the cave's mouth. After they stepped into the sunlight, Doran led Seren over to the smoldering fire where he and his fallen companion had cooked their breakfasts before her arrival. Kneeling for a moment, the soldier strung his satchel, cloak, and the rest of his few belongings—as well as his comrade's—on his marching pole.

Once he was equipped for their journey, Doran led Seren to the west instead of following the northbound path through the woods that led to where her parents impatiently awaited her return. Since his coronation, King Kadoc forbade parents from accompanying their children to the cave because his men experienced less resistance when they could spirit young elves away to the palace without tearful goodbyes and rightfully protective fathers attempting to liberate their children. Now, the distance Kadoc created for his selfish gain created the ideal circumstances for their clandestine escape.

As they crept through the underbrush, Seren wished that she'd worn a more practical pair of shoes that day, but in her vanity, she'd opted for a pair of simple sandals that were made for fashion over boots made for function. Rather than focusing on her increasingly uncomfortable feet, she thanked the gods that she'd only worn a tunic and cloak. Without her usual layers of clothing, she felt incredibly exposed, but the lighter garments allowed her to move more swiftly, and burrs and low branches didn't catch on her skirts as they usually would have.

When they reached the west side of Mount Ceallah, Doran crouched behind a tree and gestured for Seren to do the same before pulling a rope from his satchel.

"There is a toll bridge up ahead, and I need to get a chariot from one of the men stationed there. He needs to believe that I'm taking you to the king, so I have to bind your hands. I'll untie you as soon as we leave the main road."

Seren extended her arms and let Doran tie her wrists in an impressive yet surprisingly comfortable knot.

"The men may speak crudely to you, but they won't hurt you since you're the kind of girl the king likes to warm his bed with. Other than a little embarrassment, you have nothing to fear."

"How comforting," she replied grimly. "So, are you actually a soldier or are you just posing as one?"

"I was assigned to the army after my awakening, and a rebel in my century recruited me after hearing about my upbringing. I've been using my position to the rebellion's advantage ever since."

"How long ago was that?"

"Twelve years."

As Seren recalled some of the battles and intrigues that had taken place since her childhood, apprehension and doubt invaded her heart. For Doran to survive so long in the king's army not just as a soldier but as a spy for the rebels, he had to be cunning and maybe even a little cruel. Yet she couldn't help feeling compassion for Doran as she sensed the sadness that haunted his soul. Some men relished in violence and duplicity, but he clearly wasn't one of them.

"Stop reading me," he said, tightening the ropes one last time. "The longer you look, the less you'll like what you see."

"I'm sorry. I wasn't trying to pry. I—"

"But you did, and I caught you. You're using your powers instinctively because you haven't learned to control them yet... or to control your facial expressions for that matter. If you want to survive this journey and prove a trustworthy ally, you'll at least need to get a handle on the latter."

"Right... I'll keep that in mind."

With that grave advice fresh in their minds, the pair rose and continued their hike. Doran led Seren by the rope and never gave the maiden a backwards glance as he marched through the field. After passing through the tree line and traversing a small, wooded area, they reached The King's Highway. The somber soldier wordlessly turned south, and they continued their tense journey until a bridge came into view. Though she'd rarely left her hometown, Seren knew a tolling station when she saw one. The soldiers guarding such stations demanded a tax from elves who passed from district to district or crossed the border into Kadoc's kingdom. This tax collection often included pilfering the travelers' finest items in the name of additional "fees" if their owners didn't hide them well enough.

As they approached, one soldier elbowed his comrade, who was relieving himself on the side of the road. He glanced over his shoulder at Seren and nodded, laughing at whatever his cohort said as he finished his task and put himself back to rights. By the time Seren and Doran reached the bridge, her cheeks had flushed to a crimson hue under the weight of the men's heated stares.

"What d'you have for us, Doran?" The recently emptied guard asked.

"I'm taking the girl to the king because she awakened as an elemental today. And she's a pretty one by his standards, so don't touch her. Kadoc will have all of our heads if we deliver spoiled goods."

"Right, right," he sighed. "What a waste."

The disappointed guard took one last lingering look at Seren, and she caught a glimpse of the depravity in his heart. Her brows lowered and nostrils flared in anger, but she managed to hold her tongue. Alas, her indignant glare only made the solider chuckle as he opened the gate blocking the bridge and gestured for them to follow him. Like the other toll stations, it featured a small, guarded building where the tolls were stored and counted along with the other booty they extorted from travelers. Twenty yards past the edifice, a stable housed the soldiers' horses and two small chariots.

"I'll have someone prepare a chariot for you," the solider said. "Wait here."

A sigh eased from Seren's lips as he plodded away, and she turned her eyes to the bridge. She'd never been this far from home without her parents before. In fact, she wasn't even sure what river they crossed. Other than the occasional trip to the market or to visit a client with her father, she'd scarcely left their village, Gridein, and had never spent the night away from home.

Her eyes sweeping over the tolling station and the soldiers stationed here—men who had spent years traveling to other realms to fight their enemies and suppressing the rebels within their borders—Seren grasped how little she knew of the world and how much she was about to experience without proper preparation or a companion she trusted. What if Doran or the other rebels proved to be as licentious as his loyalist counterparts at the tolling station? She had powers at her disposal but neither the skill to use them nor the combat expertise to defend herself. And she'd just allowed this strange man to tie her hands and take her away from the people who loved her the most. Sweat beaded on Seren's forehead and her breathing quickened as the grim possibilities formed in her mind.

Leaving with Doran could be the biggest mistake of her life.

As the edges of her vision faded into darkness, she sensed a glimmer of something from her companion. In succumbing to her anxiety, Seren also relinquished the little restraint she had over her power and saw into his heart. Instead of perceiving some nefarious notion, Seren felt compassion mingled with protectiveness.

Heaving a deep breath, she thanked Aire for giving her the gift of empathy. The path stretching before her was no doubt a dangerous and difficult one, but she had the good fortune of being able to discern who was and wasn't trustworthy. And in that moment, she knew she could at least trust Doran for the journey ahead. She also further understood the wisdom in his earlier suggestion. Not everyone they encountered would be worthy of her trust, and revealing her knowledge of their duplicity or hostility at an inopportune time could put their lives in even more jeopardy. Mulling over that fact brought to mind a sage saying from her father:

"A small gift in the hands of a wise man can defeat even the fiercest enemies, but a great gift in the hands of an unwise one will destroy the fool and his friends before his foes even think to fear him."

Aire had given Seren three gifts: one powerful, one useful, and one burdensome. Yet each one had the power to be her undoing if used improperly. No matter where this journey took her, mastering those gifts and bringing them under the yoke of wisdom needed to be her greatest priority... even though she'd spent her life assuming that her parents or the masters at the guilds would be her mentors.

This isn't what I prepared for, but the gods will give me what I need, she reassured herself as the guard returned with their chariot.

Doran nudged Seren, and she climbed into the chariot. When he tied her wrists to the cart, she silently assured herself that it was part of their act but didn't temper her disdain. After all, her annoyance only added credibility to their deception.

"I'll return the chariot on my way back from the palace," Doran lied smoothly.

Without a single pleasantry, Doran snapped the reins, and they set off on their journey. In her naiveté, Seren had imagined that riding in a chariot would be an exhilarating experience—the wind in her hair and sun on her face as she dashed through the countryside—but the reality of traveling in the two-wheeled cart was much less glamorous than she imagined. Every bump and rock in the road threatened to knock her from her feet, and plumes of dust and dirt flew up from the horses' hooves, invading her eyes and nose while inspiring the occasional cough. A bath would *definitely* be in order whenever they reached their destination.

Being tethered to the railing also meant that Seren couldn't steady herself properly, and she lost her balance periodically. However, pride and mild frustration prevented her from asking Doran for help or leaning on him for support. The rebellious soldier was also more focused on his duties as a charioteer than making conversation or inquiring after her comfort, so they traveled in silence until the sun rose to its highest point and he brought the chariot to a stop. The instant they were still, he turned his attention to her for the first time since they started their horse-drawn travels and promptly untied her hands.

"We will be traveling on foot for the rest of our journey to Agron."

"*Agron?* Why would we go there?"

"Because the king can't track us within their borders... and because Fedhlim's army is stationed there."

"How can he fight King Kadoc and the ogres at the same time? They hate elves."

"They don't *hate* elves. They resent elves who act superior to them and like to humble us every now and then. But they do see Kadoc as a threat. After all, the ogres will be his first target if he ever decides to expand his kingdom, and he would simply take their freedom or their lives since they have neither power to steal nor beauty to behold."

Her whole life, Seren's elders had woven frightening tales about ogres, who were known for their great strength, lack of refinement, and penchant for devouring their enemies… sometimes while they still lived. The prospect of leaving the safety of her own people behind to lodge with the brutish beings didn't bode well with her, but neither did being subjected to the king's advances again. Remembering their brief yet intense encounter, Seren shivered and turned her eyes to the east.

"Then to Agron we go."

After driving the chariot off the road and into the sparse wooded area on their right, Doran unhitched the horses and sent them galloping to freedom westward while Seren stepped out of the cart. She wished they could have kept the majestic steeds for their journey, but the warding on the animals would have helped the king's minions find them with little effort.

"We're about two hours from the border," Doran said. "The king won't expect you at the palace for another three hours, so we should arrive safely in Agron before he sends a search party."

Seren pursed her lips to silence her disbelief upon hearing the words "safe" and "Agron" uttered in the same breath.

"Lead the way," she said.

With a nod, Doran walked eastward, and Seren followed his lead. There was little conversation for the first hour of their walk. The soldier warned her about large rocks on the ground, low hanging branches, and other obstacles in their path, but he never inquired as to whether she was tired, hungry, or thirsty. Despite having Doran less than a stride away and exchanging a few curt phrases during those interactions, Seren felt incredibly alone. However, as she watched her dark-haired savior marching several feet ahead, she remembered a comment he made after they met.

"I would recognize it anywhere. I was beaten by the shrew that wore it so many times that it's haunted my dreams more times than I'd care to admit."

Is he being standoffish because his heart is hard or because I look like the woman who tormented him as a child? She wondered with sinking spirits.

She didn't necessarily need to laugh and converse with Doran on their journey to Agron, but she hated that her appearance likely inspired unpleasant memories of his grim past. As those thoughts drifted through her mind, she fought the temptation to reach out with her power and discern just how much her presence vexed him. He'd already endured too much at the hands of the king and queen. The last thing he needed was his tormentor's lookalike violating his privacy.

"How much time have you spent in Agron?" she asked.

"A little."

"What do you like about it?"

Doran took a few steps as he contemplated her question.

"I like seeing elven families living without fear."

"Families?"

"Yes, many people fled to Agron after the king's massacre of male infants, and they never came back. So, a whole generation of children has grown up in our little settlement, and some are now starting families of their own."

"But what about their awakenings? Do they still try to go to Mount Ceallah when they come of age even though they can't register with the king's stewards?"

"They don't, and Fedhlim and the elders have been trying to sort that out for several years. Short of ambushing the guards and using the cave without the king's permission, which a few foolish boys have done, there isn't anything they can do."

"How do they survive without having their gifts?"

Doran rolled his eyes.

"The same way young elves do before their awakenings: manual labor. But the older settlers and people who fled to Agron after their awakenings do have powers. Theirs just weren't unique enough to tempt Kadoc."

"What are your powers?"

"Weapons mastery and healing."

"Healing yourself or others?"

"Both. I heal quickly, but that ability is stifled when I heal others."

Glancing at Doran's face again and numbering his scars, Seren surmised that he'd either endured those painful encounters before his awakening or had chosen others' health over his own healing many times in the past.

"It seems like Aire gave you the first gift so you could help others more freely with the second one."

"Yes... that's what I like to think. My gifts are the reason I was forced into the army. Being one of the few healers in the army has allowed me to gather information for Fedhlim that would be nearly impossible to glean otherwise."

"It's so reassuring when we can clearly see why the gods bestowed specific gifts on people. It's a small reminder that they haven't abandoned us."

"Well, you'll find many in Agron who believe they have. Kadoc's tyrannical reign has stripped the hope from many people's hearts, but your awakening may be a sign that it's coming to an end."

"That's not what the king believes."

"What do you mean?"

"When I met him, he seemed to think that the gods were showing their approval instead of their disdain."

Doran mulled over her words for a moment.

"Do you know why Kadoc killed the sons of Eaiven?"

"To discourage the rebellion, but that obviously didn't work."

"That's what he *wanted* the people to believe," Doran corrected. "I was able to recognize you so quickly because I grew up in the palace as the seer's servant. My parents served the royal family and died when I was a child, so Aled took me in until my awakening. One night, a fierce vision roused him from his sleep. He seized and convulsed, groaning in the ancient tongue as his eyes went white as snow. I'd seen Aled have physical reactions to visions before, but nothing had ever been that severe. Nevertheless, I was too paralyzed by fear to do anything until he came to his senses and sent me to alert the king. When Kadoc came to him, he shared his prophecy. In his vision, he saw a child's birth and a rebel sitting on the throne before hearing a voice say: 'A new light dawns in the east, and its light will cast out the darkness forever.' They both assumed that the child who would defeat Kadoc was a male, but I'm starting to believe we were all wrong."

"When did this happen?"

"Almost twenty-one years ago."

"How is Queen Neassa involved in all of this?"

"Well, Aled advised Kadoc to increase his power, and the only elf strong enough to add to his power was his wife."

Seren's stomach dropped.

"He killed her."

Doran nodded.

"When Kadoc steals an elf's power, he can choose to spare them by leaving a single gift behind, but in his fear and greed he drained every bit of power from her and blamed her death on a rebel assassin—using it as an excuse to intensify the conflict that had already been brewing in the kingdom for years and execute the innocent children who may rise up against him."

"I had no idea…"

"Few elves know what truly happened that night. He may see your existence as a blessing from the gods now, but I see it as a sign of judgment. He abused the power and position they gave him and even betrayed his own wife. Now, the gods have reincarnated the victim of his greatest treachery to be his undoing."

"You're expecting too much of me. I'm terrified of Kadoc and wish someone would overthrow him, but I don't have the skills, heart, or gifts to be a warrior. I'm afraid I won't be 'undoing' anyone any time soon."

"If the gods needed a warrior, then you would've been raised as one or you'll become one. Besides, we have plenty of men who are equipped and willing to fight and die for our people's freedom."

Seren bit her bottom lip as she ruminated over Doran's unexpected narrative. As much as she loathed and feared their king, she couldn't quite see herself being an instrument of his destruction. Toying with the onyx token in her pocket, Seren turned her thoughts to her brief time with Kadoc hours before. The king had clearly been in anguish since he murdered his wife and feared that the King of the Gods had judged him. Could his reign end not because of his death but because he became grieved enough by his own barbarism to turn from it?

No matter how much fear and regret have haunted him since that dreadful night, it wasn't enough to make him change. And he somehow saw me as a sign of approval *not condemnation. If anything, my running off with his enemies may increase his savagery.*

Shaking her head, Seren released the necklace and removed her hand from her pocket. After she made it to Agron and met the rebels, she would discern how to best use her unusual token. Until then, the necklace would stay out of sight.

★   ★   ★

When they neared the forest's edge, where vine-laced trees gave way to swaying wheat, a massive wall of moss-covered stone came into view. Towering about twenty feet high and topped with spikes of iron and jagged stones, the wall was more crudely made than anything even the greenest of stone-working apprentices created, but beholding the elven skulls stacked on one especially tall spike reminded Seren that the wall was not of her people's creation. Just before they broke through the tree line, Doran stopped and motioned for her to do the same.

"The border is ahead. Be silent and on your guard in case Kadoc's horsemen were able to travel ahead of us." He pulled a dagger from his belt and handed it to her. "If anyone comes for us, run toward the skulls, and don't stop. That portion of the wall is an illusion that only elves can see, but you should be able to pass right through it."

Seren nodded and took the blade, her pulse accelerating as Doran unsheathed his sword and advanced toward the wall. Always little more than a footstep away, Seren crept to the border, feeling especially vulnerable once the forest's fragrant canopy no longer concealed them. Though summer's heat was three months away, sweat that had little to do with the afternoon sunshine broke out on Seren's knitted brow. However, her fear proved to be all for naught when they reached the wall without incident. Before they stepped through the magically cloaked border, Doran took her hand in his.

"Don't let go of me until we're on the other side."

"All right."

Heaving a deep breath, Seren let Doran lead her into the false wall. The instant she passed through the border, everything bled to black, and searing pain set every inch of Seren's body ablaze. Before she could even attempt to exercise restraint, a shriek ripped from her throat, and she loosened her hold on Doran's hand. Even in her pain-induced haze, she felt Doran grasp her wrist. With his grip came a pricking sensation that spread from her extremities to her very core. Being attacked by a swarm of the red wasps that insisted on nesting in her father's prized apple tree would have been less painful.

The pain stopped just as quickly as it began, and Seren's vision returned. Instead of seeing another empty clearing or forest, she beheld a wall of another kind. Ten ogres stood shoulder to shoulder, surrounding her and Doran with their clubs raised and their leathery gray faces contorted in rage. Some simply sneered at her through clenched, stone-like teeth while others audibly growled, drool dripping from their cracked, trembling lips as uninhibited rage darkened their hearts.

"Don't you dare raise your weapon against me, Engar," Doran barked at an ogre whose face was covered in streaks of black and blue paint. "I'm a member of the rebellion and friends with your chief Anrek."

"What is a friend of Anrek doing with the whore of Kadoc?" He growled. "Why do you defile our land and endanger our children by bringing Neassa into our homeland?"

"This isn't Neassa. Her name is Seren."

"She may call herself Seren, but wards and ogres aren't deceived by doe-eyed wenches as easily as elves are."

"I'm not being deceived. I personally witnessed this girl step into the scared pool this morning and emerge with gifts that Neassa never possessed."

"That's because she bewitched you!"

Engar advanced, brandishing his club, but Doran darted in his path quick as lightning and placed himself between Seren and the ogre.

"If you hurt her, you'll have to answer to Fedhlim."

The ogre shifted his yellow, snake-like eyes in Seren's direction and gripped his glass-studded weapon more tightly, his scaly chest heaving, and his top lip curled in a silent snarl.

"I spent the first twelve years of my life enduring Neassa's wickedness as a servant at the palace in Riamon. Do you truly think I would be naive enough to be fooled by her?" Doran snapped. "I swear by Millam's stars that Seren is no danger to you, but if you feel threatened, simply send two of your men with us to the settlement."

Engar locked eyes with Doran, who remained unshaken by the ogre's imposing form and unveiled hostility while Seren silently shuddered from her place in the dirt.

"You're no fool, but neither am I. *I* will escort you with Unok and Malor," he grunted. "May Millam cast *both* of you into Ifryn if you're wrong."

Ignoring the ogre's curse, Doran turned to face Seren as Engar unleashed a fierce growl and maintained his fighting stance, ready to bash her head in with his massive club at the most infinitesimal sign of aggression.

"Are you well enough to walk, or do you need a moment to rest?"

"I-I can manage."

Doran helped Seren stand, and they set off down the road. Though the rebel remained silent, she sensed that he was on high alert, ready to defend his life and hers at a moment's notice even if it meant harming his unconventional acquaintance. Seren wordlessly berated herself for using her powers without his consent, but she wasn't so quick to suppress her gift. Instead, she reached into Engar's heart. A chaotic mixture of rage, grief, and loyalty cluttered his soul, and Seren found herself wondering if he hated Neassa on principle alone or based on personal experience.

As they continued their travels through the ogre kingdom, Seren shifted her focus from her companions to her surroundings, trying to spot the differences between her homeland and the strange kingdom she walked through. Ogre stonemasons had paved the roads with rough, irregular stones, and the crudely painted signs marking various forks in the road looked as if they'd been fashioned from driftwood... a stark contrast to the smoothly sanded, artfully painted oak signs marking elven roads. Somehow, the ogres were able to trudge along the paved path unaffected while she periodically stumbled and frequently had to turn her eyes downward to find her footing. Whether intentionally or accidentally, the brutish creatures had created what would surely be an effective defense against the elves if they ever chose to invade Agron.

When she chanced a glance upward, Seren smiled upon seeing familiar trees and flowers lining the road. They hadn't been trimmed and pruned like the ones on The King's Highway, but she recognized the dimpled blue berries and verdant flowers all the same. The air even had the same fresh, lightly floral aroma that she adored, and that bit of familiarity cheered her troubled heart despite the increasingly pungent stench that joined it. Thinking of Eaiven also reminded Seren of her parents.

By then, Kalbhac and Inley no doubt learned of their daughter's disappearance, and they had no way of knowing that she was safe… if her current travel arrangements even counted as such. Even if they or Kadoc's soldiers surmised who she was with, she'd never expressed even an inkling of interest about joining the rebels' cause after she awakened. They probably assumed she was a rebel hostage and feared for her life as much as they would have if she'd been spirited away to the royal palace.

"Doran?" she whispered.

"What do you want?"

"Is there any way I can send a message to my parents once we reach our destination? Even if I can't tell them where I am, I at least want them to know that I'm safe."

"I'll see what we can do when we get to Aden. There are a few elves who slip between the two kingdoms to spy on Kadoc and his men, so I may be able to talk one of them into conveying your message if it doesn't endanger his mission."

"Thank you."

"Don't thank me unless it happens."

"I'm not just thanking you for that. I can't imagine that anything good would have happened if you hadn't intervened at the cave or protected me at the border. I owe you my life."

"You're welcome. I only hope you won't regret trusting me with it."

"And I hope you won't regret helping me. I'm sure you're leaving a lot behind in Eaiven."

"Nothing that I can't live without. Aled was the closest thing I had to family, but he is unnervingly loyal to the king, and our relationship has been strained at best for ages. We haven't spoken in at least five years, and even that conversation was borne from obligation, not affection."

"I'm sorry to hear that."

Doran shrugged.

"You've removed my lifelong burden of having to feign allegiance to the crown. I feared Kadoc and Neassa as a child, and my fear turned to hatred as I became a man. Leaving my home and the king's service isn't something I anticipated doing yet, but it's a change I've longed for since I was a boy."

"I'm glad you can see the good in this."

"You can't survive as an orphan in Riamon without seeing even the smallest glimmer of good in the bad. Without that sliver of hope, you either wither away or become like the wicked people mistreating you."

"Well, maybe their wickedness is finally coming to an end."

"Let's hope so."

★   ★   ★

Two hours into their tense trek, the traveling party reached a fork in the road, and Seren's heart warmed upon seeing the sign pointing to Aden. Unlike the ogres' rustic signs, this smoothly sanded sign bore the town's name in an elegant script, and a delicate vine of green paint encircled the town's name. As they turned down the road to the settlement, Seren noticed that the road was much more even than the ones created by the ogres. Elves had even pruned the greenery lining their path and draped the branches with thalsach vines to attract luminescent butterflies, which would light travelers' paths at night.

Before Kadoc's prophecy-inspired paranoia, the kingdom's spell-casters had lined the roads with enchanted lanterns that gently pulled magic from passing elves to illuminate their paths. Those beautiful, multicolored lanterns lit every main road in Eaiven, and made traveling at night delightful and even romantic. But the power-hungry king viewed spellcasters as a threat and now deprived each one that awakened of that glorious gift. So as beautiful as the vines and butterflies were, they served as a reminder of Kadoc's cruelty and the countless lives he stole during his reign.

However, the resentment that usually flashed within Seren as her gaze traced the carefully draped vines was strangely absent. Rather than silently raging because of how Kadoc harmed her people and denied them the chance to use their gifts, she felt curiosity. What events or fears inspired Kadoc's sadistic rule? Though Kadoc's father reigned long before her time, King Brinnac had ruled Eaiven with valiance and benevolence. So, what had sparked the oppressive king's wickedness? After all, bad fruit didn't spring from a good tree without someone poisoning its roots.

"Seren, what are you doing?"

Seren shook off her contemplative daze and looked at her travel companion.

"What do you mean?"

The rebel-soldier gestured to her hands, and Seren noticed that she'd been fiddling with her broken necklace.

"I didn't even realize I'd taken it out," she marveled softly.

"What were you thinking about just now?"

"I was wondering why Kadoc is so different from his father. How could a man so evil be the son of someone who was so good? That's not a bad thing to ponder, is it?"

"Bad? No, but it is a waste of time. That son of Malok is a murderer at best, and his depravity has only deepened over the years. You should spend your time thinking of how you can help us end him instead of wondering why he's such a despot."

Seren nodded, still not putting the token away.

"Do you have anything more secure that I could keep it in until we can speak with Fedhlim? Magic items always seek to be used, and I'd prefer not to wind up in the palace again if I can avoid it."

Doran called ahead to Engar. "We need to stop for a moment."

The ogres stopped, but instead of relaxing or conversing amongst themselves, they turned to face their elven companions, clutching their weapons as their flashing yellow eyes settled on Seren. A shiver running through her body, Seren focused on Doran as he opened his satchel and pulled out a small wooden box.

"You can place it in here, and I'll carry it with my things."

"Thank you."

Seren placed the necklace in the box, smiling as she recognized the earthy scent of medicinal herbs, which her mother routinely used to cure their family's ailments. While Doran's box was empty, the aroma still clung to the wood long after the leaves and stems had been used. The instant the piece of jewelry touched the fragrant wood, Doran cried out in pain and crumbled to the ground. Seren dropped to her knees to help him but was immediately pulled away by an ogre as Engar raised his club.

"Witch!"

"I swear I didn't do this on purpose," Seren said, trembling as a snarling ogre pressed the tip of his sword into her neck. "Why would I hurt him when he's protecting me from you?"

"Because you make people suffer for sport!"

"Stop it!"

Doran climbed to his feet and drew his sword again, his stance considerably less threatening than it had been when they first crossed into the ogre kingdom.

"The gods did this, not her," he rasped. "And remember what I said about Fedhlim! Your lives will be forfeit if he finds out that you killed our only hope against Kadoc."

"And *yours* will be forfeit if she scratches a single scale on my men's heads."

"Would you feel better if my hands were tied?" Seren asked, careful to remain immobile under the ogre's uncomfortably close blade. "Most elves need their hands to use their gifts, so if you tie mine, I'll be less of a threat."

"Don't be ridic—," Doran started.

"Tie her hands *tightly,*" Engar snarled to the pot-bellied ogre beside him.

Another ogre dropped his iron-spiked club on the road and pulled a rope from his belt as Seren pocketed Neassa's necklace once more. The frayed, unrefined cord was so rough that it made Doran's rope feel like silk, but Seren resisted the urge to wince as he confiscated her dagger and secured her hands behind her back with a tight knot that she was certain would leave a mark long after she was freed.

"You're lucky Doran's a friend. If he wasn't, you would've been dead hours ago," Engar grumbled.

With a grunt of disgust, Engar shoved Seren in Doran's direction and the group continued their journey.

"You shouldn't have done that," Doran hissed.

"Do you want to know what I felt when Engar grabbed me?"

"No, because it doesn't change how stu—"

"Fear. He was angry and *grieving* when we first arrived in Agron, but when he thought I used magic, he was terrified not only for himself but for everyone here. No one has ever had a reason to fear me, and I hate the way that felt. He's still scared, but he feels more at ease than he was a few minutes ago. They all do."

Doran opened his mouth to speak but shut it and shook his head with a sigh.

"Inspiring fear is something you'll need to get used to. The ogres aren't the only ones who suffered and died at Neassa's hands while she was on the throne, and you can't let every trembling elf, ogre, or faery disable you."

"I know, but at least this way we can get to Aden without incident. I'll figure out how to approach people without terrifying them once I'm settled there."

"Or we'll have to find a mask for you to wear."

"We?"

"The gods let me hear Aled's prophecy *and* brought you to the cave when I was on duty. That can't be a coincidence. Whether it's for a few days or for a season, it seems they want me to help you through this."

"Thank you."

"You're welcome. Just don't make me regret it. I like a good row as much as the next solider, but I'd rather not spend my final moments looking at one of their ugly mugs."

Doran's lips curved into a hint of a smile, and relief flooded Seren's heart. Though she'd been grateful for Doran's intervention at the cave and his protection on their short journey, she hadn't experienced any camaraderie with him until that brief exchange. His friendly sarcasm and unsolicited pledge of support showed that he could potentially be not just an escort or protector, but a friend… something she desperately needed if she was to survive the journey ahead without losing heart.

While friendly conversation didn't mark the rest of their journey, Seren's disquiet about her predicament lessened thanks to Doran's presence—his hand on his sword's hilt and his watchful honey brown eyes trained on the ogres for the entire trip. Thankfully, they reached Aden without another confrontation, but Engar insisted on staying with them when they spoke with Fedhlim. Rather than sending him away with his comrades, Doran welcomed the ogre's company but freed Seren's hands once they entered the city despite his adamant protestations.

As they walked through the surprisingly developed city, passing fountains, a market, and temples to the gods, Seren marveled at their uneventful experience. If an ogre had set foot within a watchtower's view in Eaiven, the watchman would have sounded an alarm, archers would have been poised on the walls with scale-piercing arrows, and able-bodied young men armed with swords would have surrounded him in minutes. Yet in this city, the strongest response she saw to Engar was a merchant glaring at the ogre because he jostled his merchandise as they passed through the market. One woman even greeted Engar from afar and offered him a drink as she drew water from the well! The oppression-borne proximity to the ogres had birthed unprecedented tolerance that Seren had never imagined possible.

Happier still was that no one batted an eyelash at her presence. Either the people they passed didn't recognize her resemblance to their deceased queen or they simply didn't care. As they snaked through the city center, she hoped the lack of response was due to the latter and not the former. When they reached the tower's entrance, Doran placed his right fist over his heart to salute the two soldiers standing guard.

"What brings you to Aden? We weren't expecting you back for months," the young man on the left asked.

"I have private, urgent news to share with Fedhlim."

"This news wouldn't happen to be why the wards sounded earlier today, would it?"

"Fedhlim will share my intelligence with the rest of you as he sees fit."

The soldier rolled his eyes, but Seren didn't detect any animosity in him… just the slight annoyance that often welled up within her when her older siblings lorded their seniority over her.

"He's in the hall with Toren."

"Thank you, Ullam."

When they entered the building, Seren breathed a sigh of relief. Not only had they successfully completed their journey to Eaiven, but she also finally had a bit of relief from the springtime sun. The warm rays didn't burn her bronzed skin as they did her mother's fairer complexion, but the unseasonal heat was downright oppressive even though she only wore her tunic and cloak. And if she hadn't felt so exposed wearing only her ceremonial attire on their unexpected excursion, she would have left the outer garment at the cave hours ago.

Pushing the day's discomfort aside, Seren squared her shoulders and lifted her chin as they entered the hall. There, two men loomed over a table, studying a large map anchored in place by a knife, a cup, and a few rocks. The man on the left looked to be in his forties, but even Seren could appreciate that he was a handsome man. His dark waves were pulled back in a low ponytail that slightly covered his pointed ears, giving her a clear view of his intense hazel eyes and thick, straight brows, which would have given him a brooding appearance even without his attention focused on the map. His tunic's short sleeves also showed off a pair of tanned, muscular arms that had seen their fair share of battles judging by the shiny, raised scars marring them. Yet as telling as his appearance was, his heart was curiously silent. She couldn't glean even a hint of emotion from the rugged warrior.

His younger companion, however, was easier to read. The curious, concerned youth wore a pristine, white toga and sported the stylish short haircut that many of their peers wore. While his skin was smooth and free of wrinkles and blemishes, the blond elf's hawkish nose and weak chin made him the least attractive of the men in the room. In addition, his slight form and poor posture made him considerably less intimidating than his rugged counterpart. But based on his presence in the watchtower and the quiet confidence emanating from his heart, his strength—whether intellectual or magical—lie within.

Never underestimate an awakened elf, Seren reminded herself.

Just as she finished her assessment of the two men, the elder elf shifted his focus from the map and promptly adjusted his posture, his legs slightly bent and hand resting on his sword—ready to spring into action at the slightest sign of aggression. Seeing his change in demeanor made Seren's spirits sink slightly, but she refused to shrink back in fear or shame.

I might have Neassa's face, but I don't have her shortcomings, she reminded herself. *I am my own woman, and I have two decades of right living to prove it.*

"I see you've brought me a guest, Doran," he said. "A guest with a very familiar face."

"A familiar face but a foreign spirit," Doran replied. "This is Seren, daughter of Kalbhac. Seren, this is Fedhlim, son of Abban, and Toren, son of Kaanh."

"How did the two of you meet?" Fedhlim asked.

"I was on duty at the sacred cave during her awakening today."

The imposing leader came forward, peering down at Seren with an inquisitive gaze while she struggled to maintain her composure and resisted the instinct to wipe away the sweat that beaded on her brow and moistened her palms.

"Is Seren truly your name, and is Kalbhac truly your father?"

"Yes."

"What gifts did you receive today?"

"Power over water, empathy, and the third..." She retrieved the necklace from her pocket and showed it to Fedhlim. "Doran said that it was a gift from Kadoc to Neassa. When I wore it, I was transported to the palace."

"Where in the palace?"

Seren's eyes dropped to the floor at the memory of her brief but impassioned encounter with Kadoc.

"The king's bedroom."

"Was he there?"

"He arrived a moment after I did."

"And what happened?"

"Does it really matter?"

"Only if you wish to gain my protection, and you'll certainly need it with a face like that."

The maiden's cheeks burned under the weight of Fedhlim's piercing stare. After flicking her eyes in Engar's direction and sensing the menace radiating from the massive creature, she indulged the rebel's impertinence in hopes of forging an alliance through honesty instead of justifying his suspicion.

"He thought that I was his wife and kissed me."

Annoyance pricked Doran's spirit at Seren's admission, and she winced upon recognizing his altered mood. She'd withheld that small detail from her traveling companion out of shame, and her omission may have damaged the little trust she'd earned. After all, Neassa was almost as notorious for her duplicity as she was for her savagery, and Doran would have witnessed her multifaceted wickedness more than most.

"How did you respond?" the leader pressed.

"I pushed him away, ripped off the necklace, and found myself back in the cave at Mount Ceallah."

"Did you feel any fondness for him?"

Gathering her courage, Seren lifted her chin to fix her eyes on Fedhlim once more.

"A little, but it was shocking and *completely* unfounded. My family has never rebelled against the king, but we *certainly* aren't loyalists. We've always obeyed him from afar out of respect for the crown and fear of his retribution but never with even a flicker of admiration. He's a tyrant and the worst of elven men. I have zero desire to see him again."

The infamous dissenter scrutinized Seren for a long, painfully silent moment before a hint of a smile dawned on his lips.

"Thank you for your honesty. Did Doran tell you what my gift is?"

"No, he didn't."

"Just as you can discern people's emotions, I can appraise their honesty. The fact that you were forthright with me due to your character instead of obligation means that you have my trust and a place in the city for as long as I watch over it."

Despite Fedhlim's preliminary approval, Seren couldn't completely shake the disquiet in her soul. Within the span of a few minutes, she'd fallen out of favor with Doran yet earned the trust of a stranger whose heart was completely closed off to her. While she'd exchanged the soldier's confidence for his leader's, she felt no more secure than she had when she stepped into Aden. If anything, her changed fortunes left her feeling more vulnerable than ever.

"I shared Aled's prophecy with Seren on our way here," Doran said. "Many elves believed that the child he spoke of would be a warrior who would lead us to victory on the battlefield, but I think she is the one he foresaw all those years ago."

"A woman fulfilling the prophecy wouldn't be inconsistent with what Aled saw or my own visions," Toren said. "She could be the one."

"What do you think, Seren?"

"Even if I'm the person in the vision, I've led a simple, sheltered life and have only possessed my gifts for half a day. I'm not equipped for whatever the gods want me to do."

"No one is on the day they awaken, but that's what apprenticeships and training are for. Besides, our people have suffered under Kadoc's oppressive hand for over a century. We can wait a little longer if it means breaking his yoke for good instead of adding a greater burden to it," Fedhlim said.

"But we do need a plan for whenever our new Neassa is ready."

Seren bristled slightly at the label Doran bestowed upon her, but she calmed herself with a deep breath rather than correcting him.

"And a good plan can't be formulated in a single day," he reminded the soldier before turning to his new guest. "Have you eaten anything since leaving the cave?"

"Only a few berries we found while we were still in Eaiven."

"Then let's remedy that before we finish planning your whole life for you. Toren, please go to my home and ask Horam to prepare a small meal for all of us. We will join you there shortly. Doran, I'd like you and Engar to head to Sarec's booth in the market and purchase a few changes of clothes for Seren. Tell the Sarec I'll pay her tomorrow."

The two men grumbled their obedience—one noticeably more agitated than the other—and left the watchtower with Engar. Realizing that she was alone with Fedhlim, Seren placed some distance between them by walking over to the map and strategically standing near the knife that was holding down the front left corner. As her eyes roamed over the map, she noticed a marker near the part of the border she and Doran passed through.

"Did you know that we were coming today?"

"Yes and no. Toren had a vision when you crossed into Agron. He didn't see your face or Doran's, but he said that whoever entered the land today would repair broken hearts and free us from the darkness."

"The expectations just keep growing," she grumbled.

"But you don't have to meet them alone. We have been waiting and preparing for our deliverer to rise ever since Doran shared Aled's prophecy with us, and even more will join the cause when they learn that Kadoc didn't extinguish our last flame of hope during that brutal massacre twenty years ago."

"And I'm sure they'll be *so* eager to support me when they see my face."

"Elemental powers may be the most coveted ones amongst our people, but your face may be the most powerful gift the gods bestowed upon you. You could make the king drop his defenses like no one before you ever could, and thanks to the necklace Aire gave you, you can confront him without a watchman seeing you approach."

Seren furrowed her brow and turned her attention to the map again, and her eyes were immediately drawn to the royal palace in Riamon. While she had no qualms about protecting herself—whether from the mad monarch on the throne or the strange warrior across the room—she couldn't fathom stealing into the palace wearing the necklace Kadoc gave his dead wife, intending to end his life like a cold-hearted assassin. Either her heart had a lot of hardening to do in its future or the rebels would have to come up with a different plan.

"And by confront, you mean kill."

"Perhaps, but many a man has fallen into ruin because he was blinded or led astray by a beautiful face. You may be able to help us kill him without getting blood on your hands."

Seren nodded.

"How long have you been part of the rebellion?"

"Almost twenty years."

"Everyone in their right mind whether elf, ogre, or faerie detests Kadoc, but most elves don't have the courage to oppose him as boldly as you have. What made you strike out against him?"

Fedhlim heaved a sigh and crossed his arms.

"After my awakening, I was stationed at Mount Ceallah's sacred pool like Doran. My heart grew more bitter toward Kadoc every time I witnessed his selfishness tear families apart, but the fires of hatred didn't blaze their brightest until five years after my awakening. I'd had my heart set on marrying a maiden from my village, and I planned to ask for her hand in marriage after her awakening in accordance with our traditions. But when she emerged from behind the curtain with the gifts of fire and foresight, we knew that our plan would never come into fruition. She was powerful and beautiful, and her life was now in the king's hands. She panicked and tried to run only to meet her end on the tip of my partner's sword. As her blood dyed my tunic red, hatred and rage darkened my heart. I killed him without a thought, fled the cave, and have thirsted for Kadoc's demise ever since."

Even though Fedhlim told the story with perfect calmness, Seren's heart still ached for him. Losing her grandmother to prolonged sickness had been incredibly difficult, but she'd lived for centuries and passed into the afterlife surrounded by two generations of her descendants. To witness the person you planned to spend your life with breathe their last breath the day their life truly began… *that* was true heartbreak.

"I'm so sorry for your loss. I can't even imagine how hard that must have been."

"I hope you never have to find out. Have you lost anyone to the mad king?"

"No. My family's gifts and trades have always been humble enough to escape his notice."

"Until now."

"Until now," she echoed. "Is there any way I can relay a message to my parents? We've never been apart for this long, and I don't want them to worry about me any more than necessary."

"Where do they live?"

"In Gridein. It's a half day's ride southeast of Riamon"

"One of my spies is scheduled to return to southern Eaiven in a few days. If you write a letter to your family, I'll have him deliver it after he completes his mission."

"Thank you."

Fedhlim glanced at Seren's hand, which was resting a little over a foot from the knife.

"You're welcome. I hope you'll come to trust my people and I as you spend time with us. We aren't the barbarians that Kadoc makes us out to be."

"I know, but barbarians or not, I won't feel completely safe until I truly know who I'm trusting my life with."

The sound of paper moving reached Seren's ears, and she turned her attention to the map just in time to see the corner near her curl up as the knife lifted from the table and floated to her side.

"Then think of this as a welcome gift. You won't need it as long as you're within these walls, but it's yours at least until you believe me."

Resisting the urge to duck her head in shame, Seren simply took the knife by its hilt and nodded in thanks before changing the subject.

"Would many people here recognize that I look like Neassa?"

"No. Most of Aden's residents were able to flee here because they lived in the country like your family, and as you know the royal family never deigned to visit rural villages in those days. Only the men my age or older who fought against or served the king in their youth would be alarmed by your appearance," he answered, his lips turning up in a half smile. "My guess is that you'll have more trouble from the younger men than the older ones since there aren't many awakened women your age here. Power from the gods is more enticing than any dowry in this city. Do you have anyone waiting for you back in Gridein?"

"Not as far as I know."

"That's surprising."

Advancing footsteps and annoyance filled the tower as Doran returned from his errand, his arms laden with a variety of women's garments and his wrist entangled by several necklaces. Engar was considerably less agitated than his elven counterpart thanks to the roasted turkey leg he silently savored. Yet the ogre's eyes gleamed with a silent threat as he tore into the tender meat and crushed the bones with his jagged gray teeth, his glare never leaving Seren's face.

"Sarec insisted on giving these to you free of charge," Doran said. "You might want to have a few words with her next time you're in the market before she starts spreading rumors about the nature of your relationship with Seren. She was practically salivating when I said you needed these for a guest."

Fedhlim chuckled and shook his head.

"That woman won't be happy until I'm married and have as many children as she does. I'll speak with her later. In the meantime, please come with me so I can show you to your rooms."

"I'll be fine staying in the barracks with the other soldiers."

"Are you sure?"

"Yes, and I can show myself there if you have no more need for me."

Fedhlim studied Doran for a moment before coming closer to the soldier and speaking to him in a hushed tone too low for Seren to hear. With a curt nod and a flash of humiliation, Doran set down Seren's new garments and left.

"Engar, can you please let Anrek know that Seren passed my assessment and is not a threat to your people?"

Glancing from the rebel to the young woman and back, he devoured the last of the meatless bone with a single, unnervingly effective bite. Then, with one final grunt, Engar was on his way, and Fedhlim turned back to Seren, offering his arm.

"Shall we?"

Suppressing the gradually quieting fear in her heart, Seren placed her hand in the crook of his arm and accompanied him out of the watchtower.

*   *   *

Seren's first afternoon in Aden passed in an unexpectedly pleasant blur. Fedhlim's cook Horam, an elderly woman whose deep wrinkles accentuated her warm smile, had cooked a pot of stew that simultaneously strengthened Seren's spirit and put her mind at ease. Rather than leaving her employer alone with his two guests, the colorful cook joined them at the table, telling the tale of how Toren nearly ruined her precious stew by adding mint to the broth instead of bay leaves when she asked for his assistance. The seer blushed from his neckline to his hairline and muttered an excuse that was barely audible over the sound of Horam's throaty laughter. Fedhlim chuckled along with his cook but gave the young man a reassuring pat on the back and praised his willingness to help.

Quietly observing the dynamic between the three, Seren couldn't help smiling. Seeing the man whose name was sneered with derision or whispered with reverence by many of her people teasing and laughing with his friends brought her far more comfort than their tense first meeting had. By the time the meal ended, Seren's eyelids had grown heavy with physical and emotional fatigue, and she felt safe enough to sleep in the guest room Fedhlim provided. After giving her weary body a half-hearted scrub in the bath that his servants prepared for her, she collapsed onto her bed and swiftly succumbed to her exhaustion.

CHAPTER 3
Unexpected Joy

Despite waking up multiple times in the night and spending an hour pacing the floor by the moonlight, Seren still awakened just as the sun peeked above the horizon the next morning. The bed in Fedhlim's guest room was much more comfortable than the one she crawled into every night at home, but her fear of Kadoc and guilt over the distress she caused her parents kept her from truly enjoying the surprisingly lush mattress. And she had no doubt that worry and grief made their sleep just as fitful if not nonexistent.

With that sobering thought fresh in her mind, Seren closed her eyes and prayed for Millam to comfort her family and protect them from Kadoc, whose interrogation methods often left his unwilling informants mutilated or dead. Upon finishing her brief entreaty, Seren rolled over with a sigh only to spring out of bed and clumsily snatch Fedhlim's knife from her bedside table. Sitting on the windowsill with his dark brows knitted together in contemplation as his prismatic eyes followed her every movement and expression was the elven king himself.

"How did you get in here?" Seren asked.

Kadoc pointed to the dried laurel wreath on his head.

"Since my engagement present to you brought you to me, I decided to see if the reverse was true."

The king rose from the windowsill and Seren stepped backward, eyeing the door and gauging if she could make it into the hallway if she leapt across the room quickly enough.

"I'm not here to hurt you, Seren. I've come to apologize for my behavior yesterday. I dishonored and frightened you with the intensity of my affections, and my actions were inexcusable."

"I wish your so-called affections were all I have to fear," she said, her voice trembling even more than her knife-wielding hand. "How long have you been here?"

"Long enough to hear an ogre's mating call in the distance and know that we're not in Eaiven, but that won't be an obstacle for me. Ogres fear me more than I've ever feared them."

"Have you hurt anyone since you've been here?"

"Not yet. I've only watched you sleep, so no one even knows about my clandestine trip to Agron yet. Now, put down the blade and come here."

Kadoc took a step forward, prompting Seren to move closer to the door.

"No."

"I mean you no harm. I only wish to bring you back home so we can talk."

"The palace is not my home. If you want to talk, we can do that here with plenty of space between us."

"I'm not leaving without you."

"And I'm not leaving *with* you."

"You're forgetting that I can read people's emotions just as you can. Part of you may be afraid of me, but you haven't cried out for help because fear isn't all you feel," he said, extending his hand. "Regardless of what these traitors have told you, would the gods have given you these affections if you were meant to be my enemy?"

"You killed the woman who you supposedly loved. Why should I trust that you won't end my life as well the moment I displease or inconvenience you, especially since I only share her face and not her devotion?"

Kadoc's shoulders slumped as self-loathing rolled through him.

"I've already ruined our relationship once. I swear to Malok that won't make the same mistake again. Please come with me."

"Swearing by that cursed name is further proof that I cannot trust you, and you are too tainted by darkness to see it."

"Seren, is someone in there with you?"

Relief burgeoned in Seren's heart at the sound of Fedhlim's voice.

"It's Kadoc!"

In an instant, Fedhlim ripped the door open with his power as he drew his sword. Kadoc raised his hand to attack Fedhlim as the renegade lunged forward. When not even the smallest spark or flame leapt from the Kadoc's hands, the king's eyes widened in alarm, and he darted out of the way just in time to evade Fedhlim's attack. Before the rebel could advance again, Kadoc removed the wreath from his head and winked out of sight with a flash of light, leaving the seething dissenter alone with his guest.

"Did he hurt you?"

"No, we only talked," she said, lowering her weapon slightly.

"How did he get in here?"

"A laurel wreath. Apparently, it was Neassa's engagement gift to him."

Fedhlim lowered his sword but didn't sheath it.

"Well, now that he knows he can get to you so easily, he'll surely try it again."

"Maybe, but it looked like he couldn't use his powers. I doubt he'll return until that's sorted out."

"Powers or not, we can't underestimate him. He's had over a century to hone his skills as a warrior, and you don't even know how to wield a weapon or water yet. I'm going to have one of my men guard you when you're alone until you can use your elemental gift to defend yourself."

Seren nodded in reluctant agreement, running a hand through her tangled locks.

"I still need to dress for the day. Could you please give me a little privacy?"

"I can give you more than a *little* privacy."

With a simple gesture, the door lifted from the floor and floated back into place.

"Someone will have to replace the hinges later, but you'll be able to dress without prying eyes," he said. "I will be right outside the door if you need anything."

"Thank you."

Fedhlim stepped back into the hallway, making the door open and shut behind him without even grazing the knob. As Seren crossed her room to pick an ensemble for the day, she noticed a small scroll resting on the windowsill. While she wasn't eager to learn the scroll's contents, she also didn't want to alarm her host once more. So, after eyeing the unopened epistle for a few heartbeats, Seren tossed her cloak over it and got dressed. She would contend with the mysterious message after she broke her fast.

Once she was decent, Seren emerged from her room, and Fedhlim escorted her downstairs. Even though his hand remained by his sword, the friendly conversation he initiated left her feeling like a treasured guest instead of an unwanted ward or a prisoner. By the time they reached the dining room, his thoughtful inquiries and terrible jokes inspired levity and chased away some of her unease. Toren had gone back to his home after dinner the previous night, so Horam was their only company. And good company she was, buzzing about in her maternal manner to serve her employer and his unexpected guest with a cheerful grin on her wrinkled face.

After the meal, the cook retired to her domain to clean and take the remaining food to a widow across town, leaving Seren alone with Fedhlim yet again. As he unrolled and scanned the scroll a messenger delivered during breakfast, conviction gnawed at her stomach. While she hadn't wanted to dwell on Kadoc any longer than necessary after their waking encounter, she had to admit that concealing his message could potentially cause harm whether to the people under Fedhlim's roof or to their fledgling friendship.

"Fedhlim?"

"Yes?"

"Something else happened this morning."

"And what was that?"

"I think Kadoc left a note for me. He didn't mention the letter when he was here, so I didn't notice that it was in my room until after you left, but I haven't read it yet."

Fedhlim nodded, staring at his guest thoughtfully as he processed this new information.

"I'm sorry for not telling you sooner. I just wanted to start my morning and enjoy a meal without whatever he wrote haunting my thoughts."

"I understand, and I forgive you. But you *must* be honest with me. I cannot protect you from him if I'm not equipped for the job. I also can't vouch for your character to people who recognize you if I'm not confident that you're trustworthy."

Seren looked down at the steaming, aromatic beverage that had been slowly unravelling the knot of tension in her stomach… tension that was rapidly transforming into shame.

"I know. I'm sorry."

Fedhlim reached out and covered Seren's left hand with his, making her jump slightly at his unexpectedly tender gesture.

"I do have some good news that may cheer you up a bit. While there isn't anyone else here with power over water, there is a fire handler named Malan who may be able to help you master your element. She was lucky enough to escape Kadoc's soldiers and flee to Aden about fifteen years ago, so she's one of the few elementals left in the land. If that sounds acceptable to you, I can introduce you to her and see if she's willing to train you."

"I'd love that!"

"Perfect, and since both of us have gifts that are rooted in understanding, I can help you master your empathic powers and keep others from invading your heart."

"Is that why I can't discern your emotions?"

"Yes, I tend to keep my heart guarded around elves I don't know and especially around empaths. I hope that doesn't offend you."

"It doesn't. I would probably do the same if I could."

"And with practice, you'll be able to."

"Thank you again for taking me in and being so understanding. I hope my family and I can repay your kindness one day."

"The gods brought you to Aden for a reason. I'd be a disobedient fool to turn you away," he joked, a pair of dimples appearing in his unshaven cheeks as he smiled. "And the gods will settle the debt if there is one to repay."

Falling prey to the contagious nature of his grin, Seren glanced down and realized that he still held her hand. Remembering her vulnerable position, she removed her hand from his and tucked a dark lock behind her ear as she swallowed the lump in her throat. Fedhlim was certainly handsome and possessed both the vigor of youth and the wisdom that came with age, but he was a stranger. His reputation was vastly unknown to her, and she was without her father's trusted protection and guidance. She needn't give him a reason to believe that she was open to anything more than being friends and allies.

"I should read Kadoc's letter before the day gets away from me. Do you mind sitting with me here while I read it?"

"Not at all."

"I'll return in a moment."

Seren abandoned the kitchen to retrieve the mysterious epistle from her room. When she spied the scroll on the windowsill once more, she hesitated before tentatively picking it up with only her thumb and forefinger. Seren halfway expected the scroll to hum with magic or burn her, but all she felt was the impression the king's signet made in the wax seal and the papyrus it held in place, which was far smoother than the rough material she wrote on at home. Rather than breaking the glossy black seal in the privacy of her room, she darted back downstairs, where she found Fedhlim pouring himself another cup of Horam's fragrant tea.

"Would you like me to read it for you?" he asked, seeing how her face had blanched since she left the room.

"I should do it myself. When Doran tried to carry the necklace for me, it nearly brought him to his knees. I don't want the same to happen to you if it's enchanted in some way."

Before Fedhlim could agree or argue, Seren carefully broke the seal and unfurled the scroll. Unwanted familiarity gnawed at her heart as she recognized Kadoc's graceful yet bold handwriting, but she steeled herself for the king's message and pressed on.

> *Dearest Seren,*
>
> *I am truly sorry for my impertinence when we met yesterday. The instant I saw your face, I went half-mad, half-joyful with disbelief, and in my elation, I lost all self-control. You did not deserve the indelicate way I treated you, and I would like to ask for your forgiveness. By now you've probably realized that you bear my late wife's likeness, but your appearance and my relief are no excuse for my actions. However, I'm certain that you share so much more than her*

*beauty based on what I detected in your heart
during our brief interlude. I can't pretend to
know what the gods' intent was in bringing you
to me or even understand the extent of your connection to Neassa, but I cannot simply leave this
matter alone.*

*If you would like to explore this unexpected
connection, you need only don your necklace and
join me in Riamon. I trust that you won't harm
me, so I won't hinder your coming or seek to en-
trap you against your will. As always, my home
is your home, and you may come and go as you
please.*

Yours always,

Kadoc

By the time Seren reached the king's signature, her hands trembled, and her heart ached with unwarranted longing. Kadoc was correct. There was more to her connection with Neassa than their shared looks, but her knowledge of the king's malice and debauchery eclipsed the curiosity and endearment that waged war against her reason. Seren needed to explore her purpose and fate apart from him, and the gods themselves would have to force their paths to converge again if that was their will.

"Are you all right?" Fedhlim asked.

"I'm as well as one might expect," she grumbled, handing him the scroll. "Would you like to read it."

"Would you like me to?"

"If there's something of importance in here that I'm not perceptive enough to pick up on, we'd all benefit from a second set of eyes reading it."

Seren placed the scroll on the table and watched the rebel read the message, nibbling on her nails and attempting to gauge his reaction with her eyes since she couldn't do so with her power. Unfortunately,

Fedhlim's expressions were as intentionally unreadable as his heart, forcing her to wait for a more audible reaction to the letter.

"I take it you're not going to go to him."

"Of course not. I don't have the history with him that you have, but I *do* know that he's incredibly dangerous. I can't risk my life by going to Riamon."

"I agree," Fedhlim said with a nod. "Now, if you're ready, we should make our way to Malan's inn. She's thrilled to meet a fellow elemental."

★   ★   ★

After cleaning up after their meal, the two left Fedhlim's house and walked across the small town to the inn. As they passed through the market and strolled down the streets, people of all ages greeted Fedhlim with the joy and reverence that their king failed to inspire in his subjects' hearts. Though they offered their leader warm smiles, a bit of that warmth chilled when he introduced his guest to some of the townspeople… elves old enough to remember or to have experienced their former queen's cruelty. With each strained encounter, Seren resolved not to violate their hearts as Neassa once ravaged their lives by reaching inside and discerning what unpleasant emotions her presence inspired.

Fortunately, Malan and her husband Kilyan greeted both elves with genuine enthusiasm when they reached the Aden Inn. Once they exchanged pleasantries, Kilyan excused himself to continue his work at the front desk while his wife led their visitors into the office.

"Thank you for agreeing to see us on such short notice," Fedhlim said. "I stumbled upon a unique situation yesterday, and you're the only elf equipped to help me."

"So I've heard. Sarec came by yesterday evening and told me all about your new guest."

"I hope you will put whatever she said out of your head and let my friend Seren make her own first impression. Doran brought her here after she awakened as a water elemental yesterday, and I would like you to instruct her. Are you interested?"

"Well, I've never trained another elemental before, and it's been years since I studied under one."

"However long it's been, you're still far more experienced than I am," Seren said. "I could tell based on the crowd in the dining hall that you already have a lot of responsibilities to tend to, so I could help around the inn in exchange for your instruction if that would persuade you."

"Having an extra set of hands could definitely help... How are you at cooking?"

"Decent."

"Can you read and write?"

"Yes, and I'm also fluent in the high elven tongue."

"You won't hear much of that here unless someone is singing from the Book of Songs or courting a maiden with fine poetry," she chuckled. "How many other gifts will you need training for?"

"I have two more gifts, but you needn't worry about those. Fedhlim will be training me."

"You're a lucky one to get three gifts. The gods must highly favor you."

"I don't know if I'd call it luck. The more they give us, the more they expect of us, and I'm not sure if I'm up for the task yet."

Malan relaxed slightly as a grin spread across her freckled face.

"Now that I know you have a good head on your shoulders, I'd be more than happy to train you," she said before turning to Fedhlim. "How many hours a day can you spare her?"

"Four... for now."

"Four is plenty. Your work can double as your training some days, so we'll make the most of the time we have together. If you don't mind, I'd like to see how the gods gifted you. Most elementals can only manipulate their element if it's nearby, others can control it at a distance, and fewer still can create it from thin air. It's why elves with air and earth gifts are typically more fearsome than ones who can control fire and water like us. Come with me."

Malan stood, and the trio ventured outside. The innkeeper led them to the stables, stopping beside the stone troughs, which had been recently filled with food and water for their guests' horses.

"Close your eyes and focus on the sound of my voice."

Seren did as Malan instructed while Fedhlim silently observed their interaction. Malan took Seren's right hand and placed it in the trough, immersing it in the tepid water.

"Call to mind the angriest you've ever been, and don't fight your rage as is rises within you. Just sit in it for a moment. Remember what was done to you… what was said to you… what was taken from you…"

While tragedy and rage weren't regular occurrences in Seren's life, one memory quickly came to mind. In an instant, she was back in Eaiven, manning her parents' booth in a neighboring town while they paid a brief visit to a friend. She preferred working at home, whether dying fabric with her mother or—if she was lucky—copying scrolls with her father, but as her siblings matured and struck out on their own, her work went from being based on her preferences to being defined by her parents' needs. Thus, she sold the flowing fabrics with a smile on her face, enduring baseless insults from cheap old women and entitled young women who sought to purchase the textiles for far less than they were worth. Even though the stingy shoppers tested her patience, the man who visited their booth that day had made her skin crawl and ignited the fury within her.

As she finished selling several yards of yellow linen to a widow, who spent the better part of their interaction pointing out imaginary flaws in it, Seren noticed a man watching her from across the way. He was easily older than her father with his tawny, weathered skin and graying hair, but he lacked her father's comforting, paternal warmth.

Instead, his roaming eyes appraised her as if she were a prized mare that he was considering purchasing. When her customer moved onto another booth, the determined man hobbled over, undeterred by his slight limp and the cane he leaned on for support.

"Hello, my dear, may I see you in my office?"

"I'm sorry, sir, but these are my parents' goods. If you'd like to purchase something, I'm happy to help you, but you'll need to return later if you need to discuss other business about their wares."

His thin lips stretched into a grin, revealing yellow teeth that were blackened with decay.

"I don't mean to discuss business… at least not the goods you're selling for your parents. If you give me a moment of your time in private, you'll make more gold in ten minutes than you ever could selling fabric and scrolls."

Seren recoiled and would have laughed at his proposition if she hadn't been so disgusted by it.

"I wouldn't let you touch my littlest toe for ten years' wages."

"You clearly don't know who I am."

"Nor do I *care* who you are."

"You should. I am the master of this town, and I could make things incredibly unpleasant for your family if you deny me or I could put in a good word for you with the king," he said, lowering his voice. "I can tell by your rounded ears that you haven't had your awakening yet, and I could encourage the king to grant you mercy if Aire gives you a covetable gift. 'Tis better to warm my bed for a few years than wind up drained by the king and dumped in an unmarked grave."

"Fortunately for me, I'm not a resident of this town, and I'd rather die by that tyrant's hands with my dignity intact than live because I was violated by yours. Now get away from my booth before I scratch your beady little eyes out, you ill-mannered son of Malok."

The lascivious master's craggy face reddened as he lowered his graying eyebrows, and he whirled around only to plow right into Seren's laughing parents, who had returned from their visit. Before either elf could beg his pardon, he was limping down the aisle as quickly as he could, glowering and snapping at anyone who dared crossed his path.

By the time that infuriating moment faded from Seren's mind, her hands were clenched so tightly that she could've drawn blood had her nails been any longer, and her chest heaved as newly awakened ire quickened her shallow breathing.

"Do you have the memory?"

Seren nodded sharply.

"I want you to imagine your anger traveling from your heart to your right hand and flowing from your fingertips. You should feel the water swirling around your hand."

She did as Malan instructed, but the water was as still as ever, only gently moving as she adjusted her hand's position in the trough. Alas, her sight confirmed what she already knew before she opened her eyes. The water was as stagnant as it had been the moment she placed her hand in it.

"Am I doing something wrong?"

"Well, I can tell that you're plenty angry from here, so no. Most elves can call on their power by channeling anger, but another emotion may be the key for you. Let's try joy instead. Close your eyes again and remember the most joyful moment of your life."

Ever the eager student, Seren closed her eyes again and tried to recall the most pleasant memory she could dream up. No one memory stuck out to her the way her encounter with the lecherous leader had, but she let her mind drift from memory to memory in search of her most joyful moment. Birthdays, festivals, time with her loved ones, achievements in her schooling, and more passed through her mind, but her heart was drawn to one unfamiliar yet exceedingly fond memory.

She stood beside the sea with her eyes trained on the setting sun, enjoying the refreshing breeze and its salty aroma as the waters twinkled in the sun's dwindling golden light. As she let the cool, invigorating air fill her lungs, an easy smile stretched across her lips, but the soft crunch of footsteps in the seashell-littered sand inspired far more delight than the beach's sights and sensations.

"Thank you for accepting my invitation," her companion said.

"How could I not? I've heard tales of Brigh's beauty for years, but I'd never seen it with my own eyes until today."

Seren turned to her right and her heart fluttered as she met his deep brown eyes. Even though the raven-haired young man before her with his impeccable posture towered over her as he always had, she detected a hint of fear in him. His deeply tanned skin was a bit paler than usual, his eyes darting from her to the seaside palace every few beats, and beads of sweat moistened his forehead.

"Is something wrong?"

"No… or at least I hope not. May I sit with you for a moment?"

The pair lowered themselves onto the cool marble bench a few paces away.

"Getting to know you this past year has been such a privilege. As I've witnessed your kindness, strength, intelligence, and humility, you have changed from a stranger to a friend and now to the person I cherish and regard more highly than anyone I know… even my father."

"I don't deserve such praise, Your Highness. I'm only—"

"Please call me Kadoc. There's far too much between us for such formalities to continue."

"All right… Kadoc."

The prince smiled for the first time since he approached her and took her hands in his, which trembled slightly as he spoke.

"I love you more than anyone in this world and would be honored if you would allow me to spend the rest of my days loving you with all my heart and protecting you with all my strength. Will you marry me?"

"Of course I will."

The words had scarcely left her lips before Kadoc swallowed her answer with a slightly clumsy yet endearing kiss. Seren shuddered slightly as his lips caressed hers for the first time and melted into the lamentably brief embrace. When Kadoc ended the kiss, they were both breathless, their cheeks flushed and hearts roaring in their ears as they gazed into one another's eyes.

"I have a present for you."

Kadoc reached into his pocket and placed a small wooden box in her hands. She lovingly traced the smooth, curling pattern of vines, leaves, and grapes on the polished lid with a smile on her face.

"It's beautiful."

"The real gift is inside."

When she opened the box, she beheld an ivory and onyx cameo with a woman's smiling face etched into the surface. The figure's eyes were closed, and her cheeks turned a pinkish hue as the jewel absorbed the heat from her hand. As Seren's eyes drank in the pendant, distant shouting reached her ears. If the frantic cries were meant to capture her attention, they failed because the beaming man by her side and the gift he clasped around her neck held her attention completely.

"It's an artist's rendering of Inneh. I hope having the Goddess of Love near your heart will remind you of how much I adore you and carry you in mine."

"I love it… and I love you," she said, relishing in how delightful and freeing it felt to finally express the affection that had gone unsaid for so many months. "Thank you, Kadoc."

The fragrant breeze ruffled the sleeves of her tunic and carried the louder yet still indiscernible voices to her ears.

"We should tell your parents the happy news," he said.

After one final kiss, the lovers rose to their feet and strolled back to the seaside palace hand-in-hand. Without warning, searing heat radiated from the ground the moment Seren's feet touched the mosaic-tiled walkway. Feeling as if her whole body was suddenly ablaze, she squeezed her eyes shut and cried out to the gods for relief.

"Seren!"

Seren's eyes flew open with a gasp, and she found herself back outside Malan's inn with flames licking at the hem of her dress. Yelping in shock, she instinctively called upon her elemental power to put out the fire. As she extinguished the flames and looked up again, Seren saw that Fedhlim and Malan were sopping wet, and the ground was a messy slurry of mud and grass from where she stood to the inn.

"I did this, didn't I?"

"Yes, you did, and I'm sorry for scorching your dress," Malan said, placing her flint and steel back in her apron's pocket. "You didn't respond when I shook you, and it was the only thing I could think to do to bring you back to the present."

"It's all right," Seren said, the unexpected memory still plaguing her. "I'm sorry for not responding."

"Don't worry about it! Now, I'm happy to report that you can do more than just manipulate water. You can create it from thin air… a lot of it. And joy seems to be the key to wielding your element. Now, you simply need to learn how to control it."

Malan explained her plans for Seren's training, but the shaken ingenue tuned out her teacher's enthusiastic explanation. Disquiet filled her heart as she grasped that the memory she'd conjured up undoubtedly belonged to Neassa, but more disturbing were the questions and greater fondness for the king that the recollection inspired.

The elf she beheld and kissed with such elation was nothing like the one she'd fled her homeland to avoid. So how did Kadoc regress from the tender, innocent man in her memory to the draconian ruler her people loathed today? Even his eyes haunted her, dark eyes that overflowed with love and lacked the cold, prismatic appearance and predatory gaze that had sparked trepidation only hours before.

"Are you occupied for the rest of the day, or shall we begin your training now?"

"She'll begin tomorrow," Fedhlim said, observing his guest's silent distress. "I need to introduce her to the elders first, and they should be arriving at the agora soon."

"All right. I'm *really* looking forward to this."

"As am I! It's been an exciting first lesson," Seren lied, her voice a bit higher than usual. "Thank you for your time."

After exchanging pleasantries, Fedhlim and Seren left the eager innkeeper behind and walked to the agora. The two were no more than a few footsteps down the street before Fedhlim broke the uneasy silence.

"Are you still up for meeting the elders? You're clearly shaken by what just happened."

"I think I can manage… The memory I recalled wasn't mine. It was Neassa's."

"Has that ever happened before?"

"No, but it certainly explains why the gods chose her necklace as my token. Apparently agreeing to marry Kadoc and receiving it as a betrothal gift from him was her most joyful memory."

"But maybe not just hers. I'm beginning to wonder if you have the late queen's face *and* her soul. If you do, that memory may eclipse every other happy moment in both of your lives."

"Well, if I'm Neassa reborn, that means that I possess the same capacity for wickedness that she did. I could do horrific things to our people."

"Yes, but since you've seen where that path leads and have witnessed the tragedy it causes, so you're more likely to reject whatever drew her into the darkness."

"I hope you're right. I'd rather die than hurt people the way she did, but I fear I wouldn't have the courage to end things if I started down that path again."

"That is a decision I pray you never have to make. You must have the humility and vigilance to surround yourself with wise counselors who can help you avoid your past transgressions instead of people who hate or idolize you too much to help you down the right path."

"Yes, but not everyone is worthy of being trusted with such a delicate secret."

"I agree, which is why I will introduce you to elves who are. And I'll also look into bringing your parents to Aden if you'd like their company. Being reminded of who you are now may keep you from slipping back into who you were before."

"Thank you. Having them here would be such a relief."

"And I will help you experience that relief as soon as I can," he smiled.

★   ★   ★

"I sincerely hope my vision is failing me or that this viper on your arm is using a glamour spell," a craggy-faced old man growled as Seren and Fedhlim approached the marble steps of the agora's temple complex.

"Neither is the case, Aeton. This is Seren, daughter of Kalbhac and fulfiller of Aled's prophecy. One of my most trusted spies witnessed her awakening yesterday, and I intend to train her here in Aden so she can help us defeat Kadoc once and for all."

"More like the daughter of Malok," Aeton's gray-bearded comrade sneered.

"I understand your apprehension, Sinam, but she has passed my initial test, and what elf could survive a second immersion at Mount Ceallah? Aire would strike them dead on the spot for entering the sacred pool again…"

As Seren listened to Fedhlim try to calm the elders' fears and field their insult-laden questions, her entire body tensed, but she held her tongue and maintained a calm façade. Rather, she chose to release her power and reach into the men's hearts. The terror and rage swirling in their troubled spirits far exceeded hers. The two men before her and their two silent counterparts, who fixed her with equally baleful gazes, were more than old enough to have lived through Kadoc's massacre as well as the atrocities that preceded it. And while Seren could easily bow up with indignation at their remarks—calling her a daughter of the Cursed One being the most offensive one—that morning's revelation stopped her tongue.

Even if she hadn't murdered, tortured, and abused elves and ogres for her advancement and amusement in this life, she had in a previous one. The least she could do was endure a few old men's wrath knowing she deserved not just their judgment but an eternity in Ifryn for her past brutality.

"Please stop arguing," Seren interrupted. "You four have every right to be suspicious of me because I don't just share Neassa's likeness. I am our late queen reborn, which means that I once brought the people of Eaiven and Agron unimaginable pain. I have no reason to believe that I'm immune to whatever drew Neassa into the darkness all those years ago, but I could learn from her mistakes and help undo them."

"What makes you think you could break free from your wicked ways?" Aeton asked.

"I can surround myself with wise people like yourselves who can keep me from the darkness and pull me back if I begin to stumble."

"I'll do more than pull you back if you harm another elf while I lead this city."

Fedhlim glared at the grumbling elder, but Aeton continued before the rebel could admonish him.

"I'm willing to see where this goes, but I need some assurance that the people of Aden will be safe while you skulk about my city."

"I'm guessing my word won't mean anything to you, so what do you have in mind?"

"There is an ancient relic that makes one elf's elemental power subject to another's will. If you and Fedhlim will wear the Cuffs of Harreb for the duration of your stay in Aden, I for one will sleep *a little* better at night."

"But how will I learn to use my powers if I'm wearing that? Surely you don't expect Fedhlim to watch over me every time I train?"

Fedhlim opened his mouth to speak, but the head elder found his words more quickly.

"This is the only way we'll tolerate your presence in the city. Refuse our terms, and we'll cast you out or worse."

Seren's jaw tightened for a moment as she contemplated their request. While she could sympathize with their fears, she also had her own to contend with. Being so far from home and surrounded by strangers was unsettling, but she'd comforted herself with the idea that she could eventually wield water well enough to defend herself. Less than an hour had passed since she first unlocked her power, but she already couldn't fathom being without it.

Every drop of moisture around her from the sweat beading on Fedhlim's furrowed brow to the unshed rain in the stormy clouds above called to her… begging to come under the yoke of her newfound power. That newfound connection with nature and her ability to create water with a thought was exhilarating despite the unnerving memory that unlocked it, and she couldn't wait to call on her element again.

And yet I robbed so many people of their powers during a life I only remember a glimmer of, she realized. *Perhaps the gods are repaying me for my past transgressions.*

"Fine. I'll wear the cuff. Where is it?"

"It's in the cave that the Brohnn River springs from. The cave is almost a half-day's ride from here, so you'd best be on your way if you want to return by nightfall."

"Why by nightfall?"

"Aglocs only fly by night, and a bloodthirsty wake of them lives in the forest," Fedhlim muttered.

"And I don't suppose we can wait until dawn tomorrow to go on our journey."

"Not unless you want to sleep outside the city walls," Sinam urged, his dark eyes gleaming with hatred. "I'd be impressed if you survived the night out there alone."

"It sounds like I have some appointments to reschedule," Fedhlim said, regarding the four elders with unveiled annoyance. "We will return with the cuffs tonight."

Without another word, Fedhlim plodded back down the steps, and Seren followed suit. Despite the rebel's ability to block her empathic powers, Seren could still feel the rage radiating from him, and guilt plagued her as she realized the negative impact she was already having on his life. But as soon as they were out of the elders' view, Fedhlim whirled around and chastised his impetuous companion.

"You shouldn't have agreed to wear the cuff."

"What choice did I have?"

"Waiting for my lead, for one! You're my responsibility right now, and I could have convinced them to let you earn their trust in a less daunting way. You can't let people control you with fear and guilt, Seren. You have to be stronger-willed and think about how your decision will affect those around you."

"I'm sorry. I—"

"If their emotions can influence your judgement so easily, Kadoc could manipulate you as well especially since you're still... *sentimental* about him."

"I'm sorry," she repeated. "That hadn't even occurred to me."

"And if that despot returns when I'm not around to let you use your power over water, you'll be defenseless. You're not a fighter, a charmer, or even light on your feet. You'd be dead or dragged to Riamon in an instant!"

Seren nodded, unease trickling into her heart.

"Maybe I can learn to defend myself without my powers. Could you or someone else teach me how to fight?"

"Kadoc has had over a century to perfect his skills as a warrior, and he possesses powers that enhance those abilities. You wouldn't be a match for him."

"But Kadoc isn't the only person I have to worry about. My face makes me a target for decades of pent-up rage, and while I hate what Neassa did, I don't want to die for it. That hardly seems like the means for me to fulfill Aled's prophecy."

"You're right," Fedhlim exhaled, running a hand through his dark waves. "I can't teach you much today, but I can at least get you a more effective weapon than my knife before we leave."

Though tension still crackled between them, Fedhlim softened a bit and beckoned Seren to follow him out of the agora so they could prepare for yet another unplanned, perilous journey.

★   ★   ★

After quickly perusing the armory, Fedhlim emerged with a cuirass and a dagger that was a handbreadth shy of being the same length as Seren's forearm. The rebel leader handed Seren the items, which she promptly donned, marveling at the armor's lightness before Fedhlim began his quick combat lesson.

"Your best bet at defeating your enemy with this weapon is to go for the throat or the lungs. Try to stab your opponent under the rib cage and aim upward. If you have the unhappy luck of being this close to an agloc after we leave the cave, remember that their hearts are on the right and not the left. I'll give you more formal instruction when we return."

"Thank you, and again… I'm sorry for being so hasty to agree to the elders' terms. As inconvenient as this is, I can see some good coming of it."

"And what good would that be?"

"Kadoc and Neassa stole power from their people for over a century, and if the people see my willingness to surrender mine, they may trust me more than they would have otherwise."

"Well, I hope your little experiment in magical humility pays off," he grumbled. "I'm going to gather a few more supplies for our journey. Then, we'll make our way east."

"Is there anything I can do to help?"

"Pray that we return to Aden unharmed."

CHAPTER 4
Harreb's Test

Within the hour, Fedhlim and Seren were charging toward the Brohnn River. His mind ever on the winged nuisances who preyed on nocturnal travelers, Fedhlim shunned the road in favor of a shortcut through the woods. The less-traveled path was blessedly deserted except for a few stray ogres. The first few times they passed the scaly creatures, Seren moved her right hand to the hilt of her blade, hoping she'd have the skill to use the unfamiliar weapon if she needed to, but praying the need wouldn't arise.

Eventually, she recognized that Agron's most numerous inhabitants were too busy hunting elk—ripping the majestic creatures apart with their bare hands to savor their raw, wriggling flesh and sucking marrow from glistening bones—to notice the rebel-ruler and his unsettlingly familiar companion. With that comforting conclusion, her unease about the ogres' ubiquity fell away, leaving room for her fears and concerns about their encounter with Harreb to surface.

As the daughter of a scribe, Seren had read many tales of aglocs with their great black wings and piercing shrieks. The vindictive creatures would poison their enemies with the venom in their gleaming talons, which would make their prey have waking nightmares of their greatest terrors and disappointments. Still, the aglocs weren't her greatest concern.

Harreb was.

The gods never left ancient relics unguarded. Just as the nymph, Aire, kept awakened elves and other creatures from immersing themselves in the sacred pool in Eaiven, Harreb or some creature under his authority would be keeping the cuffs safe. Some guardians demanded a price, others tested hearts and intelligence, and the most fearsome ones forced elves to prove their worth in combat. As someone who was handier with a stylus and papyrus than a sword and shield, Seren selfishly hoped that Harreb would challenge Fedhlim and not her since he would be supervising her elemental power.

Looking ahead at her companion, Seren silently assessed him. Fedhlim was tall, well-muscled, and seasoned in battle. He also seemed to have a good head on his shoulders. After all, you can't wage an ongoing war against a mad king and lead a group of displaced, disenchanted elves with brawn alone. Based on his reputation alone, she was sure that Fedhlim could fare decently well against Harreb if strength or mental prowess was the key. But his heart was another question.

She knew from reading and hearing tales about Kadoc's predecessors that even great leaders could be failures in matters of the heart. Men who singlehandedly conquered fearsome beasts from the deep had harems of mistresses and wives, while philosophers whose wisdom any elf could quote treasured their blind hatred of faeries and ogres more than the purest gold.

What is his flaw? I know he's loved someone before, but could women or strong drink be his weakness? Or perhaps he eats aeslin berries to trigger hallucinations. I've heard of many soldiers consuming them to escape the grim reality of their professions.

Even as she assessed her companion, doubts about the state of her own heart nagged at her. Despite being only a day into her unexpected adventure, she already noticed a shift in her feelings toward the king.

While she'd once felt vague disdain toward Kadoc, curiosity, confusion, and even compassion now filled her heart. And instead of fearing for her life, she feared for her soul and the impact he could have on it. Nothing was as black and white as it seemed when she arrived at Mount Ceallah the day before, and she was afraid that her life would grow increasingly gray as the days and weeks passed. If Harreb searched her heart to see if she was worthy of receiving the cuffs, she would probably fail… or be judged so unworthy of her powers that he would gleefully hand the relics over to bind them for as long as possible.

Fedhlim should be more concerned about me than I am about him.

Shaking off that disturbing revelation and her insecurities about the upcoming challenge, Seren redirected her focus to their journey and her surroundings. Fedhlim slowed his steed, and she followed suit as they neared the tree line. The solid, dry ground gave way to a wetland with a pungent accumulation of peat. Their more careful pace gave Seren the freedom to cover her mouth with her sleeve, the stench making her feel nauseated and borderline lightheaded as it overpowered the forest's usual floral aroma.

"By Millam's stars… I've never smelled something so disgusting in my life."

"Don't say that around an ogre. These waters are precious to them," Fedhlim scolded, seemingly unbothered by the eye-watering odor. "They pulverize the peat from the swamps of Agron with its waters and use it to enhance fertility."

"And by 'use it' you mean…?"

"The poorer, weaker ogres drink small vials of it when they deem it necessary or give it to one another as wedding gifts, but the more esteemed ones wear it as their daily perfume. If you encounter and ogress who smells like a thousand rotting plants, she is either quite wealthy or extremely irresponsible."

"I hope I keep the company of poor ogres during my stay here."

Fedhlim chuckled at Seren's nose-wrinkling disgust.

"They'd say the same about your perfumes and incense. They can't tolerate anything floral or fruity."

"Goodness… then what do they eat for dessert at feasts?"

"Bark bread with duck eggs."

"The duck eggs don't sound so bad, but what is bark bread?"

"The eggs are buried in the ground for two weeks then cured in sea salt until they harden and turn a deep green hue. And bark bread is made by pulverizing bark from trees and using it as flour for unleavened bread. It's actually not bad."

"Well, I can't say that I'd eat it if I had the option not to, but I certainly respect their creativity. It sounds like they take as much care with their food as we do with ours."

"They do," he said, raising an eyebrow. "While I don't like their bread enough to have Horam cook it, I do occasionally enjoy sprinkling a bit of ground bark on my meat. It adds a nice earthly flavor and a little heat."

"Interesting. What else should I know about the ogres?"

"Kadoc has harmed them just as much as the elves if not more. He's used his power to enslave some of them and force them to work in his quarries and mines as beasts of burden. He's also been known to have ogres fight to the death for his entertainment. Whenever ogres bore or offend him before falling in battle, he feeds them to the chimera."

A fierce chill came over Seren at the mention of Kadoc's so-called pet. The creature had the head and body of a lion, the wings of a dragon, and a spiked tail that was as deadly as its great fangs and fiery breath. According to the rumors, he captured and tamed the beast completely unarmed during her parents' youth. Seeing such a fearsome, legendary creature submit to the despot only fueled the people's trepidation and hopelessness. She couldn't imagine laying eyes on the chimera let alone facing it in battle.

"What about Neassa… what don't I know about her?"

"That's a tale for another day. It's hard to fight valiantly when your heart is laden with guilt."

Seren nodded, disappointment and relief swirling in her downcast soul. She knew little of the woman she'd once been other than rumors, legends, and the brief memory she experienced that morning. While she wanted to learn from her predecessor's sins to avoid falling into the same darkness, she also dreaded learning about her former depravity.

The ogres clearly loathed her, but was Neassa found guilty by association, or had she taken part in Kadoc's atrocities against them? And what evil did she commit against her own people? Elves hissed the dark queen's name as a curse almost as often as Malok's, but they spoke little of her actions since her demise. Her father rarely mentioned her because their present life under Kadoc's rule was bitter enough without dredging up unsavory memories of their oppressor's fallen consort.

Millam, please help me remember only what is helpful and protect me from whatever isn't, she prayed, hoping the King of the Gods would find little of her past life useful.

After several minutes of splashing and slopping, they reached drier land, and they allowed their steeds to run free once more. But as Seren began to savor the forest's undefiled air, she detected a fresh, familiar scent on the wind. Before she could warn her fellow traveler, the clouds released a deluge that washed the swamp's lingering stench from their clothes and left their garments sopping.

For a moment, Seren silently grieved her saturated state, but her lamentation turned into inspiration in a twinkle of her hazel eyes. Reluctantly yet curiously, the elf closed her eyes and called to mind the emotions Kadoc's proposal inspired—joy, excitement, and love—and imagined the rain emerging from her clothing and lifting away from her body. When Seren opened her eyes again, she saw the rain falling around her newly dried form yet not soaking her as it had previously. Shifting her gaze to Fedhlim, she extended her power in his direction and watched as the rain obeyed her unspoken command. The rebel glanced at the maiden, finding her grinning both because of her triumph over the rain and the memory required to control it. A smiled dawned on his face as he slowed his steed's pace enough to ride beside her.

"You're a quick study."

"Don't speak too soon. I could lose control at any moment and leave you soaked to the bone."

"I have full confidence that you won't," he smirked before turning serious again. "I'm sorry for losing my temper earlier. I could never relinquish control over my powers as you are, and I admire your humility even though I'm frustrated by it."

"Neassa stole elves' powers for her own gain, so I hope me surrendering mine for their benefit will help them feel safer and see how different she and I are."

"If they don't, they're allowing their own hatred to blind them."

"It's not just hatred. My face inspires terror greater than any fear I've ever experienced. They're frightened for themselves and their families, and I can't fault them for that."

"Well, if it's any consolation, you don't scare me in the slightest."

Something about the soft rumble of his voice made Seren's spirits lift and redness creep from her neck to her cheeks.

"Then I suppose I should be grateful that I met you first and not the elders."

"Yes, you should," he chuckled. "Speaking of the older generation, I'm sorry that we couldn't send a message to your parents today. I'll make sure they hear that you're safe before the week ends."

"Well, hopefully I *will* be safe. I have no idea what awaits us today. Do you?"

"Harreb tests the worthiness of whoever is requesting the cuffs, but the test changes with each pair. It's impossible to guess how he may test us."

"Are his tests physical or mental?"

"I've heard stories of elves enduring both. One pair had to scale a cliff with their hands tied together and another had to fight a two-headed beast like Kadoc's hound without using their powers."

"So, he forced them to complete the challenge while being disabled in some way."

"Yes, but I'm not sure if that's always the case."

"What power or skill are you the most fearful of losing?"

"I've heard enough lies to tell when people are being dishonest without my powers, so I'd be more concerned about losing my fighting ability or my strength in general. And you?"

"I don't have any well-honed skills that could help me in battle, so I'm more fearful about what I have than what I could lose," Seren said, feeling the ghost of her necklace around her neck. "At the very least, we should probably prepare ourselves to face whatever this challenge is without your strength."

"And with your fears in mind. What do you fear more: facing Kadoc or becoming more like Neassa?"

"I'm not sure."

"Perhaps we'll find out soon."

★   ★   ★

The peaceful babble of running water joined the birds' joyful chirping as Fedhlim and Seren neared Harreb's cave. Emerging from the forest, they beheld a tall cliff of sandstone and ochre hues with small niches carved into the slightly jagged façade. The largest opening lacked the manmade refinement of the smaller alcoves, and inky liquid flowed from the cave's mouth, running clearer and clearer as it joined the Brohnn River below and irrigated the ogres' untamed land.

Fedhlim dismounted, and Seren followed suit. Though the more experienced elf didn't draw his sword, he remained alert and scanned every inch of Harreb's sacred area for threats. While guardians such as Harreb didn't harm those seeking their treasures, who's to say that another elf wasn't seeking the cuffs... or revenge against his former queen?

After climbing the uneven stone steps hewn into the cliff, the pair got a better look at the cave. The cavern wasn't terribly deep, but some god or the guardian himself had placed three identical doors opposite the opening, and magic radiated from each one.

"Are we supposed to go through—?"

71

A great tremor silenced the young elf and nearly knocked both travelers off their feet. Then, the very cave itself moved, the floor remaining untouched as the walls rotated with an ear-splitting rumble that agitated their horses, inspiring flattened ears and swishing tails. When the shift was complete, the doors were at the elves' backs and the cave mouth was before them, but it revealed a setting drastically different from the forest they'd traveled through. The sky above was darkened as at twilight, and its burgundy hue was both breathtaking and unnerving. The grass was thankfully a familiar shade of green, but each blade shone with an iridescent cast that added an eerily exquisite radiance to the setting.

"Isn't it beautiful?"

The two elves whirled around to face their newfound companion. Fedhlim unsheathed his blade in a swift motion while Seren clumsily retrieved—and nearly dropped—her weapon. Before them stood a man who easily could have passed for a northern elf thanks to his unblemished fair skin and smiling blue eyes, but his hair was the same deep berry shade as the sky and shared the grass' strange luster. He also wore a pair of cuffs—one silver and one gold—each engraved with a two-headed snake that slithered within its magical borders.

"It is," Fedhlim agreed, refusing to relax his stance. "Did you create it?"

"No, but I am the master of it. Lower your weapon, Fedhlim, son of Abban. I will not harm either of you."

After a moment of hesitation, Fedhlim sheathed his blade and Seren did the same, hoping she wouldn't need to use the blade during their encounter.

"You won't, Your Majesty… or at least you won't need it on my account."

Seren bristled at the telling title and the roguish gleam in his eyes.

"I am Harreb, and am I correct in assuming that you're after my cuffs?"

"Yes, you are," Fedhlim confirmed. "What price do you require for them?"

"I require permission not a price."

"Fedhlim has my permission to control my elemental power."

"But his is not the permission I seek."

Harreb extended one graceful hand, and in a wink Seren's magically repaired necklace appeared in his palm.

"If you wish to use my cuffs, you will need Kadoc's permission to don them, and you must secure it without deceiving him."

"He won't give it," Fedhlim said.

"Then I won't give you these. Who am I to usurp a husband's authority over his wife?"

"Is there something else we can retrieve or another task we can complete?" Seren asked, combat suddenly seeming like the safer bet.

"No. Either you secure your husband's blessing or you return to Aden empty-handed and face the aglocs when the elders cast you out. It's your choice."

Harreb dangled the necklace before them, silently challenging Seren with his unyielding gaze.

Seren took a step forward only to have Fedhlim seize her by the arm and hiss, "You can't go to him."

"And I don't *want* to, but if can't face Kadoc peacefully, how am I supposed to face him in battle if that's where this journey leads?" she countered. "And if Aled's prophecy was truly about me, then I haven't served my purpose yet, which means my life is secure for the time being. Now, let me go."

Fedhlim released Seren with the shake of his head, and she strode toward the guardian. Upon taking the trinket from his pale hand, she earned a grin more perfect yet more infuriating than any she'd ever beheld.

"Your necklace, my queen."

"Your challenge, my guardian."

With those mildly embittered words, Seren clasped the necklace around her neck and closed her eyes. A gust of wind overtook her just as it had in the cave, and her eyelids blazed red as light bathed her. Rather than taking in her surroundings, Seren reached for her dagger the instant she opened her eyes only to find that it, her sheath, and her cuirass were gone. And when she turned to see if the yet-to-be-used blade had somehow fallen to the floor, she instead saw that she wasn't alone.

Kadoc lie asleep on a couch a few paces away. While his very presence sparked disquiet in Seren's heart, the king looked almost angelic with the dwindling sunlight bathing his body with golden rays and making his white hair shimmer with radiance she'd been too frightened to notice during their previous rendezvous. The king's lips were parted slightly as he breathed in the fresh air, and a half empty cup of wine sat on the marble floor near where his right hand dangled from the couch. Watching the slumbering king, Seren realized that any other rebel would have taken that opportunity to claim his life. Yet violence was nowhere to be found in her anxious heart.

And she hated it.

Seren jumped slightly as the king shifted in his sleep, rolling in her direction. As he did so, she saw that he clutched the laurel wreath in his other hand and remembered her purpose. The maiden stepped forward until she obscured the king with her shadow and reached out her hand to wake him, but she stopped just short of touching him. Shaking her head, Seren gathered her courage, knelt beside the couch, and extended her hand again. This time, her hand rebelled against her sensibilities, brushing his waves out of his face instead of jostling him out of his sleep by shaking his shoulder. The king awakened, and while his strange, prismatic eyes unnerved Seren as they had during their previous interactions, the joy in them simultaneously alarmed and disarmed her.

"Either I'm having the best dream I've had in ages or the gods finally brought you back to me."

"Neither is true. I need to speak with you, but I don't intend to stay here with you."

Kadoc sat up and observed Seren for a moment. Her very presence filled his heart with joy and weariness at the same time. He longed to take her into his arms as he had so many times in the past, but he could sense her unease growing the longer he drank in her presence. Instead of prolonging her discomfort, the king rose from the couch and offered his hand. After a moment of uncertainty, Seren took it and reluctantly let Kadoc help her up. Once she was on her feet, he stepped away to replenish his wine.

"What do you need to speak with me about?"

"I need your permission to wear the Cuffs of Harreb."

"Whose powers will you be controlling?"

"I intend to be the one being controlled."

Kadoc's eyebrows lowered as he set down his cup.

"You *what?*"

"The people are afraid of me, so I promised to wear the cuffs… at least until I earn their trust."

"And what if I don't give you permission?"

"They'll cast me out, and I'll have to fend for myself in Agron."

Kadoc tightened his grip on the cup, the precious gold crumpling like papyrus in his hand. Seren's breath caught in her throat at his unexpected display of strength, but knowing that his anger wasn't directed at her inspired barely a sliver of comfort.

"Why endanger yourself by agreeing to those traitors' asinine requests when you could live here in comfort and be free to wield your powers as you choose?"

"I can't stay here."

"If you're scared that I'll hurt you, I swear on my father's grave to never harm you."

Kadoc barely had a blink to search Seren's eyes before she dropped her gaze to her fidgeting hands.

"Please give me permission to use the cuffs so I can return to Agron. I'm not going to stay here with you."

"What are you afraid of, Seren?"

The maiden bit her lower lip, refusing to speak, and Kadoc heaved a sigh.

"Do you truly detest me that much?"

"Yes and no," she admitted. "I wish I could hate you as much as everyone else for all the unthinkable acts you've committed, but I can't. The gods awakened more than my powers yesterday, and these abominable feelings are growing even as I stand here."

The king took a step forward.

"What feelings?"

Seren turned around, cursing Harreb as she wiped away the rebellious tear that journeyed down her flushed cheek.

"When you use your elemental power, what emotions do you call on?" she asked.

"Anger."

"Well, this morning I tried anger, but that emotion didn't work. I dreamt up the most infuriating moment of my life, and nothing happened. When I tried using joy instead, I finally unlocked my powers. I should have been ecstatic about that accomplishment, but I was so shaken because the memory I called to mind wasn't what I expected."

"What memory was that?"

Seren gestured to the necklace.

"What do you think?"

"So, our engagement is your happiest memory in *both* lifetimes, but you don't want to be with me?"

"If you were still the man I saw in my memory, I might be tempted to, but you've killed countless people—including innocent children—for your own selfish gain and terrorized the rest into submission. What happened to you to turn you into such a monster?"

Kadoc's shoulders sagged, and he massaged his temples for a moment as if to cast out a rapidly burgeoning headache.

"Dinner is about to be served. Will you dine with me if I tell you?"

"Will you give me permission to use the cuffs if I do?"

The suddenly fatigued king chuckled.

"Yes, but I do hope this isn't the last time we dine together."

Kadoc offered his arm, and Seren took a deep breath before accepting it and letting the man she feared more than anyone else escort her to the great hall. As they walked through the palace, the people drew Seren's gaze more than her opulent surroundings. Older servants fought the urge to gawk, and the residents bowed as low as their bodies would allow when the two passed, greeting her as "Your Majesty" and "my Queen." Being on the receiving end of such undeserved esteem pricked at Seren's heart even more than the elders' and ogres' fear had. After all, her former self was worthy of hatred and fear, not honor.

When they reached the hall, Seren was pleased to see that no one else would be dining with them. Either the king had already planned to dine alone or he'd magically alerted his servants to their plans during their brief stroll across the palace. Once they were seated, a servant brought them plates of soft, herbaceous cheese with flat bread, figs, honey, and walnuts. Since the task at hand had occupied her mind for most of the day, she'd scarcely thought about food. And the spread in front of her inspired hunger that was as emotional as it was physical.

"Do you like it?" Kadoc asked after a few minutes of silent but smiling savoring.

"It's delicious. I've never had anything like this before."

"My cooks are as creative as they are gifted."

"Yes, they are."

"It's nice to see you enjoying yourself."

Seren looked away for a moment and stiffened a bit, remembering her purpose and how dangerous her dinner companion was.

"Now that I'm having dinner with you, will you tell me how you became as you are today?"

"Yes, I will," he said, the light leaving his eyes. "Shortly after our wedding, we conceived a child. We were both ecstatic, but as I went to tell my father about the new life coming to our family, death loomed on the horizon. A great quake shook the kingdom, leveling homes and temples and greatly damaging the palace. A toppled column crushed my father's skull while parts of a fallen frieze injured you and ended our child's life before he or she ever had a chance to see the light of day."

Seren's heart lurched, and sorrow inundated her spirit. She closed her eyes for a twinkling to catch her breath, but she found no solace in what awaited her when she opened them again. For a moment, she saw the dining hall in ruins as painful moans and grief-stricken cries filled her ears. Then, her gaze traveled the length of her body, and horror stole her breath as she saw her bloodied stola and slowly became aware of the pain radiating from her head and abdomen. Seren squeezed her rapidly watering eyes shut again, and the scene disappeared. Alas, her anguish wasn't so quick to dissipate—chasing away the little levity that the food had inspired.

"Are you all right, Seren?"

Seren shook her head, struggling to find the composure necessary to verbalize her distress. When the king abandoned his seat, she raised her hand and took a sip of her wine, which she diluted with hot tears.

"I just saw the earthquake's aftermath."

"Perhaps we should finish this conversation later."

"No! I need to know what happened."

Ignoring Seren's dismissal, Kadoc crossed the room and knelt beside her, wiping her tears and guarding his heart from the long-suppressed, paralyzing grief that threatened to rise as he saw her pain anew.

"Please tell me."

The king nodded but he remained by Seren's side, clasping her trembling hand in his as he continued the untold tale.

"Losing my father and our child in one day left me devastated, and I was terrified when a fierce fever overtook you in the days that followed. Our healer perished in the quake, so I had to rely on physicians to heal you. I was so petrified by the prospect of losing you that I refused to rest until I could ensure I never would. I spent my time alternating between being by your side and immersing myself in the oldest works in the library, trying to find a way to heal you and protect you from further harm. Then, as my eyes grew dim with fatigue, my desperation reached its peak, and I reached for the one manuscript I'd shunned in my hunt for knowledge: The Scroll of Malok."

The hairs on Seren's arm stood on end and dread temporarily cast out her anguish. Elves rarely uttered the God of Darkness' name, and even the crudest of men only used it as a curse or insult. To read his works or those of his few perverse followers was forbidden not just because of Malok's vile nature but because he was the biggest threat to their kind.

Elves, faeries, and many other creatures were children of the light, hand-crafted by Millam after he won the right to create the elves in his image by defeating the other gods in battle. His former rivals bowed before their new king and surrendered some of their power to him, but the ever-resentful Malok refused. Millam cursed him for his disobedience by stripping him of his physical form. Thus, Malok melted into the darkness, always plotting against his brother and targeting his beloved children instead of blessing them as the other gods had.

"What did you do, Kadoc?"

"The scroll claimed that anyone who completed the ritual and became the Cursed One's vessel would obtain immortality and gifts greater than what the other gods gave the elves. I memorized the ritual and acquired the necessary beasts for the sacrifice. Once I had everything I needed, I traveled to Aire's cave in secret and made the sacrifice, letting the blood flow into the pool as the scroll instructed and carefully pilfering its tainted waters. I didn't want you to suffer if my efforts did more harm than good, so I drank the elixir before I left Mouth Ceallah. Power, pain, and desire greater than anything I'd ever experienced flowed through me and brought me to my knees. My senses were so sharp that I could smell the gold coins in my purse and sense the pool's magic more distinctly than ever. But my heightened sensitivity didn't stop there. I could feel the power swirling within the two soldiers who guarded the cave, and it lured me from the darkness like a siren's seductive song."

Seren felt Kadoc's pulse hasten through their entwined hands.

"One guard bowed when I emerged from the cave, but the other gaped at me in terror. Of course, he didn't know the grim task I'd completed moments before, but his gift warned him that evil was imminent, so he instinctively reached for his sword. Unfortunately for him, he hesitated just long enough for me to seize him and consume the very power he was too slow to utilize. When his comrade sprang to his defense, he met the same end, and my newfound power intoxicated me so completely that remorse was impossible. All I felt was a desire for more power and the urge to share that exhilarating experience with you. So, I returned to the palace and gave you the rest of the potion."

"Did I know what you were doing to me."

"No, but I had to do what was best for you."

The king's eyes glowed and a shudder-inducing grin spread across his face as a strange dark haze filled the room and undulated around him like living smoke.

"And now that you've returned, we can be as we once were."

Seren stood and tried to pull away, but Kadoc tightened his grip, threatening to crush her hand if he didn't relieve the pressure.

"Let me go."

"I'm not making that mistake again."

"By Millam's stars, I command you to release me!"

The malevolent smog dissipated, and Kadoc dropped her hand as if it were a venomous snake. Then he backed away, massaging his head as he placed several yards of much-needed distance between him and his shuddering bride.

"You need to leave," the king whispered, his voice unusually strained. "And I will not give you my permission to use the cuffs. You will need every power the gods have given you to keep me from dragging you into this nightmare again."

"But I—"

Kadoc crossed the room again quick as lightning and unclasped her necklace before she could finish protesting. And with a gust and a flash, Seren was back in Harreb's domain, the necklace falling to the darkened cave's floor and the resulting clink alerting her companions to her return. The rebel leader abandoned his mission to wear a groove in the radiant grass with his pacing and rushed to Seren's side.

"Did he give you permission?"

Seren shook her head, fresh tears filling her eyes as her head throbbed relentlessly.

"Did he hurt you?"

"No," she croaked. "If anything, he was trying to protect me."

"You can't let him deceive you, Seren. Everything he does is motivated by complete depravity and selfishness, and whatever performance he put on during your time together was no different. You cannot trust him!"

Seren withdrew from Fedhlim and the guardian, who silently observed their interaction from several yards away, to take in the fresh air. Gazing at the unusual sky, she saw that it had brightened to a more crimson hue during her interaction with the king, and the heavens' new coloring reminded her of her tragic memory and Kadoc's unholy sacrifice to Malok.

As horrified as she'd been by the truth behind his descent into greed and bloodlust, grief for his soul brought forth the tears she shed in those moments, not fear and disappointment. In his mourning and desperation, the king committed an unthinkable act that claimed more lives than she could count, including the very one he originally sought to save. Malok had used his grief to bring an abomination into the land and strike out at the elves in a way he never had before.

And I'm meant to stop him. How can I defeat someone who softens my heart more with every encounter? I need righteous anger and courage, not pity and heartbreak.

"What happened, Seren?" Fedhlim pressed.

"Kadoc agreed to give me permission and tell me how he came to acquire his powers if I had a meal with him, so I did. He revealed that he obtained his power by becoming the Cursed One's vessel. As he told his story, darkness filled the room and the tenderness I saw in him vanished. I invoked Millam's name, and the evil presence left, but instead of giving me the permission I sought, he said I'd need my powers to defend myself against him and unclasped my necklace to send me away."

"By the gods… I never would have guessed that the God of Darkness was part of this… or at least not to this extent. Madness and greed yes, but pure evil…"

Fedhlim sighed and folded his arms, stroking his graying beard as he contemplated Seren's news.

"My greatest danger from Kadoc is that he would force me into bearing the Cursed One's yoke as I did before, and I can't risk being powerless if he uses the laurel wreath to come to me again."

"I agree. Contending with him is hard enough, but both of you… the people couldn't withstand that great evil again," he agreed. "We need to tell the elders the source of Kadoc's power and find a new way to appease them."

Fedhlim stepped away from Seren and spoke with the watchful guardian once more.

"I'm sorry for wasting your valuable time, but we no longer wish to use the cuffs. Can you return us to the Brohnn River?"

"You might not wish to use them, but Seren will need them to complete her calling."

Harreb extended his upturned hands, and white light sliced through the cuffs from wrist to forearm. The cuffs slid from his wrists and floated forward until they rested in Seren's hands. The cuffs, which had previously been seamless now featured a pair of hinges so an elf could don them without using the guardian's ancient magic.

"Do not wear these upon your return to the city. When you need them, place the silver cuff on the one whose powers need to be bound and the gold one on whoever will permit their use. The silver cuff will remain sealed until the one wearing the golden cuff removes his of his own volition or perishes."

"Thank you," Seren said as she placed the cuffs, which were warm with magic, in her borrowed satchel. "Did you know what would happen when I went to Kadoc?"

"Goodbye, Your Majesty."

Before Seren could repeat her question, the ground trembled violently and knocked both elves off their feet. By the time the tremor ended and they caught their bearings, the cave had returned to its previous state, and Harreb was gone. As Fedhlim helped Seren to her feet, she glanced back at the cave's inner wall, intrigued and troubled by the guardian's behavior.

"We should return to Aden as soon as possible. We stayed with Harreb longer than I anticipated, and dusk will be upon us soon."

The two quickly mounted their horses and traveled back to the elven settlement. The return trip passed more quickly than the first, but the setting sun reminded them of their winged enemies, who would rise ready to torment them as soon as darkness cloaked the land. Thankfully, the lights of Aden appeared in the distance as the sun set behind the mountains, but a dissonant trio of shrieks pierced the night as they emerged from the forest and took to the road. Chancing a glance at the sky, Seren caught a glimpse of three winged figures circling above like vultures eager to prey on newfound carrion.

"They're here," she called over the horse's thunderous steps.

"Prepare yourself for battle, but don't slow your pace," he instructed, drawing his sword. "And remember—their hearts are on the right."

As the words left Fedhlim's lips, the bone-chilling calls grew louder, and one of the flying scourges swooped down. The black creature, which had the face and body of a woman but the eyes and fangs of a serpent, attempted to scratch Fedhlim with her talons, but the warrior struck out with his blade, forcing it to fade backwards in avoidance of his blow. A second agloc descended from the sky, setting her sights on Seren.

Thankfully, the maiden perceived the intentions in the fiend's heart and called to mind her troubling yet joyful memory of Kadoc. In an instant, water cascaded from her hand and slammed the agloc into a tree lining the road. A howl of pain ripped from the agloc's lips, for the liquid didn't just overwhelm her. It also scalded her skin, melting it away with a sizzle to reveal glistening red flesh. Caught off guard by her power's effect on the dark creature, Seren's gaze lingered on her stunned victim long enough for the first agloc to advance unnoticed.

The hissing fiend knocked Seren from her horse, and she landed on her side in the underbrush by the road with an audible crack. Fedhlim redirected his steed to come to her aid, but the third agloc made her move and distracted him with her relentless assaults. Seren attempted to rise from the ground but cried out as sharp pain in her side and her aching head stole her vitality. Fighting for breath and strength, gratitude filled her heart as she saw her steed walking toward her.

Alas, before she could reach the animal, her airborne enemy slashed its talons along the length of its back. The horse reared up and whinnied in anguish before turning its attention to Seren again. The maiden took a tentative step forward, seeing that the agloc circled above again, but hesitated as she took in the horse's new demeanor.

The mare's ears were pinned back and the skin around her eyes tightened until Seren could see the bloodshot whites of her eyes. As they made eye contact, the horse lowered its head and snaked it back and forth as its tail swished violently. Then, an unsettling growl sounded from deep in its throat, and Seren's eyes widened as it slowly stalked toward her. Keeping her left hand against her right ribs, Seren lifted her right hand and slowly moved around the horse in an attempt to draw nearer to Fedhlim.

"I'm not a danger to you," she trembled in a hushed tone. "I'm sorry that the agloc hurt you, but I'm not your enemy. There's no need to fear me."

The horse shook its head more violently, flinging foam in the air before charging at his once beloved rider. But a blade sailed through the air and embedded itself in her steed's head, and the horse fell dead mere paces from her timorous target. Redirecting her attention to Fedhlim, Seren saw the agloc he had clashed with lying on the ground minus an arm and a wing. The rebel rode toward her as their final foe dove from above, aiming her venomous talons at Fedhlim.

"Duck!" Seren cried.

Fedhlim did as she commanded, and the injured maiden released her power once more, sweeping away the final agloc with an unexpectedly corrosive deluge that left it mewling and writhing on the ground by its wounded counterpart. Rather than immediately coming to Seren's aid, Fedhlim dismounted and stalked over to the struggling beasts. Once he reached them, Fedhlim cleaved their heads from their bodies before piercing their hearts. The two headless bodies thrashed about for a moment, their melting wings weakly beating against the grass and their backs arching in agony before falling still at the rebel's feet.

Satisfied with his deadly work, Fedhlim jogged over to Seren, who collapsed to her knees.

"I think my ribs are broken," she rasped, the pain in her swollen side intensifying with every breath.

"We're almost to Aden, so you'll get help soon enough," he said, lifting her into his arms. "By the time morning comes, your pain will be little more than a memory."

As Fedhlim rose to his feet, Seren's head swam and the world around her tilted perilously. Then, darkness filled her vision and swallowed her whole.

★　　　★　　　★

When Seren opened her hazel eyes later that night, the grim face that greeted her was not the one she expected. Upon seeing that his work was successful, Doran removed his hands from her head and side and stepped back, but she grabbed his arm before he could vacate the room as planned.

"Thank you for healing me."

"Thank Fedhlim. He's the one who gave the order."

Doran turned to leave again, but Seren tightened her grip and sat up.

"I'm sorry for not telling you everything that happened with Kadoc. You abandoned your life in Eaiven without hesitation to save me from him, yet I was more truthful with Fedhlim than I was with you. Will you please forgive me?"

86

Doran stared down at her for a moment, weighing her words against the comfortable bitterness he'd held so dear for what felt like much longer than two days. Seeing the pleading and sadness in her eyes, he grudgingly acknowledged that her regret was genuine and loosened his grip on the resentment churning in his heart.

"I forgive you."

Seren's posture relaxed as a sigh escaped her lips.

"Thank you."

"I heard that the elders sent you to find the Cuffs of Harreb."

"Yes, they did."

"And were you successful?"

Seren's brows lowered as she harkened back to the day's unexpected events.

"Yes, but I don't plan on wearing them yet. Didn't Fedhlim tell you what happened?"

"No, he just burst into the barracks while I was in the middle of eating dinner and commanded me to heal you. He left immediately after explaining your injuries."

The maiden finally took in her surroundings, realizing that she was lying on a crude wooden table and that broken earthenware and spilled food littered the floor. Feeling invasive and foolish, she hopped off the table, careful not to step on the mess Fedhlim made in her time of need.

"I'm so sorry, Doran."

"I'm used to eating light," he shrugged.

"Where is Fedhlim now?"

"I'm not sure. He put you on the table and fled fast as lightning before I could say a word."

"He must have gone to the elders."

"Perhaps. So, what did Harreb have you do?"

"He told me to go to Kadoc and ask his permission to use the cuffs."

"You're kidding."

Seren shook her head.

"I left my necklace here, but he transported it to the cave for me to use. So, I put it on and faced Kadoc for the *second* time today."

"Second?"

"Just as the necklace he gave me for our engagement brings me to him, the laurel wreath I gave him brings him to me. He was waiting for me in my room when I woke up today, and he wanted to apologize for how our first meeting went yesterday."

"Don't tell me you believed him."

"I was skeptical too, but I'm fairly certain that he was being truthful."

"And what of your latest interaction?"

Seren knelt beside the table and cleaned Doran's failed attempt at dinner as she told her unusual tale.

"In exchange for dining with him, he agreed to give me permission to use the cuffs and tell me how he gained his power. That unknown part of our story had been weighing on me all day."

"Because of your conversation this morning?"

"No. Fedhlim took me to see Malan so she could teach me how to use my power over water, and apparently joy is the key to unlocking it. But the joyful memory I called to mind was Kadoc proposing to me and not one of the many happy moments I had back home in Gridein. But in that memory, he wasn't the man I've lived in fear of my whole life. He was kind, gentle, and even a little unsure of himself. Even his appearance was different… his eyes were the color of the darkest of teas and filled with warmth and love that made my heart melt and strengthen all at once. His skin and hair were also darker like those of normal southern elves instead of the pale shades they are now. We were both *so* different then. Something clearly happened to change him into the man we fear today, and I underwent a similar transformation."

"What did you find out?"

"After an earthquake killed his father and our unborn child, he was desperate to keep me from dying. So, he performed a forbidden ritual to grant both of us immortality, and he's been the Cursed One's vessel ever since. Even as we conversed, the glimmer of gentleness I saw in him was overtaken by evil. The only thing that kept him from acting on those urges was me invoking Millam's name."

"And he still gave you permission?"

"No, but it wasn't to spite me. He said I would need my powers to protect myself from him and sent me back to the cave before I could protest. Even though I didn't complete Harreb's quest, he still gave me the cuffs to use later."

"Did he say why?"

"Unfortunately, no, but I'm positive that he knew what I would face when he sent me to Kadoc."

"It sounds like he did," Doran agreed. "Also, would you prefer if I call you Seren or Neassa."

"Seren, of course. Why would you ask me that?"

"When you've spoken about Neassa tonight, you've said 'I,' 'me,' and 'we.' Last time we spoke, you referred to her as if you weren't the same person."

Seren stopped cleaning and sat back on her heels, wiping sweat from her furrowed brow.

"I'm sorry. I didn't even realize I was doing that," she whispered.

Doran sat beside Seren on the floor and briefly placed his hand on her shoulder in an awkward yet genuine attempt to comfort his companion.

"Don't apologize. As much as I detested Neassa, you're not the woman who once tormented me."

"But maybe I am. The woman I am now—the one my parents raised me to be in Gridein—is more like who Neassa was as a young woman than the villain Kadoc killed twenty years ago."

"Is it possible for you to become like that again?"

"No… not willingly. I didn't choose to become what I was in my previous life, and I wouldn't choose it in this one either. Kadoc fed me the elixir without telling me what he'd done or what it would do to me. I'm more afraid of Kadoc trying to drag me into depravity with him as he did before than of being tempted to seek it out."

"We won't let him corrupt you again, and the gods have already revealed that you will be the one to defeat him."

"But they haven't said *how* I'll defeat him or what that victory will cost me."

As Doran opened his mouth to respond, Fedhlim swept into the room with the same boldness he'd used only minutes before. His dark hair was in a disarray while dirt still soiled his clothing and skin, but his grave demeanor was far more alarming than his wild appearance. The two elves stood to greet the solemn rebel, but he spoke before they could invite him into their conversation.

"The elders will let you remain in Aden without wearing the cuffs."

A smile dawned on Seren's face for the first time in hours.

"What changed their minds?" she asked.

"Follow me."

Fedhlim left the room, and Seren and Doran trailed behind him. As they exited the barracks, Seren noticed how the few elves wandering the streets watched her with curiosity and fledgling hope in their eyes and spirits. Some even greeted her with nods of deference and smiles. It was the first time since she entered Agron that someone acknowledged her and regarded her with something other than fear or scorn. Even with those wordless interactions, the streets were considerably less crowded than they'd been during the daytime, so the trio crossed Aden in a matter of minutes.

Rather than leading Seren and Doran to the agora where the elders congregated during the day, the watchtower, or his home, Fedhlim brought his companions to Malan and Kilyan's inn. When they entered the crowded guesthouse, singing and shouts of glee happily assaulted their senses, and they followed the joyful din to the dining hall, where guests and residents clapped and sang along to a merry song as a young man sang and played his lyre. Judging by his build, he was a soldier, but he performed like a true artist.

> *"By Millam's hand my enemies*
> *Fell at my ready feet.*
> *He strengthened my arm and my fist.*
> *So, I threshed them like wheat.*
> *For years and years, I wept hot tears*
> *Because of all my fears.*
> *But by his hand and with this fist*
> *My enemies were beat."*

Every elf in the room was blissfully transfixed by his talent and charisma—singing the young bard's song as if it was a familiar tune despite never having heard it before. The only people who weren't caught up by his song were Doran, who scrutinized the young man in disbelief from the first note to the last, and Fedhlim, who observed his soldier's increasing perplexity. When the young man finished the song, the crowd burst into raucous applause, and he looked upon his appreciative audience with stars—and maybe even tears—in his gray eyes.

"Kathal?" Doran asked, narrowing his eyes.

"Who is Kathal?"

"Kathal is a young man a little older than you whose parents fled to Aden during the massacres," Fedhlim said. "He's never left Agron, nor had he played the lyre until this afternoon."

"What does me not wearing the cuffs have to do with him?"

"He's always been a bit of an awkward boy, so some ruffians take pleasure in humiliating him. As a child of Aden, he's never been a match for them because of his powerlessness, and his slight build made him an even easier target," Doran said. "I've tried to teach him to defend himself when I've traveled to the city, but he's never been able to catch on or increase his stature."

"Yes, he could barely lift a sack of grain without panting," Fedhlim said. "Today, he was working at the stables when someone shoved him from behind. He landed face-first in the trough, and as they held him down, he underwent an unexpected transformation. Kathal's build and demeanor changed before their widening eyes, and he thumped the scoundrels without any assistance. Once they were gone, he looked at the empty trough and saw a wooden stone with a lyre carved into it and a stone token in the shape of a bear."

"The symbols for music and strength," she said.

Fedhlim nodded.

"The water you wielded gave him the powers that Kadoc's tyranny denied him. When Malan and Kilyan brought him to the elders and explained what happened, they finally admitted that you were sent to be a friend to the elves—not our enemy."

Seren slumped against the wall, trying to organize her thoughts as Fedhlim's unusual tale sank in. Though she'd been in the heat of battle, she knew something was different about her powers when the water ate away at the aglocs' flesh, but learning how it imbued the once gawky young man in front of her with strength from the gods added oil to the flame that already burned in her heart.

Millam, what do you want from me?

"As far as they're concerned, you are now a citizen of Aden and may dwell in the city freely as long as you like."

"Does anyone else know that I caused this?"

"Only whoever Kathal has told, and he's been too busy drinking in this newfound attention to publicly give you credit for his transformation."

"This isn't the only abnormal thing my power has done," Seren revealed. "When I tried to fend off the aglocs, my water burned away their flesh and killed one of them. I've never heard of another water elemental possessing these abilities."

"And no one has ever heard of the same elf being born twice, but these are the days the gods have appointed for us," Fedhlim said, taking her hand in his. "Even though their will is a mystery to us, you don't have to sort it out on your own. I will help you for as long as the gods allow me to"

"Thank you."

"Now, you've had quite a long day. I'll walk you back to the house so you can rest."

"Rest sounds nice."

Fedhlim blessed Seren with a small smile before turning back to Doran.

"Can you keep an eye on Kathal for the remainder of the evening? You know better than anyone how proud and senseless some elves become after their awakenings."

"I'll make sure he doesn't do anything foolish."

Fedhlim pulled a few coins from his satchel and dropped them in Doran's hand with a wink.

"And enjoy a meal on me to replace the one I ruined. I hear the lamb is delicious tonight."

"Thank you, sir."

After sending Doran on his new mission, Seren and Fedhlim left the bustling inn and returned to the warrior's home. Horam greeted the pair with a delicious dinner and warm, spiced milk that uncoiled Seren's nerves one steaming sip at a time. By the time the meal ended, she could barely keep her eyes open, but she managed to drag her way upstairs alone. There, she found that someone had repaired her door and placed a fresh nightgown on her bed in their absence. After wiping the day's grime from her face and limbs, Seren pulled on the blessedly soft nightgown and curled up in bed, letting sleep overtake her only moments later.

CHAPTER 5
Corpses and Conflict

The next morning, Seren awakened and swept the room with her bleary eyes to make sure Kadoc hadn't decided to repeat the previous day's early morning surprise. Upon realizing that she was as alone as she'd been the previous night, relief assailed her heart. Rolling onto her back and staring at the ceiling, Seren let her mind drift back to the events at the inn. Would the water she called on always awaken elves whose power lie dormant, or was Kathal's experience an anomaly? If the latter, was there something about the young elf that made her power manifest differently?

Seren groaned inwardly and pulled the covers over her head. Every new piece of information she learned led to even more questions, which were more difficult to solve than their predecessors. And while Fedhlim had been kinder to her than she deserved, even his tenderest gestures failed to comfort her as her mother's arms or father's wisdom could have.

I need to contact them as soon as possible.

With resolve in her heart, Seren dragged herself out of bed and prepared for the day. By the time she emerged from her room, Horam had already cooked and plated breakfast for her, but only Fedhlim awaited her in the kitchen. Seeing that the cook was gone and that no meal sat before her host, she braced herself for a grave conversation that she was barely awake enough to hold.

"Good morning," Fedhlim said.

"Good morning," Seren replied, salivating at the sight of the freshly baked bread and honey drizzled apples. "I take it you need to speak with me about something."

"Yes, I do. While you spent your night resting, I wasn't so fortunate. I lie awake long after I retired to my room contemplating your encounters with Kadoc. The fact that he is able to slip into Aden so easily greatly troubles me whether he has his powers or not. I went to the library early this morning and enlisted Aeton's and Toren's help. The three of us pored over the scrolls we've accumulated over the years to see if I could find a solution."

The young elf's nostrils flared at the news that they'd done such important research about her predicament without including her, but she stifled her annoyance and the sigh that threatened to escape her lips.

"Did you have any luck?"

"Possibly, but I'm not sure if you'll like our solution."

"Whether I like it or not, I still need to hear it. What did you come up with?"

"When we were in Harreb's cave, he called Kadoc your husband, and the tokens that bring you to each other are associated with your betrothal. They think that if you end your marriage to Kadoc, you may break the magical bond that ties you together."

"Well, women can't seek divorces of their own accord, and I seriously doubt he would divorce me."

"True… but entering into a new marriage may nullify the previous one."

Seren's pulse accelerated as Fedhlim took her hand in his.

"I know I'm not the kind of man that you probably envisioned for yourself, but I possess wisdom that young men your age lack and will treat you with respect and kindness as we strive to inspire the affection that usually precedes marriage," he swore. "The priest can perform the ceremony today if you consent to it."

She gaped at her host for a few beats before removing her hand from his gentle grip.

"I-I can't marry you."

"Would you prefer someone else? Doran is closer to your age, and I'm sure he would—"

"It's not about you specifically. I'm honored that you would ask me to fill such a significant role in your life even under these circumstances, but I can't marry someone without my parents' permission."

"Of course… I should have considered that before I asked. If I was able to bring them to Aden and obtain their permission, would you consider my offer?"

Seren perked up at the prospect of being reunited with her parents, but the possibility of entering a loveless marriage with Fedhlim or Doran in an attempt to end another unwanted union dampened the little levity that the question inspired.

"I'd consider it, but I can't make any promises."

"Then would you mind writing them a letter explaining your predicament? I should be able to have someone deliver it and bring them to Aden today if nothing disrupts their travel plans."

"I wouldn't mind at all!"

"Perfect. I'll get you some writing materials."

As Fedhlim left the kitchen, his concentration waned, and Seren caught a glimpse of the state of his heart. Though she only had a moment to look, the disappointment and loneliness he felt were clear enough for her to pick up on with little effort. Despite having the respect and admiration of his people as well as a noble purpose and adventurous profession that many young men likely coveted, the rebels' leader hadn't known love since his beloved died at the awakening cave so many years before. Whether his position, grief, or age prevented him from marrying, Seren wasn't sure, but her heart ached for him.

No, Fedhlim *wasn't* the kind of man she'd fantasized about marrying, but he had many of the qualities she and her parents had hoped for. He was gallant, strong, kind, intelligent, and even handsome despite the years between them. The warrior also didn't seem calloused despite spending so long waging war against their mad king. Any woman would have been lucky to be yoked to such a man.

But am I the woman he should marry? Are the gods using this strange situation not just to sever my ties with Kadoc but also to heal his broken heart?

Seren didn't have long to contemplate her predicament before Fedhlim reappeared with paper and a quill. Thankfully, her host gave her solitude as she wrote her letter over breakfast and maintained his distance for the rest of the day after escorting her to Malan's inn to continue her training.

Though their time together revolved around Malan teaching Seren the basics about elemental powers, which she was a quick study at, the innkeeper's almost maternal gentleness during that instruction put Seren at ease in ways that Fedhlim's and Doran's company had failed to since they began their brief acquaintance. The fact that Malan either had no knowledge of Seren's odd connection to Kadoc or simply chose not to mention it also provided some much-needed relief from the strange burden the gods forced her to bear. However, seeing the horses drinking from the trough she'd filled the previous day as they fetched bales of hay to use as targets made her peace ebb slightly.

Alas, the sight of the transformative water proved to be the least of Seren's troubles. After an hour of target practice, the women returned to the inn for a little refreshment—and so Malan could change into a drier dress—and found Kilyan waiting for them with a troubled expression on his sun-weathered face.

"What's happened?" the fire-handler asked, squeezing water from her hair as they neared the inn.

"Aeton just sent word that one of the guards found two women's bodies along the road to New Aden this morning."

"By the gods! Who were they?"

"The elders didn't recognize them, so they've asked us to take a look at them in case they were tenants of ours," he grumbled. "I know it's an unpleasant task, but you talk with the women more than I do. Would you mind meeting them outside the gates to help identify them?"

"I mind, but I'll do it," Malan agreed before turning to Seren. "I'm so sorry, but it looks like I have to cut your lesson short. If I knew the women, this errand may take up what's left of my day."

"It's all right. I can accompany you if you'd like."

"If you're sure you can stomach something so grim, I'd appreciate the company," she breathed. "Let's go."

Heavy hearts weighed down their steps as they plodded from the Aden Inn to the city's gates. Malan responded to the greetings she received with a tight-lipped grin and the nod of her head, but she avoided conversation on their brief journey through the small yet bustling city. Thanks to the lack of true interruptions, they reached the gates in only a few minutes and found Aeton leaning on his walking stick as he spoke with two ashen guards. Before them were two cloak-covered shapes that attracted more than a handful of eagerly buzzing flies.

Upon hearing their footsteps, the elder turned in their direction. While he didn't regard Seren with undisguised scorn as he had the previous day, his simple greeting lacked anything resembling warmth. Seren reassured herself that his lukewarm greeting was inspired by their grim predicament and not her presence, but she still shivered under his sharp gaze.

"Thank you for assisting us with this matter, Malan. I hope we won't have to take up too much of your time."

"So do I. Shall we begin?"

"Before we do, I must warn you that these women have been viciously butchered. I've never seen anything like this in all my years in Aden."

Malan nodded in understanding and heaved a deep breath. After giving the innkeeper a moment to reconsider her involvement in the grisly task, Aeton nodded to the guards, who pulled the cloaks back just enough for the two women to see that someone had severed the victims' heads from their undressed bodies. Vomit rose in Seren's throat before she could attempt to steady herself, and she emptied the contents of her stomach a few feet away, the acrid taste of bile joining the stench of death that clung to the two corpses. Thankfully, neither the men nor Malan reacted to her embarrassing display, so Seren took a few seconds to compose herself several yards away.

"They don't look familiar to me," Malan said. "Where did you find them? Maybe they were on their way to Aden from Eaiven."

"We found them just outside the city," one guard said. "They were both naked with their heads chopped off and hearts run through. One was lying on the road and the other was leaning against a tree."

Seren's pointed ears perked up at the guard's grisly description, and she reluctantly joined the group once more.

"Was there a third body or a dead horse nearby?"

"A third body, no, but there was a dead horse," the guard replied.

"Do you know these women?" Aeton asked.

"Yes and no. Did Fedhlim tell you about the aglocs who attacked us last night?"

"He mentioned that you'd been in a fight, but he didn't share any details."

"Well, I tried to use my elemental powers to fend them off, but my water burned their skin instead of just diverting them. And one agloc scratched my horse, so Fedhlim had to kill it. The wounds on these corpses match the ones Fedhlim dealt the aglocs."

"You think these women were aglocs?" the elder pressed.

"Possibly. I can't think of any other reason why someone would have found two women bearing the same wounds they had. We've already seen my water do something abnormal, so is this really that farfetched?"

"No, it's not. How much do you know about the aglocs' origins?"

"Very little."

"Well, according to Origins, a group of elven women who worshipped the Cursed One summoned him using dark magic and begged him to bed them. He granted their request, and they each conceived children. When they gave birth, their daughters were strange creatures with the forms of their mothers but the darkness and demeanor of their father. If your hypothesis is correct, the water you wield may have removed the Cursed One's corruption from their bodies."

"I wonder if it would do the same for their souls…"

"Unless you have the gift of necromancy, I don't think we'll be finding out any time soon."

"I don't need necromancy. I just needs a live specimen to experiment on," Seren said. "What if we captured a living agloc for me to test my abilities on?"

"To what end?" Aeton asked. "Securing our own freedom is difficult enough without trying to liberate our enemies."

"But are they really our enemies?" she countered. "They had no control over their creation, and the Cursed One's influence is incredibly strong. It's not easily shaken off."

As the words passed through her lips, Seren reflected on her last conversation with Kadoc. If her water did indeed cure the aglocs, could it cast the darkness out of him as well?

But would the people embrace him if he changed or still demand his life for everything he's done? And why would Harreb insist that I have the cuffs if he could be redeemed somehow?

"I'll speak with the other elders and see what they think," Aeton conceded after a moment. "I'll send for you if we decide to move forward."

"Thank you."

With the elder's slightly encouraging dismissal, the two women left the grim scene and returned to the inn. Though they continued Seren's training as planned, no amount of target practice or shape forming could chase visions of those mutilated bodies from their troubled minds.

By the time they finished Seren's training, both women were physically and emotionally spent, so they were eager to taste the stew that had been simmering for the past few hours. But when they stepped into the dining hall, it wasn't bread or meat that cheered Seren's downcast heart.

"Mama! Papa!" she cried, running to her parents and practically collapsing into their arms.

The trio stood there for several minutes, embracing and weeping as if they'd been separated for weeks instead of days.

"I'm so happy you're here," Seren said. "I missed you so much."

"We were so relieved when Fedhlim told us you were all right," her mother said. "We waited for you to return for hours the day you awakened, and when we went to the cave and saw the dead guard, we feared the worst."

"I alerted a soldier near the cave about your disappearance, but he dismissed us and said that you'd been taken to the palace," her father continued. "That alone would have broken our hearts, but it still didn't sit right with us."

"Well, the second guard at Mount Ceallah was a spy for the rebels, and he brought me here right after I awakened. He lied to his fellow soldiers to get us a chariot, so that's why they thought I'd gone to the palace."

"That's what Fedhlim said, but he wouldn't explain why you'd been spirited away to Agron of all places. He said we should hear the tale from you."

"Yes, you should," Seren sighed. "Let's have a seat. This is a very long, confusing story that not even I fully understand."

And so, the displaced family gathered at a somewhat secluded table in the dining hall, where Seren shared everything that happened from the moment Aire gave her the tokens until her unexpected revelation about the aglocs. As expected, her parents asked questions when her story was unclear or seemed preposterous and lovingly berated her when she recounted some of her more foolish actions. Despite that, gratitude and relief won the battle for their hearts as they relished in one another's familiar company. Yet one hidden detail gnawed at Seren's conscience.

Fedhlim's proposal.

By the time she finished her not-so tall tale, their stew had gone cold, so Malan kindly reheated it using her powers. Her host appeared around that time, and his eyes were weary yet attentive as he entered the dining hall. Keeping his unusual proposal in mind, Seren excused herself to greet the rebel.

"Thank you for bringing my parents here. I know it's a dangerous journey, so I truly appreciate it."

"You're welcome. It was a task I only trusted myself with."

The maiden flashed him a nervous, closed lip smile as she gathered the courage to ask her question.

"Did you tell them about your... idea?"

"No, I haven't. I thought it would be better if you did so yourself."

"You thought right. I still don't feel at ease about saying yes, but I will talk with them and seek their counsel on the matter."

"Of course," Fedhlim agreed with a nod.

"Would you like to join us for dinner? Malan made stew, and it's delicious."

"I'd love to. But there is one detail we should discuss first. Now that your parents are here, I think it would be more proper if you stayed with them. Either you can stay here or in two of the rooms in the tower. Either way, I'll make sure you have protection in case Kadoc decides to surprise us again."

"I'll ask my father which option he prefers."

With one last awkward agreement, the two joined Seren's parents once more for a satisfying meal that made their spirits rise and eyelids droop. Realizing that sleep was nearly upon them, Fedhlim made his exit, and Seren, Kalbhac, and Inley retired to their rooms in the tower, which Kalbhac had chosen after gleaning information about their options from Fedhlim. There, the family of three turned in for the night, and as Seren closed her eyes, she experienced something she hadn't felt in days.

Peace.

★   ★   ★

When morning came, Seren enjoyed the familiarity that came with starting the day with her parents. Of course, their surroundings were alien and circumstances were strange, but the company was comforting... comforting enough that she finally divulged the true reason they'd been brought to Agron.

"Do you remember when I told you about my necklace yesterday?" she asked as her mother refilled her tea.

"It takes you to Kadoc's palace," the matriarch said.

"Yes, but it was also the engagement gift I received—"

"The gift *Neassa* received," her father interrupted.

Even though the maiden had slowly come to terms with her connection to the dark queen, her parents weren't so quick to accept it.

"The necklace was also the gift that Kadoc gave Neassa upon their engagement, and the reverse is true about the laurel wreath that he used to come to me," she continued. "When Fedhlim and I went to get the Cuffs of Harreb, the guardian spoke as if I was still married to Kadoc even though Neassa's death should have severed the covenant. Fedhlim believes that us still being married may be why the two tokens bring us together."

"Well, from the sound of it, I doubt the king would give you a divorce," Inley sighed.

"I agree, but Fedhlim and the elders think entering into another marriage may break my bond to him."

"Do you have anyone in mind?" her mother asked.

"No. None of the men in our village ever caught my eye or asked to pursue me."

"What about here in Aden?" Kalbhac asked.

"The only men I've spent time with are Doran and Fedhlim, and we haven't spent enough time together for me to truly see their character."

"Did Fedhlim have any suggestions?"

Even though she'd anticipated her father's question, Seren still had to gather the strength to answer it.

"He volunteered to marry me himself."

For a moment, Seren allowed herself to peek into her parents' hearts. Worry and wonder filled her mother's, but anger welled up within her father's spirit, only to be slightly suppressed by a contemplative mood and a hint of admiration.

"What do you think?" she prodded.

"Part of me wants to strangle him for proposing to you without seeking my permission first, but I'm assuming that influenced his decision to come and get us," Kalbhac said.

"It did. I told him I needed your consent."

"Do you like him?"

"He's nice, valiant, and seems to be a good leader."

"You just gave me a list of observations and not your personal feelings," he lovingly chided. "Do you *like* him?"

"A little, but I don't know if I like him enough to do this. I hate that Kadoc can appear at my side whenever he pleases, but I'm not sure if I'm ready to take such drastic action to cut him off. Besides, if the gods still consider us married even though I died over twenty years ago and gave me the necklace as my token, who's to say that they'd take its power away so easily?"

"What about Kadoc?" her mother piped up.

"Like you said, I doubt the king will divorce me. So being able to come to me in an instant isn't something he'll easily give up. The benefits of surprising me outweigh the risk of my surprising him since my powers aren't a match for his. If I—"

"That's not what I meant. Is there some part of you that still wants to be married to him?"

Seren deflated slightly, acknowledging the weight of both her mother's question and her knee jerk answer.

"Yes… I think part of me does."

"How big is that part?"

Tears sprang forth in her eyes as shame and reason sought to silence the honest, unwanted meditations of her heart.

"Too big to ignore. I don't want to feel this way, but each time I see him or remember something about our past, those feelings grow. I don't think I love him, but I certainly don't hate him enough to do this. I'm sorry."

Inley pulled Seren into her arms, letting her distraught daughter melt into her comforting embrace.

"Why didn't you tell us this to begin with? Your mother and I would celebrate as much as the next elf if Kadoc was deposed, but we'd never force you to marry someone if your heart wasn't in it."

"I know, but my life isn't just mine anymore."

"No, but the gods gave you your face, gifts, and feelings for a reason," Kalbhac said. "Even though I can't fathom how you'll fulfill that prophecy, I can see that their will for you includes this connection to Kadoc. It could be that they gave you these feelings so you wouldn't hate him enough to sever it as many of us would."

"I agree with your father. I don't want you connected to that despot, but I'm sure there's a reason you are."

"So, I can reject Fedhlim's proposal?"

"Yes. In fact, I'll do it for you," her father offered. "If this had been done the proper way, I'd be delivering the rejection anyway."

"There's nothing proper about any of this, so don't be angry with him" Seren said, "But yes… that would be really helpful."

"I'll talk to him this afternoon."

"Thank you, Papa."

After a valiant attempt to take the conversation in a less intense direction with a question about the ogre's uneven roads, the family transitioned away from Seren's predicament and discussed the strange land they now inhabited. When they finally went their separate ways to finish preparing for the day, some of the heaviness on Seren's shoulders lifted, but uneasiness still churned in her spirit for the remainder of the day.

★   ★   ★

By the time the sun dipped behind the horizon, Seren was exhausted and exhilarated from a day of training and working. While serving and cooking at the Aden Inn didn't stimulate her mind the same way helping with her father's scribe work did, doing tasks that felt normal and learning how to use her gifts chased away some of the gravity that had lingered since the family's conversation that morning. After slinging her satchel over her shoulder, Seren stepped out of the inn's kitchen and nearly collided with a mead-drinking young man mid-swig.

"I'm sorry," she apologized.

"It's all right," he assured her with a friendly grin.

As Seren continued on her way, she recognized that patron in question was the man whose powers she unknowingly awakened. Seeing the confident young elf reminded her of a fact that neither of her instructors brought up during her day of training. The water she wielded had magic in it. Instead of leaving for home as planned, Seren walked back into the kitchen and approached her trainer once more.

"Malan."

"Yes?"

"Are you up for a bit of an unplanned adventure?"

Malan looked up from the roast she was carving, one of her brows arched in curiosity.

"What kind of adventure?"

"I'd like to try using my water on a live agloc tonight, but I'm not confident enough in my abilities to try it alone. Will you go with me?"

"Wouldn't Fedhlim be better suited for this?"

"Yes, but I... I think you'd be a better companion for this."

The innkeeper set down her knife and narrowed her eyes at Seren.

"I'm just as curious about this as you are, but I don't see the rush in figuring it out. We already know you can awaken elves' powers and fight the aglocs. Is something else driving this?"

Seren's gaze dropped to her fidgeting hands as she tried to formulate an honest answer.

"I want to find out if my water can make the aglocs human without killing them because if it can remove the darkness for them, it could do the same for Kadoc. There might be a way to end all of this without killing him."

"You don't want to kill Kadoc after everything he's done to our people?"

"Not if I can help it. I think he made a grave mistake in aligning himself with the Cursed One all those years ago, but from the little I've seen, he may also be a victim of the darkness in his own way. He went to The Scroll of Malok in desperation, and all of us have been paying the price ever since."

Malan stepped forward and placed her hand on Seren's arm, prompting her to look her friend in the eye.

"It sounds like you care about him," Malan said.

Seren nodded.

"Well, I still have a little work to do here before I can leave, but meet me outside the city gates right after the market closes for the night."

"Thank you, Malan."

"No. Thank *you* for being so honest with me. I know that wasn't easy."

With a parting hug and a shed tear that went unseen thanks to Seren's prompt cheek wiping, the maiden left the inn and returned to her parents. After supper, she wove a believable tale about returning to the inn for some additional training, clandestinely donned the weapon Fedhlim gave her before their quest for the cuffs, and dropped the necklace and cuffs in her pocket after a moment of deliberation. Once she felt prepared for the task that lie before her, Seren slipped into the night, passing the unsettlingly quiet agora on her way to the city gate.

Once she was outside of the village, Seren lifted her eyes to the sky in search of the winged scourges her people feared and turned her heart to the unwanted yet effective memory of her tender moment with Kadoc. If an agloc descended upon her, she was near enough to the city to cry for help, but she had to be prepared to fight if one swooped down before Malan arrived. Just as she pulled her dagger from its sheath, she heard someone approach.

Seren faced the city again expecting to see her friend, but Malan hadn't come alone. Fedhlim, Aeton, Doran, Toren, and a trio of guards stood with the innkeeper, who lingered at the back of the menacing crowd.

"What is this?" Seren asked, taking a step back as the men drew their swords.

"We should be asking you that question, traitor," Fedhlim seethed.

"I'm not betraying you. I wanted to see if my powers could—"

"Could help you be with that spawn of Malok that you call a husband," he cut off. "I should have known from the start that you couldn't be trusted."

"I'm not trying to reunite with him. I just want to see if we can defeat Kadoc without killing him. So many elves have died in this rebellion, and if I can free him without bloodshed, maybe we can—"

"You're forgetting my gift, girl. Whether you're lying to yourself or not, you can't lie to me. Do you still love Kadoc?"

"I'm sorry for overstepping and trying to do this behind your back. If you don't want me to try my powers on an agloc again, I won't, but—"

"Do you still love Kadoc?" he shouted.

Seren hung her head, her heart shuddering within her and hands shaking.

"You have to kill her," Toren said. "I saw her become the dark queen again, and we can't let that happen. Our people have already been through too much."

Seren's head shot up as she heard Toren's murderous counsel and perceived the violence rising in Fedhlim's heart. Though the other men stood ready for action, their hearts set on obedience and filled with anger, she detected a spark of doubt in Doran.

"I thought we were only capturing—"

"Kill her," Fedhlim roared.

The guards advanced, and Doran hesitated, his heart lurching for a moment before he grudgingly moved forward. Seren lifted her dagger with a shaking right hand and her left hand as well, which grew moist as she prepared to unleash her power.

"I don't want to hurt anyone, and I would never ally myself with Malok again. I only want the chance to save Kadoc from the Cursed One," she quaked, her pleading eyes darting from one man to the next. "If you don't want me in Aden anymore, just let me leave in peace. I'll find my way on my own!"

"The only place you're going is a shallow grave!" Fedhlim barked.

For a moment, Seren could have sworn that she saw the air darken around Fedhlim, but the inky haze dissipated as quickly as it formed. Before she could say another word, the warriors broke into a run and her body tensed in anticipation of the fray, which she would undoubtedly lose. But when the men were mere yards away, Doran turned on his comrades, taking advantage of the element of surprise to quickly disarm one and attack the next. Rather than addressing the unlikely traitor, the third guard forged ahead to end the maiden's short life.

Seren released her power, water pouring from her hands with the force of a waterfall and knocking him off his feet. Before the maiden could relish in her victory, Malan hurled a ball of fire across the countryside, forcing Seren to dive out of the way. She threw out her right hand to brace herself only to hear a telltale snap from her wrist and experience pain that seared as powerfully as Malan's fire. Seren struggled to get her bearings, but the sound of splashing footsteps stole her attention.

Rolling over with a wince, she attempted to stand without putting any weight on her broken wrist. By the time she stood on unsteady feet, the third guard had recovered and was stalking toward her. Her eyes darting to and fro across the tiny yet terrifying battlefield, she saw Doran fighting his fellow rebels and barely holding his own, Fedhlim abandoning her other accusers to approach her with his sword drawn, and heat waves surrounding Malan as she struggled to light a fire with flint and steel. Despite her little experience in battle, Seren recognized that she and Doran alone couldn't fight off their opponents and survive.

Fleeing was her only option.

Seren sent a torrent of water in Malan's direction, knocking the wind out of innkeeper and soaking her lighting tools in the process. Then, she unleashed her power on her other foes, leaving them failing and slipping in the mud as she snatched her satchel from the muddy ground and sprinted away from the city. Rather than sticking to the road, Seren darted into the trees lining it, hoping they'd provide much needed cover and that she'd gain a significant lead over her opponents despite her stumbling and tripping.

As she fled the battlefield, someone called her name, but her earsplitting pulse and thundering footfalls nearly drowned out the voice. Dashing through the trees as quickly as her frantic feet could take her, Seren's breathing turned from pants of exertion to gasps of desperation. She'd been able to place distance between herself and her friends-turned-foes, but she had neither the stamina to outpace them long term nor enough knowledge about the area's geography and mastery of her powers to truly escape them.

She staggered to a halt and sagged against a tree, praying for Millam to steady her soul and struggling to quiet her hurried breathing. Closing her eyes briefly, Seren strained to hear if anyone approached. After a moment, she heard neither leaves crunching nor twigs snapping. Either her pursuers were infinitely better at being sneaky than she was, or she'd lost them thanks to her directionless sprinting.

Yet she didn't move forward.

Seren remained still and prayerful for several silent minutes before finally peeling away from the tree and examining her surroundings. She couldn't see the road in any direction, and she was far enough from Aden that she couldn't make out the city's lights through the forest's fragrant canopy. Panic rose in her heart again and tears stung her eyes as grasped that she was lost and alone in a land where no one trusted her and even her former protectors saw her as an enemy.

Why couldn't Fedhlim see through Toren's false vision? Why didn't he believe me? Why did Malan betray me so easily?

As Seren recounted the rebel leader's ambush, she recalled seeing a strange shadow about Fedhlim and that a similar phenomenon occurred the last time she saw Kadoc. Either it was a coincidence or The Cursed One was somehow at work in both men's hearts. Fedhlim clearly hadn't taken the same elixir as Kadoc, but that didn't mean Malok couldn't influence him in some other way. And if that was truly the case, Malok wanted her dead.

If he wants the rebels to kill me, it must be because I'm a threat to him. That means I'm doing something right… or at least I hope it does.

Feeling slightly, albeit morbidly, encouraged by her revelation, Seren tentatively moved forward. While she didn't know where she was going, she didn't feel quite right remaining where she was. With that in mind, she searched for anything in nature that could indicate what direction she was traveling in. Alas, either moss didn't grow on trees in Agron or the ogres scraped it away for cosmetic or culinary purposes, so that task took much longer than it would have in her home kingdom.

Half an hour of purposeful wandering later, Seren recognized a bush of grien flowers growing at the base of a tree. Each day, the tiny, fiery flowers followed the sun's course across the sky before resting after sunset. During the spring and summer, they faced north. During autumn and winter, they faced south. Using the flowers' drooping heads, she determined which direction was north, plucked one of the slumbering blooms to serve as her compass, and re-oriented her steps, heading back to the Agron-Eaiven border to the west.

Of course, she didn't feel completely safe returning to Eaiven, but far fewer people saw her as a threat in her homeland than they did in Agron. After all, if no one had recognized that she bore Neassa's likeness for twenty years, she could surely get by without being recognized for at least long enough to formulate another plan. But her plan to make a new plan fell apart as quickly as it came together.

A jarringly familiar shriek shattered the silence, and Seren turned her gaze to the sky just in time to see an agloc crash through the trees about half a furlong away. The frightened maiden raised her rapidly moistening hands to fight, but the agloc didn't move. Seren crept forward a few tentative steps before she made out a spear sticking through the winged creature's back.

"That's my kill!" a gravelly voice rumbled.

Seren looked to her left and saw an ogre approach. When she saw the enormous bow in his scaly hands, she realized that the spear wasn't a spear it all. It was the ogre archer's arrow.

"I'm sorry. I didn't realize—"

"I've seen you before."

Seren took a step back.

"You must be mistaken."

The ogre sniffed at the air, and its hairless brows lowered as it detected her scent on the nighttime air.

"You're *her,*" he snarled.

The ogre stalked forward, uttering curses in his native tongue as he drew another arrow from his massive quiver. Without a thought, Seren took off once more, but her miniscule lead dwindled with every heavy footfall the ogre made. She wasn't fast enough to outrun him, and she certainly wasn't strong or skilled enough to fight him. Pausing for a flash, Seren released a deluge in the ogre's direction, but it neither slowed nor injured her pursuer. If anything, the watery distraction seemed to further enrage the already murderous creature.

As Seren sprinted through the woods once more, she remembered that she'd packed a certain piece of jewelry in her satchel earlier that evening. Cursing to herself, she reluctantly reached into the satchel and grasped her necklace. The instant she held the delicate token and pulled it from her bag, Seren tripped over a tree root and tumbled to the ground, twisting her ankle and slamming her head into the rain-parched ground.

With barely a moment to recover, she crawled forward, passing up her fallen dagger in favor of her necklace, which had landed several feet away, and clasped it around her neck as the ogre reached for her twisted ankle. Bright light bathed her rapidly blurring surroundings and a gust of wind ruffled her hair and clothing, but darkness swallowed Seren before she could fight it.

CHAPTER 6
The Royal Reunion

Even before Seren was fully awake, she knew that her plan had worked. A cool, soft pillow caressed her cheek instead of hard soil, and the aroma of incense filled her nostrils instead of the forest's earthy scent. Her ankle still hurt, but upon sitting up, she saw that someone had at least wrapped it in bandages. She also saw that she wasn't alone.

Instead of Kadoc hovering or sitting nearby, she beheld an elven woman just a few years her senior observing her from the doorway. Like her, the woman had dark chestnut curls and deep bronze skin, but her lips and cheeks were rouged with cosmetics and kohl rimmed her honey brown eyes, which studied her with a predatory curiosity like a snake watching the mouse it had its heart set on devouring. Despite her perfectly applied makeup and white, pleated linen dress, Seren instantly knew that the woman who'd watched her slumber was far more than a pretty face and a full bosom. She was dangerous… and envious.

"Hello, Seren," the woman said, lacking the friendly inflection that a proper greeting required. "Your arrival caused quite a stir last night."

"I'm sure it did," Seren said. "And you are…?"

"Orla," she said.

The watchful woman took a long drag from the golden, snake-shaped pipe she held as she ran her gaze up and down Seren's body. In doing so, she gave Seren a clear view of the crown-shaped brand on her forearm.

"You're not at all what I pictured," Orla continued, raising an artfully darkened eyebrow.

"How so?"

"I was expecting someone much taller or at least more warrior-like. You're so… soft and average in every conceivable way."

"And yet you're still threatened by me. If I'm average, what does that make you?"

Orla rolled her eyes.

"Enjoy your stay, Seren. I'll still be here long after you leave."

With that effervescent farewell, Orla slunk away, leaving Seren to convalesce alone. Instead of embracing her comfortable position, the young lady limped and winced to the door, where she nearly ran into the man she'd both dreaded and anticipated seeing. The king carried a tray of broth, bread, and wine, but there was nothing servile about his commanding presence and the power radiating from his stately form.

"You shouldn't be walking," he berated with surprising gentleness.

"Well, I can't just stay in bed all day."

Kadoc gestured toward the bed, but Seren lowered herself onto the couch instead. The white-haired king placed the tray on the table before them and sat beside Seren. She brazenly searched his heart, which he allowed without an ounce of resistance. Upon detecting neither malice nor lust in his heart, she relaxed a sliver.

"Thank you for taking care of me," she said.

"You're welcome, but I need to know what happened. You must have been desperate to come here after what transpired during your last visit."

"The rebels turned on me, and I had the misfortune of running into an ogre with a frustratingly good memory after I escaped. I had nowhere else to turn."

"Why did they betray you?"

Remembering Toren's so-called vision and Kadoc's desire to return her to her former state, Seren tailored her tale to be truthful yet incomplete.

"Fedhlim doesn't trust me anymore. He thinks that I'm in love with you and refuses to believe otherwise."

"Well, if it's any consolation, I'm sorry they cast you out. I didn't want you to return any more than you did."

Kadoc handed Seren the broth.

"You should drink this. It has healing properties that will help your ankle."

"Don't you have the power to heal?"

"I do, but I assumed you wouldn't want me to use a stolen power on you."

"The thought hadn't occurred to me, but no. I wouldn't have," she said, taking a sip that sent a warming sensation through her body—energizing, healing, and relaxing her with every passing moment. "Thank you."

"You're welcome, and you can treat this as your home for however long you need or want. You're the mistress of this palace whether you're here for an hour or a fortnight."

"Speaking of mistresses, I believe I met one of yours a moment ago."

Kadoc exhaled heavily and sank further into the couch.

"She doesn't mean anything."

"You don't even know which one I'm referring to."

"It doesn't matter. They were all meaningless distractions."

"They *are* or *were* distractions?"

"I haven't laid a hand on a single one since the day we met."

"But they still live here."

"Of course they do. How welcome do you think they'd be in their villages and cities after being part of my harem? I won't force them to face rejection twice, so they're free to leave whenever they please or remain in my care for as long as they like."

"That sounds… reasonable."

"Don't sound so surprised, Seren."

"Why wouldn't I be surprised? Every tale I've heard about you painted you as a tyrant. Even the last time we met, you were so terrifying."

"But I haven't always been this way. Your memory might not be as complete as mine, but you remember enough to know that I'm not the despot you were raised to hate."

"Yes, but you're not the king you were raised to be either."

"I couldn't be that man even if I wanted to. I am Malok's vessel until death, so darkness will always have dominion over my soul. The most I can do is make the most of fleeting moments when the remnants of good in me prevail."

"If there was a way to cast out the Cursed One's influence and be yourself again, would you do it?"

"Would you stay with me if I did?"

"I don't know, but surely the good of the people is more important than my acceptance?"

"Even if I could be free of Malok, the people would never let me remain on the throne. They'd put me to death for everything I've done."

"King or not, it takes time to earn back trust once it's been lost."

"And it's impossible to reclaim your life once it's been lost," he countered. "It would be easier for you to become as I am than for me to become good again."

Seren stiffened.

"But that's not on the table, is it?"

Kadoc shook his head and placed his hand on hers.

"Not at all. I was only pointing out the impossibility of what you speak of. I—my *true* self—wouldn't subject you to Malok's yoke again. Please say that you believe me."

Even without taking a glimpse into Kadoc's heart, Seren knew he spoke the truth.

"I do, but you're not always this version of yourself."

"No, I'm not. Did you bring the Cuffs of Harreb with you?"

"Why?"

"If darkness overtakes me again, you have my permission to bind whatever powers you can with them. I don't want to hurt you."

As comforting as that statement was meant to be, Seren knew that she wouldn't be able to trick Kadoc into wearing them if Malok invaded his heart once more. She'd be lucky if she escaped another encounter with the God of Darkness with her soul or her life.

"I'll keep that in mind."

Kadoc nodded and rose from the couch, his heart heavy but slightly more hopeful that it had been in quite some time.

"I'm sure you need to rest and prepare for the day ahead. This room is furnished with all of the clothes, comforts, and cosmetics you'll need during your stay. If you need anything, trace the flower engraved on your bedside table or the door and someone will assist you promptly. If you need me, trace the crown."

"Thank you."

With a small nod, Kadoc left the room, and a strange combination of relief and longing filled her heart. Instead of letting her mind wander, Seren chugged the broth and walked to her bed with considerably less pain. Within minutes of following the king's instructions for calling on the servants, she had a warm bath scented with fragrant oils and fresh flowers. Once she was sufficiently relaxed and cleansed, Seren consumed the rest of her meal and crawled under the covers once more for what she hoped would be a brief yet refreshing nap.

But what awaited her was no mere dream.

Though she was still lying in bed, the jeweled dress, veil, and flower petals strewn on the floor were far more luxurious than the modest dress she'd folded and neatly placed by the bathtub an hour before. The clothing also denoted that a very specific event had taken place the night before... and remembering that long-awaited event made her glow with joy as she rolled over to see her companion.

"Good morning, new wife."

Her cheeks reddened and heart fluttered at Kadoc's greeting.

"New wife? Is there an old wife that I'm not aware of?" she teased.

"You are my first, last, and only wife, but you're also my new wife because we made a covenant before the gods and the kingdom last night."

"We did? I had no idea."

"If we didn't, your father is going to be very unhappy with me."

"Lucky for you, my father loves you almost as much as I do."

Kadoc laughed and shook his head.

"I can't believe I get to wake up beside you every day for the rest of my life," he said. "I hope you know that I meant every vow I made during the ceremony. I will love and protect you until my dying breath and beyond."

"And I will love you and remain by your side every day of my life and beyond."

As Kadoc leaned in to seal their repeated vows with a kiss, his empty stomach growled loudly, interrupting their tender moment and inspiring quiet chuckles from the newlyweds.

"Do you love me enough to tell the staff that we're ready to break our fast?" he asked.

"Of course."

Seren began to sit up, but Kadoc gently grabbed her arm, laughing as he kissed her cheek.

"I'm jesting, my dove. I sent for breakfast when I saw you waking, so it will be here shortly," he revealed, making her hear swell as he smoothed her dark curls out of her face. "I'll find something for you to wear so we can make ourselves decent before the servants arrive. As much as I'd love to stay in bed, being waited on in my marriage bed by men and women who served me as a child isn't my idea of fun,"

After Kadoc pulled on a knee-length tunic and disappeared through the bed's drawn curtains, the vision vanished as well and gave way to the guest room. There, Seren awakened with longing and sadness pricking her tender heart. Perceiving that her ankle was fully healed, Seren vacated the bed to take a walk about the castle, hoping her impromptu stroll would help her decode whatever message the gods were attempting to tell her and cast the rapidly intensifying devotion from her heart.

The palace's staff gave her the distance she expected, and that space was nearly as distracting as their warmth would have been. Each averted gaze and hurried shuffle reminded Seren that the men and women who served her knew nothing of the woman she was. Their only experience was flinching under the shadow of their despotic queen and fleeing the wrath of their murderous, mourning king. The only person in the palace who had any fond feelings toward her was Kadoc, but he was hardly trustworthy so long as Malok had a hold on his heart.

That grim truth reminded her of Toren's supposed vision of her coming under Malok's control again. Because she'd fled so quickly, Seren hadn't been able to press him for details or even look into his heart, so she didn't know if his intentions were malicious or not. And if he truly saw her transform, was his vision a look into the past, an avoidable future event, or a fixed outcome that would hurt the very people she thought she'd been born to save? Unfortunately, she knew little about the young prophet's powers, and he was out of her grasp, so she had no way to learn more about his gift of foresight.

Yet as she passed the king's bedroom and saw the two guards flanking the entrance, she remembered the little Doran shared about his past and the night the king gave him the burn scar that wrapped around his neck. Based on the soldier's account, she knew that Kadoc still kept a seer in his palace despite his many gifts.

But can I trust him with my concerns? Seren wondered. *Then again, I can't really trust* anyone *right now.*

"Good morning, Your Majesty," a hesitant voice greeted.

Seren slowed her aimless amble and fixed her gaze on the elven woman on her right. Judging by her fine linen dress and golden jewelry, she was no servant. The absence of visible brands also meant that unlike Orla, she wasn't a member of Kadoc's harem, but she was certainly beautiful enough to be chosen for it with her thick, straight dark auburn hair and a lightly tanned complexion that spoke to her life of luxury or at least more scholarly pursuits indoors.

"Good morning," Seren replied.

As the two women studied one another, Seren saw that sadness haunted her forest green eyes and downcast heart instead of contempt or calculation.

"You don't know who I am," the crestfallen woman said.

"I'm sorry. I don't. Did we know each other in my previous life?"

"We were practically sisters," she answered. "I'm the king's first cousin Tierna. He told me that you'd regained some of your memories, but I suppose it was foolish of me to assume that any of them included me."

"It wasn't foolish. If we were as close as you say, I hope I gain some recollection of our friendship. It would be nice to remember something that inspires joy instead of turmoil."

Tierna took a step forward and lowered her voice.

"So, you're remembering events from after your change?"

"No, thankfully. Only things from before."

"Why would that inspire turmoil?"

Seren hesitated for a moment, but the true concern and warmth in Tierna's heart gave her the courage to speak what was in hers.

"If you're one of Kadoc's relatives, surely you've seen how he's spiraled into depravity since we lost our unborn child. To see how kind and innocent he was after a lifetime of only knowing rumors of his wickedness is… jarring. I would never knowingly yoke myself to the man he is now, but the gods are trying to awaken whatever love I felt for the man he was."

"Would loving the man he was really be so bad?"

The former queen opened her mouth to speak, but Tierna held up her hand and shook her head.

"You don't have to answer that. I've already asked too much of a woman who is more of a stranger than an old friend," she said with a sad smile. "I'll leave you to your morning, Your Majesty."

Tierna briefly bowed her head in deference before scampering away with her spirits low and shoulders hunched. Seeing her former in-law's woe inspired an inward groan, but Seren pressed on to find Aled. As much as she wanted to learn more about Kadoc's cousin and whatever friendship they once had, finding the prophet was her priority. While she had no memories of him, her swiftly stepping feet seemed to remember exactly where he spent his days in the palace.

After descending to the ground floor and walking past the great hall and throne room, Seren came upon a set of double doors that hummed with magic. Like her door upstairs, his featured a set of carved shapes on the frame, a flower, a crown, and a shape that made her cheeks flush with embarrassment. Apparently Kadoc wasn't the only man who used his position to his *very* personal benefit.

Shaking off her disgust, Seren squared her shoulders and knocked. After some shuffling and cursing, a thin old man with long graying black hair answered the door with a glare that would have made lesser women shrivel. Upon recognizing his unexpected guest, Aled wiped the scowl from his face and bowed.

"My apologies, Your Majesty. I wasn't expecting you."

"It's all right. I didn't exactly make an appointment. May I come in?"

"Of course."

Aled opened the door wider and gestured for Seren to enter, keeping his gaze trained on the ground. Once she was inside, Seren swept her eyes across the room. The smell of unfamiliar incense filled the seer's private library, both providing a pleasant scent and relaxing its newest guest as she noted the many unfurled scrolls, spellcasting supplies, and very feminine-looking personal items littering the round table in the center of the room. As Seren stepped closer, she recognized the bridal veil she'd seen in her dream.

"Were you trying to cast a spell on me or conjure a vision about me?"

"The latter, Your Majesty. The king is curious to see what your future holds."

"What have you seen?"

"Nothing."

"If I asked you to stop, would you?"

"No, my Queen. His Majesty's commands take priority over yours."

"Of course," Seren said, disappointment flashing in her eyes.

"If you have a request for me, I still consider myself your servant. However, I cannot go against my king's orders."

"I don't, but please tell me if you have any visions about me."

"I will," Aled said with a bow.

Since the moment he recognized Seren, Aled hadn't made even a moment of eye contact. The seer was one of Kadoc's most trusted, elevated advisors and was the closest thing to a friend that the king had, but he couldn't bear the weight of the resurrected queen's gaze. As she studied the unexpectedly meek seer, Seren felt the tumultuous mixture of fear, uncertainty, and guilt in his heart. Each time she'd detected fear in men's hearts, shame welled up in hers, but remembering the seer's deadly counsel to Kadoc aroused anger instead.

Twenty years before, Aled's vision and counsel frightened Kadoc into doing the unthinkable. With little deliberation, Kadoc murdered his own wife, the woman he'd sworn to love and protect until death and murdered countless children to preserve his position. But if Aled hadn't given that deadly recommendation, she would still be the most hated, feared queen in Eaiven's history instead of the woman her parents raised her to be. She couldn't bring back the men, women, and children who died during Kadoc's reign, but she could use her new life to end that bloodshed.

"Aled," she coaxed gently, "please look at me."

The seer lifted his chin slightly and met her gaze with troubled brown eyes.

"I know about the counsel you gave Kadoc and that you're part of the reason he killed me, but you have nothing to fear from me. I won't seek to punish or torment you for the part you played in my death, but you have a long road to walk before I can trust you again."

The elderly elf slowly knelt before Seren and kissed her hand.

"Thank you for your undeserved mercy, my Queen. I desire more than anything for our friendship to be as it was before."

"If Millam could bring peace between elves and ogres in Agron, I'm sure he could mend a broken friendship in time," she said with a slight smile. "Please stand up."

Shock flickered in Aled's heart as Seren helped him to his feet, but she thought nothing of it. Even she was surprised that more anger didn't rise in the presence of her one-time traitor. Instead of pressing him any further, Seren bade him farewell and retreated to the palace gardens. Fear, regret, suspicion, and expectation filled the hearts of every person she encountered, and fresh air and solitude suddenly seemed infinitely more appealing than seeking the few familiar faces in the palace or waiting for a former friend or foe to find her.

★   ★   ★

The rest of the day passed with something resembling normalcy. After an uneventful stroll through the gardens, Seren went to the library and perused a few scrolls, hoping for one of the holy writings to spark an idea or a memory that could help her navigate her newfound predicament. To her disappointment and slight relief, she found no inspiration from the scrolls, but the king's appearance halfway through the story of the agloc's creation distracted her from the fruitless task.

"I didn't realize you enjoyed reading so much."

"My father is a scribe, so scholarly pursuits were a large part of my upbringing," Seren said, carefully re-rolling the scroll and setting it aside. "Did you need something?"

"A rebel named Doran was captured near the Agron border. If I remember correctly, he's the one who spirited you away after your awakening."

An icy sensation shot down Seren's spine.

"Are you going to kill him?"

"Do you want me to?"

"Of course not!"

"Don't sound so shocked. You *did* say that they betrayed you."

"Some of them did, but Doran tried to help me escape."

Kadoc studied Seren for a moment, and she noticed envy bubbling in his spirit.

"There's no reason to be jealous of Doran. He's only a friend and barely even that."

"You can read hearts. I didn't expect that."

Seren furrowed her brow for a moment, realizing that Kadoc didn't know what her gifts were. The only people who witnessed her receive her gifts were Doran and his deceased comrade, so her receiving the enchanted necklace was all he knew about her awakening.

"Why is that such a shock?"

"I thought that you'd have the powers the gods gave you last time. You could inspire fear in people's hearts and control fire. What other gifts do you possess now?"

"I can also control water."

"Can you create water as well?"

"Yes, I can."

"Interesting… You couldn't spark flames until after you took the God of Darkness' elixir," he mused. "In any case, I'd like you to be present when we question the traitor."

"If by 'question' you mean 'torture,' I don't want to have any part in it."

"What if I swear not to cause any physical or magical harm to him?"

"Why are you so determined to have me there?"

"Because you're my wife and queen, and your place is by my side. You once helped me rule this kingdom, and I'd like you to do so again."

Seren drummed her fingers on the table as she considered his reasoning. The gods had been pretty clear that they still considered her Kadoc's wife, but how much did they want her to honor their old covenant if her ultimate purpose was to defeat him?

At the very least, maybe my presence will force him to be more civil.

"I will attend Doran's questioning, but my role here is not what it was before. I don't plan to remain here forever, but as long as I'm in the palace, I will only help you if it means helping the people. I won't be a party to the evil you commit."

"I'll agree to that."

Relief flooded both royals' spirits as Seren abandoned her fruitless exploration. The king smiled as Seren took his arm, and her pulse fluttered with a heady combination of anxiety and excitement. Looking into the king's prismatic eyes then letting her gaze drift to his upturned lips, she felt the inexplicable urge to close the distance between them with a brief kiss, and she detected the same amorous desire in him. Yet fear cast that impulse from her heart before she could act on it. Instead, the shaking maiden stepped away.

"I-I think I put one of the scrolls back in the wrong place. I should—"

"I'm not going to kiss you again, Seren," he interrupted, his voice just above a whisper. "I was wrong for doing so without your consent the day we met, and I swear by Millam's stars to treat you as a sister until you say otherwise. The last thing I want is for you to fear or resent me for being too familiar with you again."

Kadoc extended his hand, and Seren heaved a deep breath before hesitantly stepping forward and assuming her previous position once more. Then, the pair left the library to pay the palace's latest unwilling guest a visit.

After leaving the palace and crossing the courtyard to enter the watchtower, the foul stench of excrement, blood, and unwashed bodies assaulted Seren's nostrils, and the color drained from her face. As they walked over the prisoners' cells, which were hewn into the floor, she cautiously glanced downward to see what the crown's supposed enemies looked like. Alas, none of the palace prison's occupants crept forward to see whose footsteps echoed above. The guards, however, were far more eager to greet them.

"The new prisoner is in his cell, Your Majesty. Would you like to speak to him?" one uneasy protector asked.

"Yes, please."

The guards shuffled to the cell at the back of the shadowy room and unlocked the barred entrance. Then, one of the sentries descended into the cell. After several moments, the guard emerged with Doran, who'd been stripped to his loin cloth and bound in heavy chains. Though there wasn't a single bruise on the rebel's body, Seren knew that was no indication of how he'd been treated. After all, the former spy could heal himself quickly, which meant that someone didn't need to be skilled at torture to leave him intact enough to face the king's questioning.

Doran met Seren's concerned gaze and nodded, giving her permission to read his heart. As she reached out with her power, she felt relief and slight annoyance—hopefully, an indication that he'd been treated fairly well since his capture.

"Why did you come back to Eaiven?" Kadoc asked. "Because of your treasonous actions at the sacred pool, I could have you executed without a moment's hesitation."

Doran spat in Kadoc's direction, earning a swift punch to the face from the guard who'd retrieved him.

"Answer your king, you traitorous snake," the hostile sentry barked.

"Was that necessary?" Seren snapped.

"Fedhlim ran you out of Agron, and then one of his men appears in my kingdom the next day. Don't you want to know why he's here?"

"Not if it means acting like barbarians. He doesn't deserve to be treated like this."

"What about what *I* deserve? Aren't I still the king? Don't I deserve respect?"

Seren lowered her voice to a whisper.

"You should know better than anyone that you deserve your subjects' derision, not their respect. If you want me to believe that I can trust you, have some humility, and treat him with dignity."

Darkness stirred within Kadoc's spirit, and an accusing voice taunted him with all the reasons Doran deserved his wrath and the promise of gratification from spilling his blood. Sensing the malice lurking in the king's heart, Seren reached out and took his hand. In an instant, her touch cast out the seductive hiss, and Kadoc's mind quieted enough that only his natural vanity remained.

"I only came with you because you promised not to hurt Doran," Seren continued. "I won't stay here if you insist on letting your men bully and beat my friend."

"And if he refuses to answer my questions?"

"Let me question him on my own. I won't take part in any questioning that would hurt the elves seeking refuge in Agron, but if you want to know why he is here, I can at least ask him that. If you choose to do more, that will be on your conscience."

"Fine. My men and I will wait outside. If he tries to hurt you—"

"He won't. You're more of a danger to me than he'll ever be."

Kadoc held Seren's determined gaze for a moment before nodding reluctantly and raising his voice to command the guards.

"The queen will be questioning the prisoner alone. Let's give her the room."

The disappointed yet obedient guards vacated the room with their king, leaving Seren and Doran with only the palace's silent, unseen prisoners for company. As the maiden drew closer to her friend, she remembered how their fortunes had been reversed only days before when she was led through Agron in chains.

"Men are too quick to put one another in chains," she lamented, not knowing how to break the awkward silence. "Are you thirsty at all?"

"A drink couldn't hurt."

Seren picked up a discarded cup from the table where the guards had been casting lots earlier and used her power to fill it with water. Then, she held it up to Doran's lips so he could enjoy the drink without burdening his shackled hands. The moment the refreshing beverage touched his parched tongue, strength filled Doran's bones and the weariness his imprisonment inspired evaporated.

"Thank you," he said. "I could march to Aden and back on that cup alone."

"It's the least I could do after last night. Thank you for helping me get away. Did Fedhlim cast you out for it?"

"Not at all. He recanted his orders after he recovered from that deluge you unleashed and sent me to rescue you."

Seren narrowed her eyes at Doran's news.

"He was bent on killing me because Toren told him I'd become evil again. Why would he change his mind so quickly?"

"He told me that an inexplicably malicious sort of jealousy came over him when your father rejected his offer of marriage. When Malan came to him with your plan to capture an agloc, he saw your insubordination as an opportunity to lash out at you for rejecting him. And his enmity deepened when you couldn't deny your feelings for the king."

"Why would he be so wounded by my rejection? He barely knows me, and he seemed pretty content with his life."

"I don't know any more than he does, but he asked me to pass along his message in hopes that you would forgive him and return to Aden."

Seren turned away, running a hand through her hair as she contemplated Doran's tale. She wanted to believe that Fedhlim's madness had left as quickly as it came, but she'd be risking her life if she returned to Agron and placed herself under his suddenly unstable leadership. Just as she began to weigh her options, her mind turned to their brief confrontation the night before. After Fedhlim gave the order to kill her, she noticed a shadow like the one that emanated from Kadoc during their ill-fated supper undulate around the rebels' leader.

Is Malok influencing Fedhlim too? If so, did my water set him free?

"He came to his senses when I used my powers on him, correct?"

"Yes. I think hitting the ground knocked some sense into him."

"Did he tell you about the dead women that were found outside the city?"

"No, he didn't."

"Someone found three women's corpses near the road, and they bore the same wounds as the aglocs we killed on our way back from Harreb's cave. I had a hypothesis that my water purged the darkness from them just like it awakened the boy at the inn. I left the city last night thinking that Malan would help me test my powers on a live agloc, because if I could turn a daughter of the Cursed One into a normal woman, I may be able to remove the evil from Kadoc as well."

"Interesting…"

"If Fedhlim was also being controlled or influenced by the Cursed One, the magic in my water may have been what stilled his hand, not just a knock on the head."

"Then will you return to Aden?"

"I can't leave Riamon without trying to set Kadoc free. The gods may have brought me back to cure Kadoc—not kill him."

"And if it doesn't work?"

"I don't know. Even without drenching him, I've seen flickers of goodness and remorse in him. Kadoc isn't the irredeemable monster we think he is."

"He has massacred *countless* innocent elves, ogres, and faeries, and he even gave me this blasted scar as a child!" The fuming rebel's chains clanging violently as he gestured to his neck. "He has to be held accountable for what he's done, and death is the only sentence he's worthy of."

"But what about me?"

"This is bigger than your ridiculous feelings, Seren. He's a murderer and tyrant."

"I'm not talking about my feelings, and I'm talking about *me*... the woman who was his consort in the bloodiest reign our people have ever seen. I don't know how many people I killed or even remember my final victim, but I was just as evil and under the Cursed One's influence as Kadoc. Yet the gods gave me a second chance and a gift that may do the same for him. Do you think I deserve death?"

The soldier opened his mouth to speak, but Seren didn't give him the opportunity.

"And what about you? Even though you were spying for Fedhlim, I know that you committed acts that you're ashamed of while you were in the royal army. Why else would you have told me that I wouldn't like what I saw if I looked into your heart?" Seren took a step forward, defiantly holding the spy's steely gaze. "What would I see if I could see not just your heart but your memories as well? Would I see anything that would be deserving of a sword slicing through your neck?"

Doran clenched his jaw for a moment.

"He can't just go free and stay on the throne after everything he's done."

"I agree, but that's not a decision for either of us to make in this dungeon today. The gods have orchestrated this at least since the moment they gave Aled his prophecy. If Kadoc can be freed of Malok's influence, then that can be the first step in pursuing justice. If all the gods wanted was swift judgement with a sword or club, I don't think they would have given me these specific powers and memories. Killing him would have been much easier if they'd given me different gifts or a even desire for revenge over my death."

"But are you willing to end his life if you're wrong and that *is* what they intend?"

"I will submit to whatever the gods' will is no matter how hard it is. Will you?"

Doran fixed his narrowed eyes on the closed door behind her.

"You should fetch your husband. I've said my peace."

Dejection invaded Seren's spirit at the sound of his chilly tone, but she nodded.

"All right. I will do what I can to make sure they treat you well."

When the soldier-spy didn't respond, Seren walked back to the door with a sigh and stepped into the hallway.

"I'm done questioning the prisoner, I'd like to speak with the king alone."

"Yes, Your Majesty," the guards chorused before entering the depressing chamber.

"What did you find out?" Kadoc asked.

"Fedhlim sent him because he recognized that attacking me last night was a mistake. He wants me to return to Agron."

"The man tried to have you killed, and now he expects you to leave your homeland to follow him again? He must be mad!"

"He's not mad, but I'm not returning. I'd like to stay here at least for a while."

A joyful smile lit up Kadoc's pale face, and his grin melted her defenses a bit even though a twinge of fear still pricked her spirit.

"That is the best news I've heard in years."

"I do have a request though."

"Name it."

"Set him free, and consider him forgiven."

"I can't do that. He has committed treason, and according to our laws, he deserves death."

"The law also gives the king the right to grant clemency according to his own judgment. If you did this, it would send a message to your people here and in Agron that you're not the irredeemable oppressor they've trembled under all these years."

"One act of compassion won't wipe away a century of misdeeds, and it certainly won't reverse what I've done to myself."

"But what if something could? What if there was a way to cast out the Cursed One's influence and make you yourself again?"

"Have you found this supposed cure, or are you speaking in hypotheticals?"

"Both. I've seen it work on other creatures he created, and I believe it could do the same for you."

"I've accumulated many powers over the years because of my bond with Malok. If I lose them, I will be defenseless against those who hate me."

"Maybe they'll forgive you once they learn why you changed."

"Or maybe they'll slice through my neck with a sharpened sword and burn my lifeless body to light their celebrations," he muttered. "No one will let me live in peace if I surrender my power."

"The people are scared and angry. They'll want justice and vengeance, but—"

"Am I correct in assuming that my current state is so offensive to you that you'd never truly be my wife again so long as I'm under Malok's influence?"

Seren held her tongue as she detected the dejection, fear, and rage in the king's narrowed, prismatic eyes. Yet she knew that the truth—as disappointing as is may be—could push Kadoc to consider her offer.

"Yes," she sighed. "I may not be free to marry another, but I cannot act like a wife until I can see that you are a man I can trust and submit to in good conscience."

"Well, I hope your conscience will keep your bed as warm as my concubines will keep mine tonight, because I see no reason to forsake them anymore."

A sharp, unexpected pang struck Seren's heart as Kadoc stalked past her. Though she wasn't completely shocked by his response, she was taken aback by the sting she felt at the prospect of him lying with Orla or another recently shunned concubine. She had no desire to be intimate with Kadoc despite the tenderness in her heart, but knowing that he resided only a few doors away and spitefully satiated himself with someone else made her face flush and her body quake with rage.

Seren clenched her hands into fists and took a step forward as her pulse roared in her ears, but hearing the guards taunting their prisoners brought her back from the brink. She couldn't let her anger and unanticipated jealousy drive her to further damage her relationship with the hotheaded king. So she closed her eyes, took three deep breaths, and left the dismal corridor with the same levelheadedness and poise she arrived with.

★　　　　★　　　　★

After spending the rest of the afternoon attempting to dampen her jealousy and wrath by reading every scroll she could find on Malok, Seren returned to her room with weary eyes and a heavy heart. As she dragged herself through the hallway, Seren caught sight of a familiar face and braced herself for another unpleasant interaction.

"Well, well, well, if it isn't the most frigid wife in Eaiven," Orla taunted.

"Shouldn't you be enjoying your return to the king's good graces instead of tormenting me?"

"Good graces?" she snorted. "Our *magnanimous* sovereign just announced that he's relocating the whole harem to the winter palace immediately. I'm being exiled to that dismal stronghold because all he cares about is plowing your precious garden."

Seren gaped at Orla, dumbstruck by the seething concubine's news.

"I didn't ask him to do that."

Orla took a step forward, her lip curled and eyes flashing with rage.

"Killing you was the best decision he ever made, and I pray to Malok that he sucks the life from you again at the most painful, unexpected moment possible."

Much like her former lover, Orla stormed past Seren, pushing her rival into the wall in the process. Yet this confrontation inspired hope instead of anger. Despite Kadoc's harsh words during their argument, he'd taken another step away from debauchery instead of seeking solace in it once more. Rather than returning to her room, Seren made a detour to the king's. At her request, the guards announced her presence to their master, who quickly had them usher her inside.

"Your timing is impeccable because I was about to come find you," Kadoc said. "You answered me honestly when I asked you a question, and I rewarded your vulnerability with spite. Will you please forgive me?"

"Of course. I know you're fighting more darkness than most elves can fathom right now."

"Thank you," he breathed. "I was foolish to expect your acceptance when we are so different now. It's a wonder that you would remain here of your own free will after everything I've done to you."

"I don't know what to say."

"Say that you'll have dinner with me at Brigh tonight."

"Brigh? As in…"

"As in where I proposed to you, yes. But I assure you my intent is not to seduce you… only to spend time with you in a place that hasn't been tainted by our darkest years. I have business to tend to outside of the palace, so we can even travel there and back separately."

Seren considered Kadoc's invitation for a moment, questioning if the night out with the king would compromise her safety or her virtue. But as she gazed into his pleading eyes, she acknowledged that distance and location had no bearing on her wellbeing. Kadoc was the most dangerous man in Eaiven and he could appear at her side without warning whenever he wished, but unquenchable affection resided within his darkened heart. His tainted yet genuine love and the regret it inspired would protect her more than a palace full of servants or settlement filled with soldiers ever could.

"All right. I accept your invitation."

"Then my men will have a carriage waiting for you in an hour."

"Thank you."

Delightfully bewildered by the king's change of heart, Seren returned to her room. Minutes later, a servant appeared with a selection of dresses and jewelry for the night's excursion. As Seren ran her hands over the soft, delicate fabric and inhaled its light, floral scent, ease and familiarity invaded her heart. Though she couldn't recall the times when she'd worn the queenly garments, she could easily imagine herself wearing the linen, gold, sapphires, and diamonds in the palace and beautifying herself with the perfume and cosmetics set before her.

The absence of hesitation in her heart was a welcome change, and she couldn't help entreating Millam, asking the King of the Gods to give her wisdom and grant her a peaceful dinner with the vacillating king.

After settling on a white stola and a scarlet palla, which were both embellished with golden embroidery, Seren donned the expensive garments and let the eager servant curl and braid her hair into a regal yet simple updo before applying a bit of rouge to her lips and cheeks. As she gazed into the mirror, the reflection she beheld was as uncannily familiar and comforting as the clothing and routine had been. Even without clear memories of her time on the throne, she acknowledged that some long-dormant part of her spirit missed the pampering and prestige that came with being a queen.

When the time finally came to leave the palace, Seren boarded the horse-drawn carriage and used the hour-long journey to Brigh to simply enjoy the rhythmic ride and watch the passing countryside. The artisans who crafted the carriage had employed a spellcaster to enchant its exterior. So while Seren could look outside through the window and feel the fresh air on her smiling face, all anyone along the road could see were wooden walls.

As the carriage traveled down the road, Seren admired the blossoming trees and the enchanted lanterns that adorned them. Kadoc's paranoia about spellcasters hadn't stopped him from giving his surroundings their magic touch. However, once she left the royal estate the magical lanterns gave way to thalsach vines, where luminescent butterflies gathered to feed on the orange flowers' sweet nectar. The sun was still high enough in the sky to light their way, but the butterflies' delicate wings and slender bodies gently illuminated the shadowy tree line with a warm glow. When the sun dipped behind the horizon, the fluttering insects would reach their full brilliance and provide enough light to help elves travel without darkness concealing their path.

Seeing that transition from the magical to the mundane forced Seren to remember the tragic, stifling effects of Kadoc's reign. The king's greed had robbed the elves of the magic the gods intended for them to have and so much more. Yet she couldn't even pretend to hate him. Mistrust kept her from humoring the love swelling in her heart, that growing affection kept her from leaving his side, and fear kept her from acting on her hypothesis that she could purge the evil from the king's body. If her untested plan didn't work, Kadoc's wrath and wickedness could manifest in a way that she couldn't survive. And if her water killed him instead of cleaning the darkness from his soul, her heart would be broken—maybe beyond repair.

Shrugging off that chilly thought, Seren focused once more on her homeland's natural beauty, recalling wisps of verses that poets and lyricists wrote about the fragrant, deep green leaves, sighing flowers, and humming vines. By the time the shore came into view, her heart was more settled but still uncertain. Rather than praying to Millam as she often did, Seren clutched her amulet in her trembling right hand and asked Inneh to bless their time and let love reign in their hearts instead of fear and evil.

When the carriage rolled to a stop, the driver hopped down from his post, opened the door, and helped her to the ground. Lit torches cast a golden glow on the marble walls, but the sea's salty scent overpowered the aroma of burning wood. For a moment, Seren closed her eyes and breathed in the refreshing seaside air, briefly lamenting that her parents had always been too concerned with selling their wares at the market and academia to enjoy the gods' beautiful creation. Most of her childhood was spent indoors or in a stall surrounded by merchants, so she'd never seen the sea before. As she glanced at the crashing waves, feelings of safety and belonging quieted her mind and slowed her pulse.

She felt like she was home.

With a smile on her face and peace in her heart, Seren entered the villa and followed the servant through the magnificent home, past incomparable frescos and sculptures, and back outside, where Kadoc awaited to escort her the short distance to their seaside dinner. Despite her earlier hesitation, Seren took his arm without pause and accompanied him through the small but nearly kept garden to their table.

"How was your journey here?" he asked.

"Blessedly uneventful," she chuckled. "This is my first time traveling for leisure instead of necessity, and I rather like it."

"I'm glad to hear it. This is the most at ease I've seen you since we met. Elves tend to be more comfortable around their elements, so I'm glad I suggested coming to Brigh."

"I hadn't even thought about that," she marveled as he pulled out her chair and she took her seat. "Were you originally an elemental?"

"Yes, wind was one of my original gifts, so I feel the most peaceful in the plains or in the mountains unless there's a storm brewing."

"Can you control any other elements now?"

"Everything except water, but I don't feel the same serenity around fire or earth that I do around the wind. The gods don't reward theft with peace."

"Of course..." Seren scanned the tablescape for something they could discuss outside of Kadoc's iniquities. "Your servants put together an impressive array in a such a short period of time. They're very talented."

"And very motivated. Everyone knows how much it means to me to have your company again, and your presence has reawakened parts of my soul that I thought were lost forever," he said pouring her a cup of wine. "This used to be one of your favorite wines. It has hints of blackberry and honey."

When Seren took the first sip and tasted the sweet, fruity wine, her taste buds practically danced with delight. While she'd only tasted wine that fine during their previous dinner, something about the full-bodied beverage was unexpectedly familiar. After taking a second sip, she glanced at Kadoc again and saw him smiling at her positive reaction to the drink.

"It's delicious," she praised.

"I'm glad you like it," he said, raising his cup. "To new beginnings."

"To new beginnings."

After the simple toast, they began their modest feast. The first course of cheeses, bread, honey, and boiled eggs inspired the same feelings of comfort and familiarity as the wine, and her defenses gradually lowered with every sip and bite. By the time the main course of deer, lamb, and turtle doves was served, Seren felt more safe in Kadoc's presence than she ever had before.

"My father would be so jealous if he saw this," she divulged as a servant carved the roasted meat. "He always loved your cook's lamb, and—"

Seren stopped herself, realizing she was speaking of Neassa's father and not her displaced patriarch in Agron.

"Is something wrong?"

"No, I just... Never mind."

She dabbed away the sweat that rapidly beaded on her forehead, and the edges of her vision blurred and darkened. As Seren's gaze rested on the lamb again, she saw the blood that pooled as the servant carved it, and the world around her fell away. Instead of the sunset seascape, hundreds of corpses and writhing elves filled her vision. A flicker of movement caught her attention, and she crossed the decimated battlefield in a wink before placing her foot on the crawling rebel's bloody back.

"P-Please... h-have m-mercy," he blubbered as blood bubbled from his chapped lips.

"If you wanted mercy, you should've stayed still."

Without hesitation, she drove her sword through his heart, grinning as the light went out of his eyes.

"You're too kind," Kadoc teased, coming to stand beside her. "I would've spilled his entrails and let him die more slowly."

The vision vanished as quickly as it appeared, but vomit rose in her throat and throbbing pain assailed her head when the beach reappeared. Seren leaned over and emptied the first courses of their feast onto the sand, which bucked and tilted as her dizziness intensified.

"Something is wrong," she panted as tears wet her cheeks. "The memories haven't felt like this before."

"Nothing is wrong. This is a perfectly normal reaction to the potion."

"Potion?"

"I'm helping you return to your former self. We can never be together so long as you're detached from who you once were, so I'm giving both of us what we truly desire."

"You treacherous..."

When Seren attempted to stand, her legs lost their strength as another gory scene passed before her eyes and she collapsed to the ground. Kadoc abandoned his seat and knelt by her side, pulling her into his arms.

"I promise you'll be all right. Just be still and stop fighting it."

Piercing pain shot through Seren's skull, causing her to cry out in pain and dig her nails into his arm. Realizing that she had neither the strength nor the skill to fight the potion, she decided to fight back in the only way she could. Closing her watering eyes, Seren called to mind the last time she was at Brigh.

She pictured Kadoc as the gods created him—innocent, loving, and untouched by Malok's corruption. She embraced the adoration, anticipation, and joy that filled her heart when he made his life-altering proposal. And she grudgingly acknowledged within that the same love that allowed her to enthusiastically agree to marry the unaltered prince was the force driving her unwillingness to end his life or their seemingly irreparably damaged marriage.

In that moment of torment and surrender, Seren used the last of her strength to pull Kadoc toward her for a kiss. As their lips touched, water seeped from every inch of her body and covered the king, soaking his immaculate clothing and even pouring from her mouth into his. Under normal circumstances, Kadoc would have sensed and defended himself against her powers, but his surprise, overconfidence, and elation prevented him from recognizing her stealthy attack until a strange burning sensation began in his core and spread to the rest of his body. Steam and vibrating black mist rose from his flesh, and he collapsed beside Seren, arching his back and clawing at his throat.

"What have you done?" He rasped, his eyes black as oblivion.

"Just be still and stop..."

Before Seren could finish mocking the writhing king, the world was plunged into darkness, and she prayed that her soul wouldn't follow suit.

CHAPTER 7
Light Dawns in the East

When Seren joined the waking world again, she didn't immediately spring out of bed. Instead, she kept her eyes squeezed shut and searched her heart for any signs of evil. Of course, fear was her closest companion followed closely by fury toward her duplicitous husband, but her anger was neither murderous nor calculating. Hesitantly satisfied with that brief assessment, she reached up, took a lock of hair between her unsteady fingertips, and opened her eyes. Upon seeing the same dark ringlets she'd possessed hours before, she threw her arm over her eyes and wept in relief.

Kadoc's plan had failed.

Yet as Seren recalled the previous night's events, dread invaded her soul. If Kadoc's potion had failed to change her and her water failed to change him, it was only a matter of time before his single-minded pursuit or searing rage caught up to her. After nearly a century of marriage, she knew better than anyone how relentless and ruthless her husband could be, and she had no intention of being his victim again.

With that in mind, Seren slipped out of bed as quietly as possible, put on her sandals, and walked to the window. The guest room she'd been placed in faced the sea, and unless Kadoc had the estate redone, the stables were downstairs and around the corner to her right.

Momentarily lamenting her fine ensemble's decline, Seren used her belt to gird her loins before tying her discarded stola around her neck in a manner that would have made both of her mothers cluck their tongues in disapproval. Then, she swung her legs over the side of the balcony and began the brief climb down. Though she'd last made the climb many decades before to steal away for moonlit, chaperone free walks with Kadoc, her hands and feet still remembered every ridge and handhold.

When the queen's feet touched the mosaic-tiled porch, satisfaction and confidence emboldened her, and she turned to continue her journey to the stables. Unfortunately, a familiar voice caressed her ears before she could take another step.

"Did you really think I would leave you in a room that wasn't warded?"

"Did you really think I would wait for you to—?"

Seren turned around to face Kadoc, her hands raised in anticipation of another less than friendly confrontation, but she stumbled backward with a gasp upon seeing her husband. Though he still possessed the same impressive height and warrior's build, the king's hair had darkened from its hoary hue to the chestnut shade he was born with. And his eyes were the deep brown shade she once drowned in and dreamed of as a maiden. Even his skin had deepened from alabaster perfection to its former tanned tone. But the greatest change was his heart, which was burdened with trepidation, longing, shame, and self-hatred. Not a single wisp of malice or calculation remained.

Sensing her lowered defenses, Kadoc took a step forward, but Seren lifted her hands once more.

"Stay where you are."

"I've changed, Neassa. I'm not the man I was last night."

"Don't call me that. I am still Seren, the daughter of Kalbhac."

"So you didn't regain your memories?"

"I did, and you're lucky that's all I regained. If the Cursed One had his claws in me again, you would be the first of *many* dead elves right now!"

"Seren, I wasn't trying to complete Malok's ritual again. I was only trying to restore your memories."

"Which is still an enormous violation," she screamed, tears springing into her narrowed eyes. "I could have happily gone my entire life without remembering the atrocities I committed. You had no right!"

Kadoc's shoulders slumped as he turned his gaze downward.

"I know."

"You can't just use magic on people without their permission because it suits you!"

"I know," he repeated tremulously. "I've committed so many wrongs against you and our people that I couldn't count them even if I tried. I don't deserve your forgiveness, so I won't ask for it or ask you to stay. But if you're going to leave, you should at least have an escort. I can have your driver take you to the palace and release your friend so you can return to Agron safely."

Seren scrutinized Kadoc for a moment, struggling to hold onto her anger as contrition and self-hatred radiated from him and permeated her surroundings like strong incense. Kadoc loathed himself more than she ever could and craved the release that only death could bring... release not just from his guilt but from looking into the eyes of the woman he treasured more than anything and seeing only rage.

That glimpse into Kadoc's heart shook Seren to the core. No matter how angry she was with Kadoc, she still loved him, and her world would have crumbled if he took his own life because she was too lost in her own anger to extend comfort when he desperately needed it. Malok had deprived her of a loving husband and the people of a magnanimous king for so long by tainting him with darkness, and now he sought to do so by claiming his life.

Instead of proclaiming her infuriatingly stubborn affections, Seren simply pulled him into her arms. Then, Kadoc wept for the first time since their unborn child died over a century before, and his grief dismantled Seren's remaining defenses. The pair clung to one another, weeping and lamenting their tragic paths and deadly choices until their eyes were as raw as their hearts.

"I'm so sorry, Seren. This is all my fault. I willingly tainted my own soul, but I subjected you to the same darkness instead of protecting you from it."

"We lost so much the when the earthquake struck, and the Cursed One took advantage of your grief. I don't know anyone who would be in their right mind after losing a father and a son on the same day."

"That doesn't excuse what I've done," he said, wiping away her tears. "I've failed you and our people in ways I never thought possible."

"But the gods have given you a second chance, and they clearly want me to as well judging by their methods. We both need to take care that we use this gift wisely and guard ourselves against the Cursed One. He lost a powerful servant last night, and I doubt he'll be happy about it."

"No, he won't," Kadoc sighed. "This is the first day in over a hundred years that I haven't heard his voice whispering in my mind. I wish I could say that it feels peaceful, but it feels lonely instead... hopeless even."

"Well, perhaps we can fill your mind with something else. We destroyed all of Millam's temples in the capital, but there's a small one in Gridein. We should go there to make a sacrifice."

"Would he even accept a sacrifice from me?"

"I doubt he would have brought this about if his intention was to reject you," Seren answered. "Have any servants seen you like this?"

"Yes, but I told them not to repeat what happened here to anyone else. They may not understand the gravity of what transpired last night, but they still fear me too much to be disobedient."

"Do any of them worship the Cursed One?"

"No."

"Good. The fewer people who know about this the better."

"I agree. With that in mind, we should ride to Gridein alone. I never visited your town, so no one will recognize me in this state, but a royal carriage and escorts will draw unwanted attention. I'll find some servants' clothes for us to wear, and you should eat something before we leave. You barely ate anything last night, and you'll need your strength."

"All right, but you need to eat too. I'll go to the kitchen and find something for us to nibble on while you secure transportation for us."

"Perfect."

Kadoc leaned forward ever so slightly as if to give his wife a parting kiss, but ended their embrace instead of intensifying it.

"I will join you in the kitchen shortly."

Before Seren could offer a surely awkward response, Kadoc disappeared into the villa. In that brief moment of solitude, she turned her eyes to the sky and her heart to Millam.

Please guide and protect us in this new chapter of our lives, and give this kingdom the healing it needs.

After her brief yet heartfelt prayer, the uncertain queen righted her bundled dress and entered the villa once more to prepare for the journey ahead.

★   ★   ★

Thirty minutes and one modest breakfast later, the pair mounted their horses and traveled across Eaiven from their seaside escape to Seren's home village. They rejected the well-paved King's Highway in favor of a shortcut through the countryside so they could travel more stealthily and speedily. Shedding their more ostentatious clothing in favor of drab, woolen garments also helped conceal their identities, and the lack of toll bridges on the way to their destination meant that they could avoid elven contact and scrutiny during their travels.

An hour and a half later, Gridein came into view, and they slowed from a gallop to a slower, easy gait as they approached the small gate in the village's wooden walls. As planned, they dismounted just before the entrance and Seren took the lead. Both guards were too preoccupied with the adorable stray pup that begged for their roasted hare to question the city's newest visitors, so Seren and Kadoc passed through the gate without conversation. Once inside the city, Seren kept her senses sharp and face hidden as they avoided the crowded marketplace and walked through the residential area to the temple.

As they hitched their horses outside and ascended the weathered stone steps, the scent of myrrh and sandalwood tickled Seren's nose and teased her troubled heart with the promise of serenity. Once they were inside, the warm glow of innumerable lamps bathed the simple, circular chamber in light and illuminated the fresco of the elves' creation story that began with Millam's triumph over the other gods to the King of the Gods crafting the first elves from clay and breathing life into their bodies. It wasn't as grand as the artwork in the palace or the villa, but the familiar, slightly faded painting reminded Seren of the twenty years she'd spent worshipping and finding comfort in Millam with her family and friends.

She felt at home.

"Seren!" a voice called.

Seren glanced to her right and saw Aerin, a priest, entering with oil for the lamps. Abandoning composure, she quickly crossed the holy chamber and pulled the aging holy man in for a fierce hug, luxuriating in the his familiar, comforting embrace. The white-haired elf had been one of the priests for Gridein her whole life, living simply and modestly as he performed sacrifices, kept the lamps lit, and prayed for the people every day. She'd served as a lamp lighter for most of her adolescence and learned about the gods at his right hand, making him like a second father to her.

"I thought I'd never see you again," he said. "Your parents told me that you'd been taken away after your awakening."

"I was, but not in the way you think. And I'm only back for a short while. We just needed to spend some time in the temple today before returning home."

Aerin glanced behind her at Kadoc, who'd turned away slightly, giving the priest a side profile view as he admired the simple clay lamps.

"Is this young man the reason I haven't seen you?" he asked with a twinkle in his gray eyes.

"Yes, but—"

"You have no idea how happy this makes me! I had a vision the day of your awakening of you with child, but I knew that none of the men here had caught your eye. Where did you meet?"

Slightly shaken by Aerin's vision but driven by purpose, Seren gently took the priest by the arm and led him to the small alcove where the temple's supplies were stored in baskets, chests, jars, and more.

"I need your word that you won't tell a single soul what I'm about to tell you—not even the other priests."

"I swear on Millam's stars not to break your confidence."

"Thank you," she sighed. "The man with me—my husband—is King Kadoc. I found out after my awakening that I'm Neassa reincarnated, and the gods gave me the power to cast the Cursed One's influence out of his heart. He is a free man, but his soul is weighed down by the wrongs he's committed. He needs your help."

"Either one of your gifts is lying or the gods are greater than I imagined."

"They are so much greater."

Aerin turned his eyes to the king again, studying him with the same power that Seren possessed and sensing the heavy burden on his heart. His brows drawn together in concern and compassion in his spirit, the priest met Seren's gaze once more with a nod.

"I can't do much, but I will help you—both of you. If you truly are Neassa reborn, I'm sure you could also use a purification ritual yourself. Each of you dress in the ceremonial gowns and meet me by the altar. I'll close the temple and prepare the sacrifices."

"Thank you, Aerin."

With a kind smile and a gentle hand pat, the priest went about his work. Seren knelt by the largest storage chest and fetched two ceremonial gowns before gathering two sprigs of hyssop that Aerin had cut earlier in the day, the shallow purification bowl, and anointing oil—an aromatic mixture of olive, rosemary, and frankincense oils. She also grabbed two braided cords of red, which Aerin and the other temple attendants fashioned with clasps made with gold from old prayer lamps. Then, she carried the items over to Kadoc and handed him a gown.

"If you get dressed behind the curtain, I'll set these up for Aerin and do the same when you're finished."

"Thank you."

Aerin reappeared with two doves in a cage and a curved knife of gold as Kadoc disappeared behind the screen, and he and Seren arranged the supplies around the altar. When the king reappeared in the long, shapeless white gown and delicate red cord around his neck, his stance was as regal as it had always been, but his two companions could sense the uncertainty and guilt swirling behind his proud visage. Instead of addressing the state of Kadoc's heart, Aerin simply knelt before him.

"Thank you for choosing this modest temple for your purification, Your Majesty. It's an honor to play a small part in your restoration."

"Please don't kneel before me. I sullied my soul of my own volition, and Seren cured me without my permission. I deserve no praise."

No more words passed between the two men as Seren quickly disappeared behind the dressing screen to change into her gown, place the red cord around her neck, and remove the combs and pins from her dark locks. When she joined them by the altar, Aerin instructed her and Kadoc to kneel. Then, the priest raised his voice, taking on a more powerful, reverent tone as he sang the sacred song associated with the purification rite.

"Purge me with hyssop.
Wash away my wrongs.
My soul now is weary.
Yet I'll sing Your song.

Blot out my darkness and all of my shame.
Restore my light with Your stars' holy flame."

Images of carnage came to the surface of Kadoc's troubled mind—warriors falling by his skillfully wielded sword, ogres and faeries succumbing to his elemental powers, his unsuspecting bride dying by his hand, and innocent infants dashed against rocks and thrown into rivers on his orders. The king shuddered and bile rose in his throat as he unwillingly recalled his most heinous deeds, and the massacre of his people's sons weighed the heaviest on his downcast soul. Hot tears moistened the black stubble on Kadoc's unshaven face and dripped onto his gown, but he remained tremulously silent.

"Cast me not away from You.
Draw me closer into Your light.
Reignite my joy in You,
And make my wrongs right.
Then I will teach my kinsmen Your ways.
Bow down and worship for all of my days."

As those last notes faded into silence, Aerin took the doves and slit their throats over the altar, letting their blood drip into the bronze receptacle before placing their limp bodies into the fire. Then, he took the hyssop and dipped the vibrant violet flowers into the blood before sprinkling it one each of his parishioners.

"You are forgiven."

"I am forgiven," they chorused.

Kadoc's voice cracked as he spoke those three words, but Seren resisted the urge to comfort him, keeping her eyes closed and head bowed. The priest took the purification bowl, filled it with water from the bronze laver, and used the second sprig of hyssop to sprinkle the water on them.

"You are washed."

"I am washed."

Finally, Aerin took the anointing oil and drew the shape of a star on each elf's forehead.

"You are radiant."

"I am radiant."

As Kadoc and Seren finished the affirmation, the blood on their clothing evaporated and their cords lightened from scarlet to white, signs that Millam had found their hearts truly contrite and accepted their sacrifices.

"Rise as children of Millam. May your latter days be brighter than your former ones."

The two royals rose to their feet and opened their eyes. When Seren gazed upon Kadoc's face, she saw tears intermingled with the droplets of holy water but gratitude and relief inspired his silent display of emotion instead of shame alone. Seren wordlessly reached over and took his hand in hers, giving him a small smile when he lifted his eyes from the floor to meet her gaze. Rather than intruding on the touching moment, Aerin simply smiled and cleaned up after the sacrifice as they wrapped their arms around one another for a long, silent embrace.

"Thank you for suggesting this," Kadoc murmured into her hair.

Seren pulled away slightly, wiping the tears from his face and wishing she could chase away his sadness as easily. But hearing villagers conversing as they passed the temple reminded her that they needed to do more than a repentant ritual to make things right in Eaiven.

"We should change back and return to the palace," she suggested.

"What if we didn't? What if we stayed here or built a home in some remote part of the kingdom and lived a simple life together?"

Seren looked away for a moment, chewing her bottom lip as she contemplated his response. Was she happy that he was free of Malok's influence? Absolutely, but she didn't fully trust him, nor had she fully forgiven him. She didn't enjoy the distance between them and knew she was a hypocrite to accept forgiveness from Millam yet deny Kadoc absolution, but her heart hadn't quite caught up to her head. Knowing she had a lifetime of violent, depraved memories to sort through didn't help matters either. Even with Aerin's vision of her with child fresh on her mind, she wasn't ready to embrace Kadoc as her husband… only as a partner in restitution.

"There's far too much between us for me to return to wedded bliss like nothing ever happened. Even if I wanted to, we can't abandon the people we hurt without trying to make things right."

"Of course. I shouldn't have asked," he murmured. "But yes, we should return to the palace quickly. Would you like to change first?"

"No, you go ahead. I need to speak with Aerin."

With a curt nod, Kadoc disappeared behind the dressing curtain and Seren approached the priest.

"Thank you for performing the sacrifice. It means a lot to both of us."

"It was my pleasure, my child," he grinned.

"I do have a question though," she continued, lowering her voice. "Can you tell me more about the vision you had of me?"

"There isn't much to share. I saw you with child—likely close to giving birth—and you were standing in a field of flowers."

"Was there anyone with me?"

Aerin glanced at the dressing screen.

"No, there wasn't. Are you feeling hesitant about reconciling with the king?"

"Yes, I know that the gods brought us together again, but I can't see myself settled with him. It also doesn't seem fair for us to be happy together and have a family after everything we've done."

"The rite we completed a few moments ago is proof that the gods' definition of fairness doesn't always match ours. Many of our people have trouble forgiving even small offenses like making a cutting remark or forgetting a birthday. It will take time for your relationship to be fully restored. In the meantime, be patient and trust that the gods will guide you and give you purpose."

Seren gave him a smile that didn't quite reach her eyes and nodded.

"I'll try."

"Good."

"I don't suppose you'd be interested in joining us in Riamon…"

"The people here need me, but perhaps I can visit once you're more settled."

"I'd love that."

Kadoc reappeared wearing his common clothing, and Seren also donned her simple garments. After thanking the priest once more, they left the temple. As the pair stepped outside, Kadoc spied storm clouds brewing in the distance, and his eyes brightened from deep brown to a silver hue before darkening once more.

"This storm will make the Kaell River overflow, so we won't be able to cross it today," he said. "I know water is your element, but you're not experienced enough to tame such a flood. We should remain in Gridein, then travel to the palace first thing in the morning."

"Well, unless my parents came back from Agron after I left, the house should be empty. We can stay there for the night."

"Should I stay at the inn instead?" he asked, detecting a hint of hesitation in her voice.

"No, that's not necessary. You can stay in my brother's old room. Besides, we can't risk anyone recognizing you yet."

"All right. Lead the way."

The royals set off for Seren's home, skirting the marketplace's perimeter and keeping their heads covered while they stole through the village. As they neared the residential area, a drunkard stumbled out of the inn and jostled Kadoc as he tumbled to the ground. The king moved to step around the man as he struggled to stand, but something told him to stop. Though disgust rose in him upon being jostled by the inebriated elf, Kadoc grudgingly helped the man to his feet before catching up with Seren. When he fell in step beside his distracted wife, weariness suddenly joined his slightly abated despair.

Within minutes, they reached her modest home. During Seren's childhood, the three bedroom house had been full of life thanks to her four older siblings, but with each awakening and subsequent departure due to apprenticeships, marriage, or the military, Kalbhac's abode became quieter and quieter. Now that her parents were no doubt worrying in Agron or traveling back to Gridein, the darkened home was unnervingly still, and the weightiness of Kadoc's presence didn't exactly inspire levity either.

Once inside, Seren gave Kadoc a brief tour, stopping between the final bedroom and her father's study.

"My brother's old room is at the end of the hallway. You can sleep there for the night," she explained. "I'll go to the market in a moment and get something for us to eat."

"Thank you," Kadoc said, eyeing the many scrolls tucked away in the study. "Your father is a scribe, correct?"

"Yes, he is."

The king stepped into the small chamber, admiring the many sheets of papyrus, vinegar, flour, umbilici, ivory, and other tools of Kalbhac's trade. Then, he turned his gaze to the stacks of scrolls in their cases.

"Are these his scrolls or ones he's created for clients?"

"Those are his."

"Do you have the Song of Aire?"

"Yes, we do. Many families request copies of the scroll for their children's awakenings."

Seren walked over to the shelf her eldest brother lovingly crafted years before and perused her father's collection of scrolls until she found the Song of Aire. She'd read the scroll many times as she helped her father with his work, but she'd never received her personal copy of the song thanks to her unusual awakening. Of course, the scroll was likely hidden somewhere in the house, but sneaking it away from its hiding place wouldn't be as satisfying as receiving it from her proud parents. That thwarted tradition was just one of the many ways her life had gone awry since she emerged from Aire's pool, and she suddenly longed for the simplicity she experienced living in the shadow of her parents' wings.

"Are you all right?"

Seren met Kadoc's concerned gaze and sighed as she handed him the scroll.

"My parents never gave me my copy of the song because I didn't get to see them after my awakening. My life irreversibly changed that day, and I never took the time to appreciate how simple my life was before it."

"I'm sorry, Seren. I know that I'm to blame for that. Is there anything I can do to help?"

"Don't make the same mistakes twice. If the gods put me on this path, it's clearly more important than what I planned for myself even though it's more difficult. If you went back to the darkness after everything we've been through, I don't know what I'd do."

"As I live, I will never serve the Cursed One again. May Millam blot my life and memory from the earth if I betray Him or you again."

Seren heaved a deep breath, blinking back the stubborn tears that threatened to spill forth.

"I'm going to the market. If anyone knocks on the door, ignore them."

"All right, but don't linger too long. The storm will arrive soon."

"I'll do my best."

Then, Seren left the study, fetched the coins she needed from her parents' room, and went to the market. Thanks to their afternoon arrival in Gridein, the crowd was far sparser than it was during the morning rush. So Seren was able to find everything she needed fairly quickly. As she paid for the chicken she'd cook for their supper, she noticed one of her mother's friends, Aislin, waving at her from the next stall over. The instant they made eye contact, the rotund woman bustled over with a smile on her face and excitement in her deep green eyes, and Seren inwardly cursed. The gods had blessed Aislin with a memory that never failed, which she unfortunately supplemented with loose lips that retold every juicy detail she remembered to any ear willing to listen.

"I thought I'd never see you again!" she exclaimed, wrapping Seren in the fierce hug that regularly stole her breath as a little girl. "Your mother told me you never came back after your awakening, and I've lit a lamp for you in Millam's temple every day since. When they up and left too, I didn't know what to think. Where in the world have you been?"

"I can't really say, but—"

"I heard that you came back with a young man and took him to your father's house. Did you marry while you were away?"

"He is indeed my husband, but we're only passing through."

Aislin squeezed Seren's arms and practically hopped in place with delight.

"How fantastic! I knew you'd find someone. Tell me—what is his name?"

Seren's heart raced as she weighed her options. If she said the king's true name—one that no parent had dared curse their child with since his dark reign began—Aislin would know exactly who she was yoked to. And as the town gossip, everyone would hear the truth within the hour and likely surround her home wielding weapons and magic to kill the man who terrorized them and stole their children for their whole lives.

"His name is Ribrohn," she lied. "We met the day of my awakening."

"How exciting! Most elves don't have such luck when they awaken."

"No, they don't."

"I thought you'd been taken to that tyrant in the north and drained dry like Comdhal's son. He and Derval didn't even know he was dead until six months later when they saw a soldier at the toll bridge wearing the necklace they'd given him for good luck."

"Well, I—"

"I'm surprised they didn't take you for his harem though. The king seems to like women with your look—bronze skin, dark hair, and big eyes. They say he likes the ones who look like that whore he was married to, but of course, I never laid eyes on the wretch myself."

Seren bristled with irritation, straightening her shoulders and lifting her chin as she glared at the matronly gossip.

"Neassa was many things, but she wasn't a whore. She was pure on their wedding day and never laid with anyone but Kadoc. If you're going to speak ill of a dead woman, at least insult her accurately."

Before Aislin could say another word, Seren moved past her, intentionally bumping her aside while she fled the market. As Seren stormed through the small town, she caught a glimpse of the town drunk, Enri, exiting the temple with Aerin walking beside him and patting his hunched shoulders. Seeing the usually inebriated elf with the priest cheered her heart a bit, but not enough to completely cast out the annoyance gnawing at her soul. By the time she returned to the house, slightly slamming the door gave her a bit of satisfaction without worrying Kadoc. He did, however, sense her frustration when she entered the study.

"What's wrong?" he asked, rising from the couch.

"Nothing. Some loose-lipped busy body was plying me for information and oversharing. Also, if anyone asks, your name is Ribrohn, and we met the day of my awakening."

"King of sadness… interesting choice."

"I couldn't think of anything else, and it seemed to suit you."

"Of course. To say that I've been rather melancholy today would be an understatement," he said. "I've been contemplating how I can make amends with the people, but knowing there are some things I cannot make right is very disheartening."

Seren nodded slowly, her grim mood deepening as she remembered that he'd forced decades of depraved memories on her… memories of atrocities she reveled in, both with Kadoc and independently to satiate her own bloodlust. Yes, the words she'd spoken to Aislin in defense of her faithfulness had been true, but she'd engaged in enough unspeakable acts that no amount of fidelity or purity could make her truly innocent.

Her hands were as bloodstained as Kadoc's.

"You look troubled, my dove. Did I say something to upset you?"

"I should put these things away. I'll let you read in peace."

Seren fled the room without another word, finding Kadoc's term of endearment more unsettling than comforting. He hadn't uttered those words since before Malok invaded their lives, and while it rolled off his tongue with the same ease it had before, she couldn't help feeling a twinge of guilt. She'd separated many lovers young and old by death or detainment, and they'd perished in the least peaceful conditions possible—stretched on racks, bound in stocks, and beaten with glass-embedded whips until their entrails spilled onto the ground. She didn't deserve even a hint of the tenderness that Kadoc's words signified and the once innocent love that inspired them.

Her shoulders burdened with grief and fresh tears in her eyes, Seren completed the little preparation she could do for that night's supper, crept to her room, and closed her stinging eyes to escape her mounting grief for whatever time the gods would allow.

★   ★   ★

"Have mercy on me, my Queen," the man blubbered, his tears mingling with the oil that the guards drenched his bound body with.

"Why should I have mercy on such an offensive specimen of a man?" Neassa derided from her perch a few feet away. "You've caused me great offense, and I'd be a poor queen to the men and women in my care if I allowed you to live and repeat tonight's transgression."

"Please! I have a wife and a child on the way. They depend on—"

"Then you should have considered their feelings before tonight's little performance."

He shuddered and wailed as the final drops of lamp oil trickled down his head.

"Millam, help me!"

Rage bubbled up within Neassa at the mention of the shining god's name. In a breath, she crossed the road to stand beside the trembling man, who'd been stripped down to only his loincloth, which he'd soiled during the first wave of torment she inflicted upon him that evening.

"You can cry to that cloying buffoon all you want, but he will not deliver you."

She placed her hand on his cheek in a deceptively tender gesture that inspired cringing in her pained captive.

"Millam has abandoned you."

Then, without a spark in sight, she set the man ablaze, her face lighting up with joy as his writhing body illuminated the dark road. Though the flames licked at her dress and curls, their heat warmed her dark soul instead of scorching her body. Satisfied with her work, Neassa breathed in the aroma of burning flesh and sauntered back over to Kadoc, who was finishing his wine on the other side of the road. Once she was within arm's length, he pulled her in for a deep, passionate kiss that most elves would have been chastised for sharing in public.

"Magnificent work," he breathed, basking in the radiance emanating from the man-turned-torch who now lit the road to the palace. "You always dream up the most appropriate punishments. I was ready to skewer him for ruining supper tonight, but this is so much better."

"Thank you," she smirked. "A cook who burns a king's boar deserves the same treatment he gave his meat—being slathered in oil, burnt to a crisp, and put on display for all to see."

"I couldn't agree more," Kadoc laughed. "Let's return to our guests. I'm still starving, and the lamb looked delicious."

With one last kiss, they strolled back to the palace hand-in-hand with ill-gotten glee in their blackened hearts.

★　　　　　★　　　　　★

Tranquility was far from Seren's grasp by the time she roused at dawn. Her chest heaved with gasping breaths and tears stung her eyes as she replayed the appalling memory—the joy her actions originally inspired giving way to self-loathing and guilt that devoured her soul like a vulture feasting on carrion. She'd burned an innocent man alive for nothing more than overcooking one portion of an otherwise perfect feast, and she'd delighted in his torment more than the flawless fare itself. The high she felt from cook's anguish even inspired her and Kadoc to indulge in vulgar displays of affection that bordered on indecent for the feast's remaining courses.

Why did you bring me back? Why give me life again and reunite me with Kadoc when I slaughtered innocent people with such wicked elation?

Seren sat up and became keenly aware of her amulet as it settled on her décolletage. Running her fingers along Inneh's artfully carved likeness, she wondered how much disgust she and Kadoc inspired in the Goddess of Love as she witnessed the depraved acts they committed in the name of the very virtue she was mistress over. Seren's trembling hands traced the amulet's setting and its delicate chain as wisps of darkness filled the edges of her vision. In a matter of seconds, she could be hours away from the man she once reveled in her rebellion against the gods with. But as she traced the necklace's chain, feeling a quickly forgotten but recently acquired accessory shook her from her melancholy.

The maiden pulled the cord from that afternoon's ritual from under her rumpled gown and marveled at the simple necklace. The three strands that made up the ceremonial necklace represented the bearer's contrition, a pleasing sacrifice, and Millam's acceptance. She'd seen many elves bearing the sacred accessory during her years in Gridein and had borne it herself after hurling some particularly offensive insults in her mother's direction during her early adolescence. Yet she'd never felt more burdened by the weight of her own degeneracy than she did in that moment… Nor had she felt Millam's comforting hand on her spirit more clearly.

The King of the Gods had the right to judge and condemn her for her wrongs, but he'd revived her wicked form, given her twenty years of blissful obliviousness, and showed her mercy when her transgressions resurfaced. She couldn't fathom why he chose to reunite her with Kadoc and overlook her wrongs, but she had to trust that he had good reason. Running away—whether to start her life anew or cut it short—would be more offensive than the wrongs she committed in her prior life because it displayed a deep ingratitude toward the god who overlooked her many offenses instead of giving her the condemnation she deserved.

As turmoil and thanksgiving dueled for dominance over her spirit, Seren closed her eyes and let fresh tears wet her reddened cheeks as she recited the Song of Contrition that Aerin sang only hours before. Though she'd crooned the holy song with vigor and decent but imperfect pitch for years with her family and fellow elves, the voice-cracking, heart-rending rendition she warbled that afternoon had more heart than every prior performance combined.

> *"Purge me with hyssop.*
> *Wash away my wrongs.*
> *My soul now is weary.*
> *Yet I'll sing Your song.*
> *Blot out my darkness and all of my shame.*
> *Restore my light with Your stars' holy flame."*

"Cast me not away from You.
Draw me closer into Your light.
Restore my joy in You,
And make my wrongs right.
Then I will teach my brothers and sisters Your ways.
Bow down and worship for all of my days."

After she sang the final words, Seren opened her bloodshot eyes and saw that not even a trace of Malok's darkness clouded her vision. She brought the braided cord to her lips and kissed it before abandoning her bed to prepare their evening meal, which she cooked in honor of the very cook whose unjust death inspired her woe. Kadoc emerged from the study just as she finished cooking the sweet potatoes they'd eat with the bird that was beautifully browning in the oven.

"I don't know what you're cooking, but it smells delicious," he said, his spirits much higher than they'd been that entire day.

"Thank you," Seren replied, trying to sound more cheerful than she felt.

"Do you need help with anything?"

Seren looked up from her handiwork and raised an eyebrow at the humbly-dressed king. Kadoc had been waited on by more servants and cooks than she could count for his entire life. Even when he went to war, a cook traveled with him to ensure that the king never went into battle without a warm meal strengthening his bones. The fact that he offered to help with a meal was almost laughable.

But it was also surprisingly endearing.

"No, I'm almost finished," she declined.

Kadoc nodded and turned to walk away, but Seren placed her hand on his arm, prompting him to face her once more.

"Have you been tempted to leave since you awakened today?"

The king glanced away for a moment, a sliver of shame penetrating his heart.

"Yes…"

"Well, I'm glad you didn't. The gods brought us together again, and we can't let Malok divide us. Promise me that you won't leave me."

"It's my duty to care for you until death, and I have no intention of shirking my responsibility."

"I won't leave you either."

A moment of stillness passed between them, but neither elf felt secure enough to close the cubit of space between them whether for a comforting embrace or an amorous one. They simply savored the knowledge that each had pledged renewed fidelity to one another. And while their brief exchange didn't alleviate the burdens they bore, the weight seemed more bearable thanks to the assurance that they need not carry it alone.

CHAPTER 8
A Somber Assembly

Their evening in Gridein passed blessedly uneventfully. The two enjoyed a meal with little conversation, but the quiet company was comfort enough for the two elves. After finishing supper, they went to their separate rooms and fell asleep to the sounds of falling rain and rumbling thunder. When morning came, they rose early, packed a few necessities, and left for the palace. No one interrupted their departure, but Seren caught sight of Aislin as they passed through the city and suppressed the indignation that rose in her heart. The town gossip's unintentional insult might have been untrue, but it was a mere drop compared to the downpour of wrongdoing she was actually responsible for. So she gave her mother's acquaintance a tight-lipped smile and a friendly wave as they passed.

Once they were outside the gates, Kadoc helped Seren onto her horse and mounted his steed as well before continuing down the road once more. As Kadoc predicted, the Kaell River had flooded during the previous day's storm but returned to a near normal depth by the time they reached the bridge. Twisted vines, broken branches, and other debris littered the bridge, but it was still passable on horseback.

After crossing the river, they abandoned the road once more to cut through the countryside as quickly as possible. As they traveled north, Mount Ceallah came into view, and Seren remembered her awakening only days before. She knew that her life was about to change forever when she parted ways with her parents to meet the sacred pool's guardian, but she never imagined the adventure that awaited her. The responsibility was great, the stakes were high, and her future was uncertain.

Aerin's vision of her with child should have brought her some comfort, but she couldn't quite see herself as a mother. A century before, she'd felt the stirrings of life inside her and dreamed about nursing their child at her breast and singing their son or daughter the lullabies her parents sung over her, but when Malok's influence entered her soul, the way of women ceased with her and bearing children became impossible. In her new life, she bled each month as the other young women did, but she knew that being a mother required more than a fertile womb.

Glancing at her traveling companion, who seemed far more at peace than he had the day before, Seren tried to asses him with fresh eyes. Even in his commonplace clothing, Kadoc was handsome. His dark, deep-set eyes were fringed with long, thick eyelashes that any elven woman would have envied, but his full brows and beard were unmistakably masculine as was the muscular physique both his gifts and his training afforded him. The king's tanned skin was free of blemishes and imperfections, but his cheeks had the endearing habit of reddening when he was nervous or had his fill of wine. His full, rosy lips stretched into an infectious grin or an easy smile when the right inspiration struck him, and she'd inspired plenty of smiles and laughter during their courtship and the beginning of their marriage.

Despite those beautiful attributes, she couldn't imagine holding him close as she once had and truly being a wife to him. Shame and concern had replaced the fear and revulsion she once felt in his presence, and those feelings were deafening enough to drown out the affection that she'd fought and denied since the day of her awakening. It was finally safe to love Kadoc again, but her heart was too burdened to enjoy their redemption and reunion… a reunion neither of them deserved. How could she and Kadoc move toward happiness together when so many elves were mourning and suffering because of their actions? The prospect of experiencing joy together didn't just feel unattainable.

It felt wrong.

Shaking those morose musings from her head, Seren shifted her focus to their arrival. Many elves would be relieved that Kadoc was no longer the blackguard they once dreaded, but she was certain that some wouldn't be so pleased. While many of their subjects obeyed them out of fear, she knew that some gleefully furthered their cause. Whether their darkness came from Malok himself or their own personal agendas, she wasn't sure, but Seren had no doubt that some would try to lure Kadoc into his old ways or subvert his efforts at restitution.

"Kadoc," she called.

The king slowed his horse's pace a bit and Seren did the same.

"Yes?"

"Does anyone in the palace know about the ritual you completed to become the Cursed One's servant?"

"No. In fact, I destroyed the scroll after I committed it to memory after your death. Paranoia reigned in my heart for quite some time after Aled's prophecy."

Seren nodded and brushed off the pang that struck her heart at the reminder of Kadoc's act of betrayal. "Was there anyone specific who you thought may be a threat to you? Someone who might oppose you once we return to the palace? I know many of our advisors were loyal, but it's been twenty years since I lived in the palace. Would this change be welcome or undesirable?"

"Everyone in the palace fears me to some extent except for Orla and Aled."

A twinge of envy joined Seren's disquiet, but she held her tongue.

"I think Aled's security rests in his foresight. I'd never been able to harvest the power of foresight from anyone, so his was a power I could never possess for myself. And he has the luxury of being able to see any danger he may face."

"And Orla?"

Kadoc hesitated, clenching his jaw for a moment as he searched for an answer that was truthful without being too distressing.

"Orla is more threatened by your reappearance than by my change of heart. She offered herself for the harem in hopes of becoming my queen one day, and your presence has dashed her greatest dream."

"She *volunteered* to be one of your concubines?"

"Yes. At her awakening, she told the guards that she'd like to be brought to the palace regardless of what her gifts were. I was impressed by her boldness despite how common her powers were, so I accepted her. While I'd never taken any of my concubines by force, being desired from the start instead of having to woo someone who feared me for months or years was so refreshing. I hadn't experienced that kind of acceptance since…"

"Since I was alive."

The king nodded.

"So why didn't you marry her?"

"Because even at my worst, I never loved anyone but you."

Seren's cheeks reddened at his heartfelt reply.

"In any case, she's with the others in Snechta until I can devise a better future for them."

"Right… she told me as much last time we saw each other."

"You've met?"

"Yes, and she hates me more than anyone I've ever met. The elders and ogres in Agron detested me, but they didn't initially believe that I wasn't a threat to them. She knows exactly who I am and loathes me simply for existing. I can't defend or explain my way out of that."

"Well, you have what she's always wanted, and you've never needed to prove yourself or compete to gain my affections."

"Perhaps it would be wise to have people we trust watch her and Aled in case they try to cause any trouble," Seren mused. "What are Orla's powers?"

"Charm, sleep, and song."

Remembering the many fitful nights when sleep evaded them during their bloody reign, Seren resentfully acknowledged that Orla's usefulness went beyond the carnal delights she once provided.

"Let's stop and give our horses a moment to rest," Kadoc diverted. "There's an orchard ahead where we can all have a little sustenance."

"Lead the way."

After reaching the unmanned orchard, Seren led their weary steeds to a nearby brook for a drink while Kadoc picked the best apples he could find. Then, they settled down beneath one of the fruit-bearing trees and enjoyed the crisp, refreshing snack with the bread and dried meat that Seren packed. Other than the occasional comment about how satisfying the food was or how gorgeous the scenery looked, little passed between the royals. Thus, they made their sit-down reasonably brief and continued their journey as soon as their horses seemed sufficiently rested. As they approached the palace, Kadoc led them closer to the road but paused before exiting the woods.

"I'm going to disguise myself so we can enter the palace more easily, so don't be alarmed at my appearance."

"All right."

Kadoc closed his eyes, and his skin and hair lightened to its previous pale palette in mere seconds. When he looked upon Seren again, she saw that his eyes remained their natural hue, and that subtle disparity cast out the unease that briefly crept into her heart.

"You're the only one who looks me in the eye, so no one will even notice."

"Thank you."

The king gave his wife a sad smile then straightened his back and lifted his chin to emulate his usual proud posture before venturing onto the road. As they approached the palace gates, the six soldiers standing guard recognized their king and bowed their heads slightly, standing at attention so rigidly that their fists quaked as they held them to their chests. Grief flashed in Kadoc's heart at the sight of their trepidation, but he spoke to them with the same callousness they'd come to expect from him.

"Tell Aled to meet me in the library in an hour and have the servants prepare a bath for the queen immediately."

"Yes, my King," they trembled in unison before the youngest guard sprinted inside the gates as quickly as his legs could take him.

In contrast to the soldier's quick pace, they maintained a leisurely pace trotting from the gates to the palace steps, where servants waited to take the horses and tend to their immediate needs. True to his prior character, Kadoc neither thanked nor acknowledged the servants while Seren expressed her gratitude as usual. Once inside, they retired to the safety of Kadoc's bedroom. Without his anxiously attentive attendants to worry about, he returned to his natural appearance and deflated as he lowered himself onto the foot of his bed. Despite sensing and seeing his angst, Seren stood her ground from a few feet away, fighting the urge to wrap him in a comforting embrace by clasping her hands in front of her.

"Are you all right?"

"I can't wait for the day when people no longer greet me with fear in their eyes, but I'll likely see hatred long before I see anything resembling respect," he grumbled. "I have a lot of amends to make before anyone will trust me."

Before Seren could respond, a soft clanging echoed in the room, alerting them that a guard had come to speak with Kadoc. In a wink, he assumed his frightening, fair appearance again and opened the door with a flick of his wrist as he rose from the bed. The speedy soldier from the gate entered and immediately fell at Kadoc's feet, his forehead to the ground and body shaking uncontrollably.

"A-Aled has left the p-palace, my King."

"What do you mean? Did he leave on business?"

"A servant saw him pack his scrolls and supplies, and flee with his apprentice early this morning. I will search the entire kingdom for him if you command me to. Please allow me to atone for my failure."

"You're not responsible for his departure," Kadoc assured him, growing weary of the man's groveling and the guilt it inspired. "Go find my cousin instead and bring her here."

"Yes, my King. I will not fail you again."

In a flash, the young sentry sprang to his feet, backing away several paces before rushing to find Tierna. Seren took a step forward and placed a hand on Kadoc's shoulder.

"You won't have to do this for much longer. Our lives will become very difficult once you share what's happened, but you won't have to pretend," she reminded him. "Now, do you want me here when you speak with Tierna or would you rather explain this to her in private?"

"My cousin may be the only person who celebrates my redemption, so I can manage this conversation on my own. You should rest before we speak with Doran. Tomorrow will be quite hectic, and you'll need every bit of strength you can gather."

"So will you. You'll also need this."

Seren reached into the satchel where she'd packed a new necessities in Gridein and handed Kadoc one of the golden lamps from the temple.

"Aerin a left lamp for each of us on the doorstep last night. My father once told me that Millam keeps the darkness away if we keep his lamps lit throughout the night, and I think Aerin knew we'd need a little illumination."

"Yes… we certainly do," Kadoc whispered. "Thank you."

Seren gave her husband one final, weary smile before leaving his room to wash away the day's grime, praying that Millam would wash away their guilt and repair their kingdom with the same swiftness.

★   ★   ★

By the time Kadoc knocked on Seren's door, she was clean, calm, and keen to get on with the remaining tasks for the day. Seeing Kadoc's glamour briefly unsettled her again, but the warmth in his eyes and smile on his face cast out her initial shock.

"I take it your conversation with Tierna went well?"

"When I showed her my true self, she started weeping before I could say a word," he beamed. "She agreed to help us with whatever we need and is sending messengers to every village within a three-hour ride of the palace to summon anyone who can travel to tomorrow's announcement."

"That's great news! She always tried to abate our madness even when we were at our worst."

"Yes, she did. She said that she always had hope that I'd become the man I was again... she just didn't know how."

"It sounds like we owe her both amends and thanks," Seren smiled, taking his arm. "And the same is true of Doran. Let's go see him."

Seren and Kadoc left the palace's luxurious residential wing for an area considerably less restful and aromatic. Though disgust threatened to rise within Seren as she entered the shadowy depths, memories of the torment she once inflicted sobered her revulsion for the dungeon and its keepers' depraved practices. At her worst, she'd burned elves and ogres alive one searing handprint at a time, skinned her enemies while they still lived, and gleefully employed the use of hot irons, stocks, and more to torment her prisoners, who begged her to end their lives long before she granted that dark release.

And those were the things she did without her husband's encouragement.

Shuddering at the memory of her own brutality, Seren removed her hand from Kadoc's arm and silently gathered the mental fortitude she needed to walk the path ahead of her. Since she'd died twenty years before, her cruelty was in the past, but the memories were soul-searingly fresh. Many of her victims never survived their encounters, but their wives, husbands, sons, and daughters no doubt still lived with the painful echoes of her malevolence. Millam had blessed her with twenty years of normalcy and innocence when all she'd given her people for nearly a century was pain and loss.

Sliding her gaze over to Kadoc, a mixture of sympathy and anger pierced her. The burden he bore was far heavier than hers because his most recent atrocities were committed days instead of decades before... And his actions had been the spark that lit the baleful blaze within her. If he hadn't forced her to drink the potion from Malok's scroll, she could have died a normal woman and never would have harmed let alone murdered her people. Instead, he'd betrayed her not once or twice but *three times*. Yes, he'd been under Malok's control, but could he truly be trusted?

Or forgiven?

Seren shook those questions from her mind and focused on their impending conversation. She squared her shoulders and replaced her scowl with a more neutral facial expression as the guards pulled Doran from his underfoot dwelling. Of course, the soldier stood proudly before them, his nostrils flaring and fists clenched as he stared defiantly without making eye contact with either of his royal visitors.

Blood stained his bare chest and face, but Seren couldn't make out any wounds or bruises—not even a hint of a scar from a knife's blade or whip's tail. But even without the physical evidence of his torment, the fury burning in his heart and eyes was enough to make Seren look away in anger and shame. When Doran was an adolescent, she'd delighted in tormenting him and reminding him that he was alone in the world. How he'd endured her company and helped her during her journey since her awakening, she didn't know, but his past kindness did nothing to assuage her mounting guilt.

"Doran, I'd like to apologize for the treatment you've received since entering Eaiven," Kadoc said once the guards left the dungeon. "My men have been harsh with you, and we've denied you the justice and dignity every elf deserves. I could blame them alone for their behavior, but I know my thirst for cruelty is what has driven their actions. Will you please forgive me?"

Doran raised an eyebrow at his former traveling companion.

"Don't tell me you believe this drivel, Seren."

"I believe him because he's not the man you justifiably hated before," she said, flicking her eyes in Kadoc's direction again. "Maybe you should tell him. There's been an isolation spell on the cells since before your father was even on the throne, so it's not like the other prisoners can see or hear."

Kadoc nodded in agreement and dropped his glamor, his skin and hair darkening to their natural hue before the indignant prisoner's eyes.

"A clever glamour doesn't change who he is."

"It's not a glamour," Seren said. "Two night ago, I used my powers on Kadoc and restored him to his normal self."

Doran finally looked Kadoc in the eye, suspicion still swirling in his hardened heart.

"You remember what happened to Fedhlim, Kathal, and the aglocs," she continued. "The gods gave me not just power over water but also the ability to cast out the Cursed One's influence and give elves the power we denied them. I used that power on Kadoc, and he's a different man now."

The silent soldier squinted at his sullen sovereign, mulling over Seren's claims as he took in the king's changed disposition. While he couldn't boast in possessing Seren's or Fedhlim's more empathetic powers, he was good enough at observing and judging elves to tell that the king had changed.

"I've come to give you your freedom back," Kadoc said. "You can go wherever you wish—to Fedhlim even—but I'd like you to consider remaining here as Seren's personal guard. While we're both eager to right the wrongs we've committed, we know that not everyone will be in favor of us making restitution to the people and ending Malok worship in the palace."

"I believe that this change is genuine, but I will not serve you again," Doran softened almost imperceptivity as he turned to address Seren. "I do hope you're successful in this, but my place is in Aden."

"I understand," she said. "Would you rather stay the night in a guest room and depart in the morning or leave now?"

"I'll leave as soon as I'm able."

"We'll make sure you have everything you need to travel back safely."

"Thank you."

Though the conversation had come to a peaceful end, Seren heaved a deep breath and took a few steps closer to Doran.

"I'm truly sorry for the way I mistreated you when you were a child. No one deserves to be treated so cruelly at any age let alone when they're so young. Will you please forgive me?"

Doran gave a curt nod, and his stern gesture was enough to fill Seren's soul with relief and her eyes with tears. She was tempted to say more but chose not to push her luck due to the surly disposition that his current predicament inspired. So Seren simply nodded in kind.

"Thank you. I'll have a servant bring you to a guest room so you can at least wash up and put on some clean clothes before you leave."

"Thanks."

Rather than prolonging the awkwardness, Seren joined the crestfallen king.

"Let's go."

As they ascended from the palace's ghastly depths to the shining hallways above, Seren noticed that Doran had denied Kadoc the forgiveness that he gave her. Of course, the pair knew that many elves would find him and his actions irredeemable, but facing that reality so soon made the king's spirits sink lower and resolve strengthen. While they couldn't force their subjects to absolve them of their guilt, they could strive to undo whatever damage they could and hope that their somber atonement would gradually lessen the bitterness and grief that their wicked reign inspired.

Before Malok's influence infiltrated Eaiven, assemblies at the palace were often marked by the constant, curious murmur of expectant elves, who wondered what happy news that their sovereign would soon share. Every wedding, birth, and joyful occasion had been marked by a deafening assembly at the king's residence and an announcement from the balcony overlooking its main gates. But since the gathering where

Kadoc celebrated his newfound power by choosing five elves at random and executing them with unbidden glee, every assembly had been eerily silent unless he or his bride forced the crowd to respond.

The elves' unsettling stillness also marked that morning's grave gathering, and the fearful hush was more jarring to the queen than jeers, insults, and curses ever could have been. With her guard down, Seren clearly sensed the people's trepidation, and she found herself imagining the pent-up rage they'd unleash upon hearing Kadoc's news—anticipating that hostility would win the day instead of celebration.

Recognizing the depressing depths her thoughts were sinking to, Seren rose from her couch to join the king, who paced back and forth several feet away without the glamour he'd worn every time they ventured from behind closed doors since their return.

"Are you as scared as I am?" she asked.

"I'm terrified."

"What do you fear the most?"

Kadoc sank onto the couch, massaging his temples to lessen the pain radiating from his head.

"That the people will rise up and tear me apart, then turn their talons on you."

"I'm scared that the Cursed One will somehow use this to harm the people even more than we already did."

Voicing their concerns made their anxiety abate a sliver, but the pair still felt unsettled.

"Do you remember the Song of Triumph?" Kadoc asked.

"It actually my favorite song."

"I thought Inneh's Ballad was your favorite."

"It was before, but my father—Kalbhac—liked to sing the Song of Triumph when he worked on scrolls. It reminds me of home."

"Perhaps we'd feel more at ease if we sang it now. I haven't uttered a word of it since I completed the ritual, but bits and pieces of it have come to mind since our return to Riamon."

"Lucky for you, I remember it like it's my own name," Seren smiled. "All I ask is that you refrain from judging my pitch. I spent my childhood in the temple and my father's study instead of taking lessons with a songmaster, so I don't have the skill I possessed in my previous life."

"I'm sure there's nothing to judge."

Suddenly feeling shy under the weight of Kadoc's gaze, Seren closed her eyes and lifted her voice in song. Within moments, the king's less sure voice joined hers.

> *"Millam's arm is stronger than*
> *The armies of the nations.*
> *His voice—it rumbles like the oceans—*
> *The first of his creations.*
> *With just a word, great kings will fall*
> *And every elf will quake.*
> *For Millam who we all exalt*
> *Will fight for his names' sake.*
>
> *"Though no king noble or mighty*
> *Nor priest humble and meek*
> *Deserves Millam's defense and love*
> *He shields the low and weak.*
> *With sword and bow and flaming spear*
> *He casts down ev'ry foe.*
> *And when the great day comes as last,*
> *He'll make his final blow*
> *To defeat the Cursed One.*
> *He'll cast out darkness with the sun,*
> *And light is all we'll know.*
> *He'll cast out darkness with the sun,*
> *And light is all we'll know."*

Between her lyrical memory and his natural yet refined skill as a vocalist, the song was almost as pleasant to their ears as it was comforting to their hearts, which were considerably less anxious by the time the final notes faded into stillness. Though Kalbhac sang the song in Seren's childhood home almost daily, elves also sang the song during the yearly Festival of Lights.

During that anticipatory celebration, every elf in Eaiven would bring their family's lit lamp—whether gold or bronze or clay—to the nearest temple at dusk and keep them burning through the night as they sang songs to celebrate the King of the Gods' first triumph over Malok in anticipation of his final victory. The celebratory lyrics were a yearly reminder that the Cursed One's poisonous presence in the world wouldn't endure forever. The mortal wound Millam dealt on the day the festival commemorated would pale in comparison to his killing blow, which every elf in his right mind waited for with longing and deferred delight.

Perhaps Kadoc and I being restored was another wound, Seren speculated.

A soft wind chime sounded in the room, heralding Tierna's presence shortly before she entered. The king's cousin was dressed as immaculately as always with a perfectly white stola and a bright yellow palla, but the flush in her cheeks and wildness in her eyes showed that she was as anxious about the upcoming assembly as they were.

"It's time," she announced. "Are you ready?"

Kadoc looked to Seren, and she nodded.

"Yes, we are," he said.

Kadoc stood and took Seren's hand before they stepped onto the balcony to address the kingdom side-by-side for the first time in two decades. Though no one uttered a word upon seeing Kadoc's changed appearance, elves exchanged wide-eyed glances and raised eyebrows as they stepped into view. The royals' pulses accelerated from the resting pace brought on by their musical moment to a shuddering speed, which only grew more erratic when Kadoc cleared his suddenly parched throat to begin the most important speech he would ever give.

"Thank you for joining me here this morning. I'm well aware that rumors about the queen's return have been swirling around the kingdom the past week, and I'm certain that my changed appearance has added to your disquiet. I hope I can answer the unasked questions that are plaguing you and give you the comfort and hope that I've denied you since my father's death."

Seren sensed the anxiety rising in Kadoc and fought the instinct to step forward and comfort him. Instead, she lifted her eyes to the heavens and asked the gods to give him the strength and calm he needed to continue.

"Seren, the woman by my side today, awakened at Mount Ceallah a week ago, and shortly after she completed the rite of passage, it became clear to us both that she is my late wife Neassa reincarnated. Instead of being raised as the daughter of a rich merchant or some noble elven family, the gods saw fit to give her a simple, humble life as the daughter of a scribe in a village so irrelevant to my machinations that I'd never deigned to visit it. Because she began her life as a common elf, she was justifiably horrified to meet me and discover our unforeseen connection. Thankfully, she soon learned that a new life wasn't all Millam had given her. He'd also trusted her with the power to purge the Cursed One's influence from my heart and nearly restore me to the man I once was.

"I say 'nearly' not 'completely' because while I'm no longer a servant to our people's greatest enemy, my heart is heavy laden with disgust, shame, and self-loathing due to the atrocities I committed against the people I was called to protect and to our ogre neighbors in the east. Whether I robbed you of power, loved ones, or simply the peace of mind that having a good king brings, I have stolen from and harmed every one of you. I have no doubt that it will take me a lifetime to earn even a glimmer of your trust and respect, but I swear by Millam's stars that I will do whatever it takes to right the wrongs I've committed."

As the final word left Kadoc's lips, a poorly-aimed rock sailed through the air and slammed into the wall to his left.

"You murdered my baby boy!" a woman shrieked from below, her round face almost as red as her bloodshot, tearful eyes. "If you want to make things right, you should fall on your blasted sword and send your blighted soul to Ifryn!"

No one said a word, but the elves surrounding the long-grieving mother slowly backed away from her, no doubt fearing that Kadoc's infamous wrath would consume them as well if they stood too close. But the king didn't respond as they expected.

"The prospect of taking my life has haunted me since the moment Seren severed my connection with Malok, but it would be foolish of me and an insult to Millam to give myself release by ending my life instead of using it to right my wrongs. I am deeply sorry for taking your son from you, and I will try to make it up to you in whatever way I can."

When the people realized that Kadoc had no intention of lashing out at the enraged elf, they unleashed the fury that they'd fearfully hidden for decades. Some screeched heartbreakingly true accusations, and others hurled the basest insults they knew. Only a handful of elves stood silently or talked amongst themselves, their composed demeanors and mildly sympathetic glances nearly unnoticeable thanks to the fuming majority. Kadoc attempted to answer his first few accusers and Seren stepped forward to do the same, but the assembly grew increasingly chaotic with every charge and curse.

Sensing the futility of the king's attempts to placate his subjects, Seren took his hand and pulled him into the palace, narrowly avoiding a second stone, which was thrown by an elf with far better aim than his predecessor. Once they were back inside, Kadoc and Seren sank onto the couch again as Tierna poured them each a glass of water with unsteady hands. Kadoc chugged his drink as if he'd spent his morning trekking across Agron's barren wilderness in the north instead of facing his own people. Seren barely sipped her water, instead choosing to rub the king's back as she had many times during their more innocent years.

"This is exactly what we prepared for," she whispered when he finally set his cup down. "We knew that some would react harshly, but we have to let them grieve freely if they're ever to trust that we've changed."

"I know, but 'we' aren't who they're angry with. Every allegation they shouted today was directed at me. Even if they weren't, I'm ultimately to blame for the evil you committed."

"But Millam has forgiven you, and they will—"

"Have *you* forgiven me?" he interrupted. "I can sense what's in people's hearts just like you can, and I felt your fear turn to anger when you regained your memories."

Seren dropped her hand to her lap with a sigh.

"I want to forgive you, but I'm only now remembering what I did when I was the Cursed One's vessel. You made me remember how vile I was, and I have to live with that knowledge for the rest of my life."

"In my desperation, I thought you'd love me if you remembered our life together, but all I did was deepen the chasm between us."

"It *is* deep, but I don't think I'll feel this way forever. My heart needs time to heal."

"And it will take even longer for the people to forgive me."

"Many of them have never known you as anything but the Cursed One's servant. They need to see that you can follow in your father's footsteps and be a good king."

"*If* I can."

"You can. I know it."

Instead of taking his wife's encouragement to heart, Kadoc turned to his cousin, who had been silently observing their strained interaction.

"The soldiers were instructed not to harm anyone in the crowd, correct?"

"Yes, I told them to take defensive measures only if necessary to keep them out of the palace."

"Good. I'll go supervise the prisoners' release from the dungeon and see how much of a staff I have left."

Kadoc stood and Seren followed suit, but he raised his hand to halt her progress.

"I'll see to this alone."

"All right," she agreed. "I'll look in on the scribes and make sure today's announcement and our restitution plans are sent out to every city and village in Eaiven as soon as possible."

With one final, curt nod, Kadoc vacated the room. Tierna cast Seren a sympathetic glance before trailing after him, leaving the uneasy queen alone. Though the pandemonium outside the palace still filled the air, Seren's own words inspired the disquiet in her heart. Yes, it would take time for her to forgive the guilt-ridden king, but she couldn't even imagine what it would take to fully excise the bitterness from her soul... and she feared that the ebb and flow of resentment would extinguish the tiny flame of affection that already struggled to remain alight in her heart.

★   ★   ★

Seren rose from her bench four hours later and shook her cramping right hand as she refilled her water with her left. Upon hearing and believing Kadoc's unexpected news, over half of the palace staff resigned immediately—including all but two scribes. So the maiden lent the downtrodden duo her assistance. At first, they regarded her with cordial skepticism, but the two scribes, Kahal and Eidin, warmed up slightly when she served them what turned out to be the most decadent meal they'd eaten since the last feast day.

Of course, conversation was awkward at best and little was shared of the men's true feelings, but their discomfort waned more with every passing minute. Though they never forgot that she was their queen, the pair inwardly acknowledged that the nervous woman with perfect lettering and a passion for the written word was very different from what they remembered or expected.

As she used her powers to top off the two men's cups, Seren heard hurried footsteps echoing in the hallway. After excusing herself, she peered into the hall and saw one of the few remaining servants rushing past.

"Is something wrong?" she asked.

The frazzled young man stopped and faced her with a quick but low bow.

"There's a man here to see the king, Your Majesty, and he insists that it's urgent. Do you know where he is?"

Seren had a few ideas as to where Kadoc could be, but she held her tongue. With every complaint the staff uttered as they resigned, the king's broken heart was further bruised, and not even the most gracious servants' loyalty could completely lift his spirits. If she could spare him yet another brow beating on an already grueling day, she would.

"I'll speak with the man instead and alert the king if he's truly needed. Please take me to him."

With a hurried affirmation, the servant led Seren to the great hall, which the kingdom's sovereigns had used to hear their people's concerns and complaints for centuries before Kadoc's bloody reign began. As Seren stepped into the room and walked to the dais where their thrones sat, she shrank inwardly upon remembering how they'd used the space to publicly humiliate and harm their subjects and enemies instead of to dole out justice and show mercy. In fact, her last venture to that room in her former life involved blinding a soldier who had the gall to look her in the eye as she passed through the palace gates.

She hadn't even known his name.

Shaking off the disturbing memory, Seren opted to remain standing instead of lowering herself onto her throne. As promised, a man waited for her, kneeling before the throne with his head bowed and face obscured by scraggly deep auburn hair.

"His Majesty is tending to other business right now, but I will help you if I can. How may I be of assistance to you today?"

"I fear I've done wrong to the king," he confessed, his deep voice quivering with every word. "He seized one of my powers when I awakened, but it's come back to me somehow."

He bowed his head to the floor and stretched his arms toward her.

"Please have mercy! I didn't mean to steal from him. I hadn't even left my own village for years. It was an accident or some cruel spellcaster's trick. I came to the palace as soon as I could, but I sold my horse last week, so it's taken me two days to make it here."

Though she couldn't make out the distraught elf's face, her ears perked up at the sound of his strikingly familiar voice. She stepped down from the platform and knelt beside the quietly weeping man, placing an uncertain hand on his shaking shoulder.

"Enri, is that you? Please sit up."

The man lifted his head but kept his eyes down, showing enough obedience to avoid chastisement but not being as bold as he would've been with another elf. As she suspected, the man trembling before her was from her hometown. They'd rarely spoken, but everyone in Gridein knew Enri as the village drunkard. After losing his power and his sons to the elven rulers' cruelty, he'd turned to strong drink—only working enough to ensure he had wine in his cup and food in his belly.

"Do you recognize me?" Seren asked.

Enri chanced a quick glance at Seren, his eyes widening when he finally saw her face.

"Seren! What in Millam's name are you doing here?"

The maiden weighed her words for a moment before giving the simplest answer she could.

"I'm Kadoc's wife."

"Then you can help me," he said, desperately clutching her arm. "Please ask him to show mercy. I didn't mean to offend him."

"That won't be necessary. He won't hurt you. Were you not at the assembly earlier today?"

"No, I was still walking here from Gridein."

"Well, a lot has happened that may set your heart at ease about speaking with Kadoc."

Seren spent the next ten minutes giving the flabbergasted elf a more detailed account of the past week than Kadoc gave the masses that morning. By the time she finished the unbelievable tale, the former drunk was dumbstruck with disbelief.

"I know that you're scared of Kadoc, but he is a changed man. If anything, he'd be happy to know that you regained your power," she reassured him with a smile. "If you wait here, I'll have someone wash your feet and find Kadoc so the two of you can speak."

"Thank you, Ser—Your Majesty."

With one last smile, Seren rose and left the hall. After asking the servants to show her guest some hospitality, she went off in search of Kadoc. She checked each of Kadoc's typical haunts—the theater, his room, and the baths—and came up empty handed, but as Seren emerged from the steamy bathhouse and saw the entrance to the courtyard, she realized that she'd been looking for the old Kadoc and not the new one. In the past, they'd gravitated toward anything that would amuse or empower them and shunned nature's simple joys—the very things that only Millam could claim credit for. During their courtship and first years of their marriage, strolls in the gardens, conversations in the courtyard, and picnics in the sunlight allowed them to bask in one another's company because that was all they truly wanted.

So Seren stepped through the door and into the courtyard, and her soul experienced a bit of blessed serenity the instant she stepped outside. For a moment, she closed her eyes and simply enjoyed the afternoon sunlight's warmth, the rose bushes' subtle floral scent, and the fountain's quiet babbling. If she hadn't been on a mission to find her husband, she could have remained rooted to that spot for hours. Thankfully, his voice both coaxed her back to reality and heralded the end of her search.

"I forgot how much I loved it out here," he said.

"So did I. We should come back after our guest is on his way."

"Our guest?" Kadoc echoed, rolling up the scroll he'd been reading and joining her by the door.

"A man from my village is here to see you. Apparently, he recently regained the power you took from him."

"Did he say how it happened?"

"Enri hasn't been sober in almost twenty years. I doubt he could recall what triggered this even if something did."

"Well, hopefully he can shed at least a little light on how it happened regardless."

Seren shared the rest of Enri's story as they returned to the hall, where they found the elf cleaned up and delighting in a small plate of fruit, cheese, and bread. Of course, he abandoned his seat to greet his king with the same groveling that he addressed Seren with, but his heart was considerably less fearful than it had been upon his arrival.

"Please sit and finish your meal. I know you've traveled a long way with little preparation, and you deserve some refreshment in light of your diligence and bravery," Kadoc said.

Enri flicked his gray eyes in Seren's direction and sat down after receiving a nod and a smile. Sensing that greater proximity would only intimidate his guest, Kadoc sat down on a stool several yards away instead of taking a seat with him. Once he could see the man's face, a memory flashed in Kadoc's mind. After he left the temple in Gridein, Enri stumbled into him. Despite his initial annoyance, Kadoc helped the inebriated elf to his feet and moved along without incident, feeling a bit more lethargic than he had before.

"What power did I take from you?"

"I can heal fast. I also burn through food and alcohol faster than most, but that's just an added bonus."

Kadoc walked over to a guard and asked for his knife. Of course, the warrior obliged, and Kadoc returned to his wife and guest with the recently sharpened weapon. Giving Enri his back, the king drew the knife across his palm. He didn't wince as the steel flayed his flesh, but fear and relief filled his racing heart when the wound healed much more slowly than it would have days before. Had he not absorbed another elf's resistance to pain and enhanced healing, the cut would have taken a week to heal, but now it would painlessly mend itself in hours instead of minutes.

"Well, Enri, it looks like I somehow restored your power to you when we crossed paths in Gridein. Though I'm glad I could return it, I'm sorry for I robbing you of it to begin with. You may spend the night in the palace, and I'll see to it that you have a safe journey by carriage back to Gridein in the morning."

Enri gaped at his king slack jawed for several beats, too awed by Kadoc's calm, meek response to revert to his submissive disposition.

"T-Thank you, Your Majesty."

"You're welcome. Enjoy the rest of your meal."

Instead of prolonging the conversation, Kadoc left the room. After giving Enri a rushed goodbye, Seren joined her husband outside the hall, where she found him fiddling with the scroll he'd been reading in the courtyard.

"Are you all right?"

"It seems as if the gods have given me a way to make things right with at least some of our people."

"Yes, they have. And the others may soften toward you when they hear of your willingness to surrender your power."

"I wish I could do the same for you."

"I don't need my powers back even if you could return them. The ones Aire gave me this lifetime are good enough," she said. "I should return to Kahal and Eidin. We still have quite a few copies to make."

Seren turned to leave, but Kadoc gently caught her by the hand.

"Can you add an addendum to my original message announcing that I will be returning stolen powers to elves one village at a time? I will personally pen letters to each village when their time has come."

"Of course. Would you like to see a draft before we start adding it to the letters?"

"No, I trust you."

After Kadoc gave Seren's hand a brief squeeze, the two parted ways to continue the tasks they had before them. Within a few grueling hours, every announcement was written. Seren sent the two scribes away to rest and enjoy a bit of pampering in the bath house, which had only been open to the royal family until that morning. Instead of joining them and having one of the masseuses ease her stiff right hand, she remained in the work room, cleaning up after herself and her newfound friends. As she tidied up, Seren prayed that Kadoc would soon experience the same camaraderie with his people, but she had a feeling that her hope for such a change would be deferred or dashed.

By the time Seren left the room, she was far more exhausted than she typically was in the afternoon. Deciding to rest her eyes for a bit, she ventured upstairs to the palace's residential wing. Only upon stepping through the unguarded door and beholding the large four-poster bed topped with a tempting pile of pillows and blankets did she realize she'd wandered into the wrong room. When she turned to leave, Seren collided with the equally distracted king, who quickly steadied her before she could fall.

As she met his weary brown eyes, Seren recalled the first time she'd met Kadoc only a week before. She'd been so terrified of the once tyrannical king that she was certain she'd never leave the palace alive. Now, as she stood in his gentle, secure embrace, there was no fear in her heart. The man who held her in that moment was the same man who won her heart one stroll and meal at a time before clumsily asking for her hand in marriage in Brigh. They'd both lived a lifetime—or more in his case—apart, but his love for her was the same.

After a moment, Kadoc felt the initial tension ease from Seren's body and noticed that she hadn't moved away from him. The king leaned forward slightly, lightly caressing her cheek to test her level of comfort. Instead of pulling away, she took a ragged breath and lowered her eyes to his lips, reminiscing about how blissful it'd once been to feel them pressed against hers. But as he finally began to close that precious little distance, she remembered that she could only call upon that fond memory because of his final offense against her. In that instant, their tender moment was tainted.

"I can't do this," she whispered, ducking her head to avoid his kiss.

"Did I do something wrong?"

Seren took a step backward, running her ink-stained hand through her hair.

"No… at least not now. My heart is only this open to you because you forced these blasted memories on me. If you hadn't given me that potion… I don't know what I'd feel, but I wouldn't be this conflicted."

"I understand. I mistook your willingness to help for forgiveness. One day, I hope I'll be fortunate enough to have both."

The conflicted queen took a deep breath and changed the subject.

"I need to lie down for a bit, but I'll join you for supper tonight."

"All right. Let me know if you need anything before then."

Kadoc stepped aside and opened the door for his wife. When the door quietly closed behind her, the maiden's spirits sank even lower, realizing that her honesty had wounded the king on one of the hardest days of his life. Seren faced the door again and lifted her hand to knock, but she shook her head and continued to her room. Once she was inside, Seren sat down and removed her sandals, wondering if a trip to the baths would be better before or after her nap. Just as Seren rested her head on her pillow and decided against leaving her incredibly appealing bed, shuffling footsteps reached her ears.

Fighting her fatigue, the maiden opened her eyes to see Tierna enter the room and close the door behind her. Though she only detected joy in the royal's heart, something dark tainted the smiling woman's happiness and set Seren on edge.

"Do you need something, Tierna?"

"I need you to be very quiet and very still. No one can know that she's here."

Seren's heart nearly stopped as the king's grinning cousin pulled a knife from her belt and held it up to her own throat.

"Tierna, what are you doing?"

"If you touch her, use your powers, or cry for help, she'll cut her own throat," a smooth, unsettling voice purred from the balcony.

Tearing her gaze away from Tierna, Seren looked to her left and saw Orla slink into the room. Though the same hatred oozed from the concubine, confidence and a new appearance accompanied her animosity. Gone were her flowing chestnut curls and in their place were stark white locks that shimmered in the afternoon sun. A triumphant smirk adorned her pale features as she surveyed her prey with sparkling prismatic eyes.

Millam, protect us. The people can't endure this again.

"I don't know what you hoped to gain by doing this to yourself, but I can help you—"

"I want nothing to do with your brand of help," Orla hissed. "Do you want to know why I volunteered to join Kadoc's harem?"

"No, but I'm sure you're eager to tell me."

Orla chuckled, and Tierna's unnatural smile widened as she dug the knife a bit deeper and drew blood, which flowed along the blade's fuller and pooled at the guard before dripping onto the pristine marble floor.

"When I was sixteen, Malok came to me in a dream. He told me that if I worshipped him by giving myself to the king, he would make me the queen of Eaiven," she revealed. "He showed me a taste of what it would be like to be by Kadoc's side, and I awakened from my dream with a fire ignited in me that no one could snuff out. I spent the next four years refining and beautifying myself so I could be as desirable as possible to the king when I presented myself to him, but no matter how many times I made Kadoc smile, helped him sleep, and gave him the very pleasure that you deny him, he never loved me."

"I'm sorry that the Cursed One deceived you, but Tierna doesn't deserve this. Please let her go."

"Trust me, she does, but you will both reap what you've sown soon enough," she said, glancing at Tierna. "Fetch the cuffs for me."

"Yes, my queen."

The entranced royal glided across the room, fabricated joy still in her eyes as Orla's charm propelled her forward. And the transformed elf continued her tale as Tierna rifled through Seren's few belongings in search of Harreb's cuffs.

"Two nights ago, Malok visited my dreams again. He said that he would finally fulfill his promise if I brought Kadoc back to him and made him as he once was, but you present an infuriating problem."

Tierna found the cuffs and came to Orla's side. The concubine extended her arm, and Tierna placed the golden cuff on her right wrist. As she fixed the silver one on Seren's wrist, the entranced elf drew the knife across her throat slightly, a silent but effective reminder that her life was forfeit if Seren resisted.

"Aled pointed out that Kadoc will mourn you again and hate me for ending your life if I kill you. But when he awakens under Malok's hand again and realizes that I am his only true equal, you'll be long forgotten."

Tierna set a piece of papyrus, a quill, and ink on Seren's desk, a drop of fresh blood barely missing the artfully pressed paper.

"Write a note to Kadoc telling him that you can't forgive him for what he's done and need to start anew away from him."

Though Orla's power of charm didn't force Seren's obedience, the blood running down Tierna's knife was effective enough. She sat at her writing desk and penned the note as ordered, wordlessly begging the gods to protect the kingdom and Kadoc from his former lover with every stroke of her quill. After signing the epistle, Seren held up the papyrus, which Orla snatched from her hand.

"This is truly heartbreaking… much better than anything I would have compelled out of you," she smiled. "If I don't have the pleasure of killing you the next time we see one another, I'm sure Kadoc will do the deed himself."

Before Seren could utter another word, Orla placed a pallid hand on her forehead, and darkness consumed her vision as sleep overtook her mind.

CHAPTER 9
Visions of Violence

Rhythmic bumping and clouds of dust greeted Seren when she finally awakened. Upon opening her eyes, she beheld two soldiers sitting across the cart from her as they cut across the moonlit nightscape. When Seren surreptitiously reached out with her powers, she felt only a combination of genuine excitement and alertness in the men's hearts… emotions that Orla's enhanced charisma hadn't elicited. Just as she began to wonder if Orla bought their loyalty with money or if it was inspired by the same perverse worship the concubine practiced, she heard the driver singing above the wheels' ruckus.

> *"On his day, he'll eclipse the sun,*
> *Eclipse the sun, eclipse the sun.*
> *On his day, water will run blood,*
> *Will run blood, will run blood.*
> *Then all will bow to the Darkened One,*
> *Ev'ry father and ev'ry son.*
>
> *On his day, ev'ry star will fall,*
> *Star will fall, star will fall.*
> *Oh his day, ev'ry lamp is crushed,*
> *Lamp is crushed, lamp is crushed.*
> *And Malok's darkness will cover all,*
> *Ev'ry temple and ev'ry hall."*

A deep chill rolled over Seren at the sound of the familiar song—one she and Kadoc once sang in celebration of their bloodiest victories. The rarely uttered folk tune wasn't written in any of the elves' or ogres' songbooks nor did the faeries in the north record the lyrics for safe keeping. Only the beings who made up the dregs of society sought out those words let alone sung them by heart with such gusto. Somewhere on her journey to the darkness, Orla had gained the loyalty of a few Malok worshippers, and Seren was left defenseless thanks to the cuff and ropes on her wrist. But she couldn't simply lie still and let them drive her to a prison more secure and torturous than the cart she currently resided in.

"Where are you taking me?"

The soldier closest to her, a blonde elf with a scar marring his unshaven cheek, stopped singing and turned his attention from the passing trees to his recently roused cargo.

"As far away from Their Majesties as we can."

Anger burned in Seren's heart at the royal honors the soldier bestowed upon Orla, but a particularly aggressive bump in the road shook her necklace free from inside her dress, making the amulet fall on her shoulder. In a heartbeat, a plan came to mind, and she prayed to Millam and Inneh that no one in the carriage knew the power her jewelry possessed.

"If you let me go, you can have this necklace. It was made by the finest craftsmen in Eaiven, and it bears the artisan hall's mark on the back, so you could sell it without anyone questioning its value. It's probably worth more than you make in a year."

The fair-haired elf snickered and leaned forward, letting the amulet of Inneh rest in his hand, which reeked of the hallucinogenic herbs that some elves smoked to addle their brains and escape their grim realities. Seeing Seren recoil inspired another chuckle, and a lecherous intention briefly rose in his heart before being overridden by obedience… and greed.

"I won't set you free, but I *will* take your little necklace."

He snatched the necklace from Seren's neck, and she flashed him a knowing grin just as light bathed the cart and she winked out of sight. When the radiance dimmed, Seren found herself in a moderately familiar wood, where peat's pungent odor rode on the wind and assaulted her nose. The scent was as unpleasant as ever, but the confirmation that she'd made it to Agron cheered her downcast soul a bit.

The maiden rolled onto her back and sat up before grasping her detached necklace with her shackled hands. Seren briefly considered attempting to don it once more, but logic helped her suppress that impulse. She was shackled, powerless, and alone. Even if Orla hadn't somehow forced Kadoc to complete Malok's ritual again, she would be more of a liability than an asset to the king due to her inability to defend herself. If she was truly to help Kadoc, she would need help… help that carried weapons and wielded power fit for combat. Alas, without the sun or grien flowers to guide her, she didn't know what route to take to return to Aden.

"Millam, please show me the way. I can't do this on my own."

The moment Seren's prayer left her lips, a voice cried out from several yards away.

"You, there! Identify yourself!"

Seren turned to her left and saw a rebel soldier poised to launch an arrow in her direction. Based on the confidence he exuded, either he had the gift of accuracy or the practice necessary to ensure it. So she raised her hands enough for him to see her shackles and obeyed his command.

"I'm Seren, daughter of Kalbhac, and I need to speak with Fedhlim immediately."

Much to her relief, the soldier lowered his weapon and swiftly crossed the grass and shrubs to get a closer look at her.

"My name is Rylahn, and Fedhlim said you might come back. I didn't expect you to return this soon," he said, glancing at her shackles. "I can't do anything about those here, but someone will be able to get them off once we reach Aden. Come with me."

The maiden released a breath that she'd scarcely realized she was holding and followed the rebel to where his horse happily snacked on grass nearby. After having a mildly awkward time helping Seren onto the horse, he mounted his steed behind her and began the short journey to the elf settlement. When they arrived, Rylahn took Seren straight to the watchtower and quickly found a metalworker to tend to her shackles while he hunted down his leader.

By the time the shackles fell to the floor and Seren had a cup of tea and conversation with her frazzled parents to fortify her, Fedhlim entered the room. Though Seren couldn't detect his emotions as she could with other elves, his brief pause at the door and hesitance to look her in the eye made his uncertainty quite obvious. And judging by the steely glare her mother shot in his direction as she and her father left, his shame was inspired by more than his guilt-ridden conscious.

"Toren foretold that you'd return by night, but I wondered if he'd seen his vision clearly when Doran came back with news of Kadoc's transformation. It wouldn't be the first time he was wrong about you."

Seren stood a bit straighter at the reminder of Toren's ambush-inspiring vision.

"You mean his vision about me coming under the God of Darkness' yoke again?"

"Yes… that one," Fedhlim confirmed, scratching the back of his neck.

"What exactly did he see in that vision?"

"Is that truly important right now?"

"Perhaps. What did he see?"

"He saw a young woman with dark hair drink a potion and take on your old appearance—white hair and pale skin and a heart darker than night."

"Did he see her face?"

"No, only her silhouette in the darkness."

"Well, Toren's vision wasn't false… just incorrectly interpreted. The woman he saw wasn't me. It was Kadoc's former mistress Orla. At some point between Kadoc sending her to the winter palace and this afternoon, she took the same elixir we did and became one of the Cursed One's servants… or rather she became in body what she already was at heart."

"Our people can't endure a defiled ruler again," he sighed, her news dampening his shame-laden spirit. "I'm so sorry for doubting you and running you off the last time we saw one another. If I'd taken the time to ask for more details about Toren's vision and given you the benefit of the doubt, then—"

"Then Kadoc would still be overrun by wickedness, and Eaiven wouldn't have its king back. As much as I wish this had come about differently, the gods clearly had a plan that not even the God of Darkness' influence could thwart."

"I'm glad you see things that way," he said with a smile that fell short of his haunted hazel eyes.

"I'd go mad otherwise. If my faith was lesser and I couldn't forgive or trust you, I don't know where I'd be right now."

As soon as the words left her mouth, Seren became keenly aware of the seed of bitterness toward Kadoc that she still held in her heart. She'd forgiven Fedhlim—a man who was practically a stranger—so easily, but she hadn't forgiven her own husband. She used the very bond that yoked them together to justify the distance between them. The man she loved more than anyone in the world had deceived her like no one ever had—setting her and all of Eaiven on a deadly journey that no one ever could have predicted. And though she'd committed countless atrocities during their gory reign and received a second chance from the gods, she still refused to release her gnawing resentment.

If Millam could forgive us despite the offenses we've committed not just against our kind and ogres but against him, *how can I not forgive Kadoc?*

"Seren?"

"I'm sorry. My mind was somewhere else," she said, shaking her head but not loosening her grasp on that convicting revelation. "Orla plans to give Kadoc the elixir again, and I can't use my powers to reverse the spell anymore. We have to go to Eaiven and stop her before she drags him and the kingdom into darkness again."

"And stop her we shall," Fedhlim said, standing a bit straighter. "I'll prepare the army. Your dagger and cuirass are in the armory, but take whatever else you think you'll be proficient with and meet me outside the city gates. We leave in an hour."

Fedhlim vacated the room, leaving Seren alone once more. Without delay, she finished her drink and went to the armory. As Seren donned her armor and weapon, she harkened back to Aerin's vision. So far, none of the visions she'd learned of had come back void, but the prophecy about her defeating Kadoc and becoming evil once more had been misinterpreted. Even if Aerin's revelation about her becoming a mother was true, that didn't guarantee that Kadoc was the father of her future child. The elves and ogres had striven against the vicious monarch for a century without dethroning him, and who knew how long it would take them to defeat or win him back a second time with her powers rendered useless.

Seren sank onto a nearby stool and cradled her head in her hands. Enduring only a week of the peaks and valleys attached to her bond with Kadoc and coming to terms with her destiny had exhausted her beyond belief, and the prospect of bearing that burden for months or years made her want to curl up on the cool stone floor and scream until her throat felt as raw as her soul. And she almost did as she imagined her husband succumbing to Orla's unnaturally effective allure. Alas, he'd no doubt feel as if his tainted decision was justified when she returned to Eaiven with an army of men and women who'd once sworn an oath to dethrone him.

"Millam, please protect Kadoc," she begged, her voice cracking as tears snaked down her hot, flushed cheeks. "Don't let the Cursed One claim his soul or his life."

Neither peace nor certainty flooded Seren's heart at the end of her prayer, but Kadoc's welfare alone was enough to bring the queen to her feet and get her out the door. Seren was undoubtedly the least proficient fighter who would cross into Eaiven that night, but her will to win was just as strong as theirs—if not fiercer. Fear, justice, and vengeance drove many an elf to fight valiantly on the battlefield, but as the song of Aire said, love was the strongest motivation of all. And Seren held her devotion dear as the army finally gathered and began the march to Eaiven.

CHAPTER 10
A Prophecy Fulfilled

"I didn't think I'd see you again," Doran said, bringing his horse beside hers as they watched a skirmish between a small group of rebels and the elves guarding the border. "Welcome back."

"Hopefully, it'll be a short reunion," she said. "I don't want this conflict to drag on any longer than necessary."

"I can imagine," he sighed. "Thank you for everything you did in the palace. I know I wasn't very kind to you, but things would've been much worse if you hadn't intervened."

"You're welcome, but between your intervention at my awakening and your help at the ambush a few days ago, I think we're even."

Doran's lips turned upward for a flicker, and Seren returned his brief smile.

"Fedhlim asked me to protect you during the battle. He doesn't want you fighting unless it's absolutely necessary, but he believes you'll be an important player in what's about to unfold."

"Important but inept."

"What you lack in skill, you make up for in heart… and in having Millam's favor. I've never seen the gods move more than I have since you appeared at the cave a week ago. If they needed a warrior, they would've made you one."

"Yes, they would have."

The fight ended as the rebels overtook the small company of royal soldiers by taking the final survivor captive. Though the small victory should have gladdened Seren's heart, it only reminded her of the greater battle that was sure to follow.

Once they bound their enemies and relieved them of their armor and weapons, Fedhlim's forces continued their journey to the palace. Other than two lightly manned toll bridges and a small militia stationed near Mount Ceallah, they faced no resistance, but neither the elves nor their dozen ogre comrades lowered their defenses. By the time the first glimmer of sunlight glowed in the east, the palace came into view… as did the legion of soldiers standing outside the walls. No one was surprised to see that Orla had assembled the warriors to protect the palace, but seeing the elves gripping their weapons and grimacing at the invaders through the narrow slits in their armor galvanized the rebels, who struggled to maintain their easy pace in the presence of their enemies.

Fedhlim, who rode in the vanguard, came to a stop two furlongs from the palace, and his army halted as well. Drawing a tremulous breath, he turned to face the men and women who'd followed him not just in battle but in life and attempted to rouse their spirits before they potentially marched to their deaths.

"Brothers and sisters, the moment we have all anticipated and dreaded has finally arrived. The gods have brought us out of exile and into our homeland for the first time in decades to face the very evil that inspired our fearful flight. Yet the evil we face is not the one we've stored up our wrath for all these years. We do not battle against men with flesh and bone but against an invisible evil who seeks to destroy all of Millam's creations. Our enemy this night and for all of our days is Malok."

Discomfort rippled through the crowd as Fedhlim uttered the typically unspoken name, but he pressed on with his speech nonetheless.

"I say his name tonight not out of reverence or fear, but out of defiance and assurance that we will deal him another grave wound this blessed day. No longer will he lead our homeland into darkness at the hands of cursed rulers nor will he divide our people with fear and hatred. His malevolent grip on the throne will be broken today with your swords, spears, arrows, and clubs. His influence on the crown will be forever cast out with your valor and skill. And his venom will bleed out one drop of blood at a time until not a trace pollutes our people's hearts!" Fedhlim drew his sword, still bloody from the previous frays, and thrust it into the air. "Are you ready to take our kingdom back?"

"Aye!"

"Are you ready to put that scourge in the abyss where he belongs?"

"Aye!"

"Then follow me into battle! Whether you fall by the sword or stand victorious when this is done, glory will be yours!"

With a primal yell that would have intimidated even the most seasoned soldier, the rebels charged forward. Just before they reached the royal army, their ogre allies broke through the crowd, sweeping the front lines of the half-spelled army aside with their clubs as if they were nothing more than a child's toy soldiers. The elves who weren't injured or worse by the ogres' attack defended the palace with whatever powers and skills they possessed—unleashing arrows with deadly accuracy, attacking the invaders with enhanced speed, and commanding poisonous snakes that nipped at the rebels' heels and rendered them immobile.

Rather than focusing on the carnage before her, Seren followed Doran's lead and moved around the palace to the garden entrance with about fifty soldiers and two ogres. Engar had decided to join their small yet fierce crew, and sensing the lack of revulsion in his heart cheered Seren just a bit. When they reached the north gate, Doran turned to the elf on his right. At his silent command, Eila closed her eyes and lifted her ebony face to the sky as she unleashed her quiet yet effective power.

"Kadoc is in the assembly hall," she said after a moment, "and the little agloc is with him."

"Are any soldiers guarding them?" Doran asked.

"Only ten. Nothing we can't handle."

Doran turned to Seren, whose breathing quickened at the sound of the king's name.

"Are you ready for this?"

"No," she answered, raising her dagger, "but when have I ever been ready for anything the gods have had me do?"

"Then let's go."

A second elf raised his hand and the iron gates groaned as the rebels' armor shook. When Ilrath opened his fist, the neatly wrought gate peeled up from the ground until a breach large enough for them to pass through opened. The small company ducked beneath the gate, which was warped and curled like great iron eyelashes, and passed onto the palace grounds. The moment they crossed over the first ward inside the estate, the ground shuddered beneath them. A low growl rumbled from behind the garden's hedgerow followed by dissonant duet of howls.

"Remember what I told you," Seren quavered as the rebels closed around her. "The hound's heart is between its heads. You'll need something stronger than wood or an arrowhead to pierce its flesh."

A breath after the final hurried instructions left Seren's lips, the hound burst through the carefully manicured greenery. The creature was as tall as an ogre with a thick coat of black fur that no one but the royal couple had ever caressed. The two wolf-like heads growled and barked with equal ferocity, their ears flattened and sharp fangs barred as blood dribbled from their thin black lips onto the ground below. Without delay, the hound charged forward, disappearing right before it could rip into the elves at the front of the crew and reappearing at the rear. The hound's left head sank its teeth into one elf while the other took a beating from Engar's brother.

As the ogre's metal-embedded club crashed into its massive head, the hound threw the elf across the palace grounds and winked out of sight before terrorizing the elves on the right. After ripping an ogre's arm from his body and sending Ilrath soaring back behind the gate with a flick of its barbed tail, the hound appeared in the center of the company and snapped at Seren, who faded backwards scarcely in time for Engar to steal its attention by swinging his club into the left head's left eye. The hound sprang at the ogre for revenge just as a particularly agile elf vaulted onto its back and attempted to sink her sword into the hound's leathery flesh. When it reared up with a bone-shaking roar, the elf tumbled off its back, losing her sword in the process.

Seconds before the hound's massive paws came into contact with the hand-manicured grass again, a piece of iron sailed through the air and struck the beast between its heads. When Seren glanced behind her, she saw Ilrath, the elf who'd opened the gate, panting at the rear of their company with blood on his armor and a ghost of a smile on his face as the hound collapsed with an earth-shaking thud.

Instead of congratulating themselves, the group quickly took inventory of their company. The two elves who the hound threw across the yard were limping back to their allies with scratches and knifelike wounds from their encounter with the beast, and the ogre who lost his arm brushed off their concerns with grunt. Despite that perturbing interlude, they forged ahead and entered the palace, attempting to be as quiet as their heavy breathing and metal armor would allow.

Though they never voiced it, the less seasoned elves were shocked that no soldier lie between them and their targets, but Seren and Doran knew more than anyone not to underestimate their enemy. The hall's open doors came into view after a few minutes, and out came the guards. Half of their hearts hummed with the same unnatural joy and conformity that Seren saw in Tierna the previous day, but the remaining elves had given themselves over to Malok, untainted hatred and violence swirling in their spirits at the sight of the insurgents.

Ilrath raised his hand to strip the soldiers of their armor, but an enemy elf was quicker, sending a knife of glass in the metal master's direction. He moved aside in time to avoid a fatal blow, but the gleaming blade nicked his arm, and a paralyzing venom shot through his body before he could comprehend the peril he was in. As the knife sailed back to its grinning owner, Engar swung his club and slammed the overconfident elf into the fresco to his right with a roar that shook his enemies' confidence. With that tit for tat combat, the fray began.

Doran stayed by Seren's side, keeping any elves who came for her occupied with his gods-given skills while she defected the few blows that made it past him with her dagger and shield. Even though she kept her focus on preserving her life and helping Doran keep his, seeing his agility, strength, and expertise made her realize how lucky she was to have such a gifted ally. Despite the dark, painful history between them, which she now remembered with unwanted detail, he still fought heroically on her behalf and defended her as if she were his sister and not his childhood tormentor.

Just as the venomous elf who Engar thumped retrieved his fallen blade and stalked in their direction, Orla emerged from the hall, and Seren's heart filled with hatred. Yet her loathing bled to despair when Kadoc exited three steps behind her, his hair as stark as the marble floors and prismatic eyes even colder. When Seren reached out with her powers and detected undivided devotion dwelled in the king's heart, rage joined her animosity, and only self-control kept her rooted to Doran's side.

"I need to get to Ka—"

"Stop fighting."

Orla's voice filled the hallway, her power caressing every soul within earshot and inspiring obedience. Every elf, Doran and Seren included, stood perfectly still, but the ogres weren't so obedient. Engar's brother charged at Orla, who simply grazed Kadoc's shoulder with her graceful touch. The king gestured toward the ogre, and fire from the nearby torch consumed him. While the flames didn't burn the ogre's scaly hide as it would have scalded an elf's skin, the force and relentless nature of the fiery onslaught kept him occupied long enough for Seren's entranced protector to stride forward and cleave the ogre's head from his body the instant the flames ceased. Engar, who lie on the ground with the enemy elf's venom coursing through his veins, let out a ferocious snarl that would have shaken every elf's confidence had they not been bespelled by their sneering mistress.

"Come here Seren," Orla beckoned.

Seren walked forward, trying to overcome the compulsion but succumbing to it bodily despite her heart being far from obedient. Once Seren stood within arm's length of Orla, the empowered elf reached into Seren's satchel and retrieved the necklace Aire had given her.

"Is this it, my darling?" she asked Kadoc.

"Yes, that's the necklace."

Orla placed the magical token on the floor in front of Kadoc.

"Destroy it."

The maiden's heart lurched in horror as Kadoc crushed the amulet underfoot, a wave of power rippling through the palace as its enchantment came to an end. When Kadoc stepped into place beside Orla, only a golden chain and beautiful rubble remained. Not even the greatest artisan could reassemble the amulet, and an insubordinate tear escaped from Seren's eye as she grasped that Orla had severed her connection to Kadoc. Gone forever was her ability to move in and out of Kadoc's presence whenever her heart desired. If they were separated again, she would have no way to be by his side. And if she needed to flee his presence, there was no magical escape route.

Even as Seren inwardly mourned the amulet's destruction, she knew that the latter was far more likely than the former. Kadoc was lost to her, and not even she could withstand the spell binding him to his triumphant concubine. The siren herself grabbed Seren by the throat with a vile grin gracing her lips before tossing her rival across the room. Seren landed at Eila's feet, but neither elf moved until their mistress commanded it.

"Pick her up and remove her armor."

Eila and another elf helped the stunned maiden to her feet and removed her cuirass, helmet, greaves, and arm guards until only her tunic and sandals remained. Once Seren was stripped of her protective garments, Orla glided toward her. Though there was no menace in her graceful stance or steps, murderous intentions churned within the elf's soul.

"In case you couldn't tell, I've already gained more power than I had when we last saw one another. It's so refreshing to be not just irresistible, but strong as well."

Orla punched Seren in the gut, and the queen nearly vomited as she crumbled before her enemy. Taking advantage of Seren's lower position, Orla followed up by kneeing her in the face. The injured maiden collapsed again with blood dripping from her broken nose, but she simply scowled at Orla, unable to even wipe the blood away without her permission. But Seren's reprieve on the cool marble surface didn't last long. The elves drew her up once more, holding their panting, pained ally by her arms as she sagged between them.

Rather than striking her rival again, Orla wiped the blood from Seren's face and closed her eyes in prayerful ecstasy as she licked it from her fingers.

"Thank you, Malok, for delivering my enemy to me and fulfilling your promise. I will be twice the daughter to you that she ever was, and I will make your name so great that your darkness will blot out the sun itself."

Orla placed her hand over Seren's heart, and terror gripped her as she recognized the unyielding grip of power on her soul. The queen had wielded that power so many times that her once incalculable evil still troubled her renewed heart, but she'd experienced its deadly tug only once before.

When Kadoc stole her powers and her life.

Undulating darkness, visible as smoke, poured from Orla and sur-rounded Seren, but she couldn't even turn her head to silently plead for help. She could only watch unblinking as Orla slowly, torturously drained her might. Searing heat and pain crept from her extremities to her shuddering heart, leaving a chilly tingling in its wake. When that icy sensation barely caressed her heart, a different kind of heat filled the palace.

Fire shot across the hallway and consumed Orla, who screamed in pain as she dropped her paralyzed victim. Before the seething concu-bine could recover, lightning struck her and threw her against the wall. Though Seren still couldn't move, warmth returned to her limp limbs, and her heart smiled when she saw Kadoc stride forward, trembling with rage as he closed in on his former lover. Using the little restraint he possessed, the king seized Orla by the arms securely enough that she could move but without injuring her. Sensing their mistress' desperation, the spellbound elves advanced.

Kadoc released his power in response by sending a tremor through the palace that knocked the elves from their feet. Before they could recover, lighting crackled from his free hand and struck them enough to stun but not to kill.

"What did you do?" Orla screeched in Seren's direction as she clawed at Kadoc's unyielding arm.

"My wife didn't do anything," Kadoc seethed. "You brought me back to my senses all on your own by trying to kill the woman I love. I refuse to be responsible for her death a second time."

"You may love her, but she'll never accept you as long as you bear Malok's likeness. And with her powers under my control, she won't be able to turn you back again."

"She doesn't need to."

As Kadoc spoke, magic rolled through his body, and his stark locks, eyes, and skin darkened to their natural coloring.

"I altered my appearance to please you because you entranced me, but the elixir didn't work on me. I will never serve the Cursed One again, and *you* will never manipulate my people again. Now, remove the cuff so Seren can cleanse you."

"I won't betray Malok like you did."

"Remove it!"

A gasp escaped Orla's lips and her back arched as heat emanated from Kadoc's hands and lightning crackled over her body. While the concubine squirmed in his grasp, her grip on Seren's soul loosened, and she was able to move once more. Clawing her way to her feet, Seren fastened her belt around her waist with half-numb hands.

"Stop! I'll remove the cuff. Just let me go," she wailed, panting as sweat beaded and instantly evaporated from her brow.

Kadoc released Orla's left hand, which she promptly placed against Kadoc's forehead. The king collapsed into a deep sleep, and Orla rose from the floor, trembling as she recovered from Kadoc's attack. Her servants didn't recuperate so quickly, but without the rebels' and Kadoc's protection, nothing stood between the corrupted concubine and her powerless prey.

"I won't bother charming you this time. I want you to run as fast as you can only to writhe in agony as I fall upon you and suck the life from your broken body."

"I'm not going to run," Seren said, pushing through her pain to focus on her increasingly limber hands.

"Have it your way."

One by one, the elves roused as Orla walked past them, obedience still in their faint spirits as they drew their weapons with quaking hands to defend her honor. Yet she silently commanded their stillness and chose to confront her rival without their aid. When she was a few paces away, Orla armed herself with Engar's discarded club and lunged toward Seren. The maiden barely dodged Orla's blow and fell on her back in the process. Instead of scrambling to her feet again, Seren swept her legs under her enemy's, bringing her to the ground as well. As Orla recovered from the unexpected blow, Seren attempted to kick her in the face, but she was neither quick nor strong enough to land another strike.

The concubine caught her ankle and snapped it effortlessly, pulling a scream from Seren's lips. Stubborn tears poured from her eyes, and she vacillated between begging Millam for mercy and cursing Malok as Orla rose to her feet with unsettling poise and clucked her tongue in disapproval.

"I can't blame you for fighting, but that was positively pitiful."

Orla kicked Seren in the stomach, her blow far more effective than her opponent's had been. The maiden slammed into the wall beside Doran and yelped in pain, continuing her silent entreaties to Millam as Orla melodically laughed at her misery. When Seren rolled over, fighting to catch her breath, she noticed her discarded dagger next to the wall and cast a furtive glance at her opponent, who knelt beside the sleeping king. Gathering the paltry strength she possessed, Seren slid the dagger under her right thigh and sat up, resting her back against the wall.

"He won't remain asleep for long. When Kadoc awakens, you'll be dead."

"Perhaps, but you'll be in Ifryn long before I make an appearance there."

Abandoning her slumbering sovereign, Orla snatched a sword from one of the elves, crossed the hallway, and seized Seren by the throat again. When Orla drew her opponent up from the floor, Seren took hold of her dagger and slipped it into the woman's body, twisting the blade once it found its home deep in her chest. Orla released her grip on Seren and both women tumbled to the floor at Doran's feet. The gasping wretch reached out to the healer, but he simply backed away, no longer a slave to her broken compulsion. The other elves also shrugged off her magical yoke, and Kadoc awakened from his brief slumber as Orla's blood oozed from her wound and onto the once immaculate tile.

The king shook off his grogginess and looked to Seren, who Doran was already healing. After Kadoc caught her gaze and she gave him a brief, permissive nod, he knelt beside Orla.

"If you release Seren from the cuffs, we will heal you and free you from Malok's curse."

Instead of accepting Kadoc's mercy, Orla spat in his face, marring his bronzed skin with blood before turning her eyes to the ceiling and lifting her failing voice in song.

"On his day, ev'ry star will fall,
Star will fall, star will fall.
Oh his day, ev'ry lamp is crushed,
Lamp is crushed, lamp is crushed.
And Malok's darkness will cover…"

Orla's eyes bled from silver to black and the same malevolent mist that enshrouded her before eased from her mouth and nose with her final breath. That darkness dissipated like vapor in the wind, leaving its once zealous host devoid of power and life. The instant her heart stilled, the Cuffs of Harreb opened and tumbled to the floor.

After closing his concubine's wide, lifeless eyes, Kadoc came to Seren's side and let her sag against him. Though not even a bruise remained on her sweat-slicked skin, Seren still felt not the pain but the weight of the battle. But seeing that the once spelled palace soldiers and rebels held the Malok-worshipping insurrectionists at sword-point cheered her heart a bit.

"Take them to the dungeon, and don't harm them unless necessary. I need to make sure the madness outside ends as quickly as possible," Kadoc ordered. "Seren, would you rather join me or rest?"

"I'll come with you."

By the time the king and queen stepped out of the palace, the conflict had come to an end. Just as their once charmed comrades had, the members of royal army who were freed from Orla's grasp turned on the Malok worshippers they once fought beside. And only a few misguided dissenters were able to flee by dawn's burgeoning light. A combination of soldiers and rebels chased them down at Kadoc's command while the remaining warriors cleaned up after the bloody battle, mourning the elves and ogres who fell because of Orla's brief but deadly coup.

As the men and women cleared the battlefield and tended to the injured, Fedhlim finally broke away from his men and approached Kadoc. Both men regarded one another with suspicion—Kadoc's apprehension infused with shame and Fedhlim's tainted with lingering aversion. Seren's dark eyes darted between the two elves, praying that bloodshed lie behind them and not before. After several tense moments, Fedhlim finally spoke.

"I will not bow to you, Kadoc."

"Nor do I expect you to. I haven't earned your respect, but I hope to one day."

Fedhlim nodded, unsure of how to respond to Kadoc's unexpected humility.

"You have done a better job leading and loving the people since you took the mantle of leadership in Agron. Thank you for serving the kingdom while I was too busy terrorizing it," Kadoc continued. "I would be honored if you would help me right the wrongs I've committed. The people trust and look up to you, so they'd be more willing to accept your kindness than mine."

"I'd need to straighten out some of my affairs in Aden, but I'll help the citizens of Eaiven as long as I can find a suitable substitute… and as long as I'm free to step away whenever I see fit."

"That's perfectly fine with me. I may also need your assistance smoothing things over with the ogres."

"I'm not sure that they'll be so forgiving, but I'll help where I can."

With that tense but genuine agreement, the two former enemies briefly shook hands and began surveying the damage and injuries caused by the fray. As Kadoc sought Fedhlim's council about how to move forward with the people, a hint of a smile graced Seren's lips. Turning her eyes to the east, the maiden realized that they weren't simply starting a new day in Eaiven. They were ushering in a new era.

★   ★   ★

Hours later, once the soldiers had set up camp and the injured warriors were under the care of healers and physicians, Seren finally indulged in the palace's baths. Instead of lingering in the tepidarium at the beginning of her excursion, Seren immediately passed into the caldarium. After massaging fragrant oils into her sore muscles and scraping away the day's soil, she reclined on a couch and closed her eyes to enjoy the heat and steam radiating from the mosaic-tiled floor. Several minutes into her rare moment of leisure, Seren heard the door open. When she lifted her head from the couch and saw Tierna enter, she greeted the king's cousin with relief rather than irritation.

"How are you feeling?" Seren asked. "I came by your room to see you earlier, but you weren't there."

"I'm far better than I was last night," Tierna said, instinctively touching her neck, which the healer had seen to earlier. "I heard that you're the one who defeated Orla."

"Barely. She would have killed me if I hadn't been able to use my dagger."

"But you did, and we have you to thank for ridding us of another of the God of Darkness' minions. Kadoc didn't tell me much more than that because he and Fedhlim needed to talk about some pressing matter, but I know that the kingdom and I owe you thanks."

A gentle chime that only Seren could hear resounded in the room, signaling the end of her time in the caldarium and giving her the chance to recover alone once more.

"It's time for me to move into the frigidarium, but I'm sure we'll chat over dinner later."

"I'll see you then."

With those parting words, Seren finished her time in the baths with a plunge in the chilly water, quickly dressed herself, and retired to her room. When the time came for supper, Kadoc and Fedhlim sent their apologies, so the two ladies dined alone, choosing to discuss lighter matters instead of the past two days' harrowing events. After dinner, Seren changed into her nightgown with heavy eyelids and fell asleep before the sun even set.

CHAPTER 11
The Lights of Iacha

Thanks to her early withdrawal the evening before, Seren's dreamless slumber ended minutes before the sun made its daily ascent. She rolled out of bed and stretched her stiff limbs then covered her mouth with her hand, using her powers to quench her early morning thirst. Satisfied with that bit of refreshment, she walked toward the balcony to watch the sunrise. Just before she passed through the doors, she noticed something unusual on her desk.

When Seren drew near the table and she saw a dried, deep green laurel wreath atop a sheet of neatly rolled papyrus, her stomach dropped. Though the wreath's familiar earthy scent called to mind the celebratory feast when she placed it on Kadoc's head and danced under the starlight until her feet ached, the keepsake failed to comfort her. Instead of dwelling on the distant past, she retrieved the small scroll, broke Kadoc's seal, and steeled herself for the message inside.

Dearest Seren,

After we parted ways yesterday, I realized that once again, I placed you and our people in danger. Good men and women perished and you nearly did as well because of the Cursed One's unwillingness to let me go and the destruction I caused during my reign. Every day that I sit on the throne, I silently challenge the God of Darkness because I am a living reminder of his most recent defeat. I know better than most that his pursuit is as relentless as his vengeance, and I refuse to let any more elves pay the price for my misdeeds.

Therefore, I have named Fedhlim as my successor and abdicated the throne. He is an honorable, upright man who cares for our people deeply, which makes him the perfect person to lead the kingdom into a new era that I pray will be marked by peace and healing. And I will spend however many days or years I have left doing my best to restore what I've stolen from the people in whatever way I can. My hope is to do more good for Eaiven as a common man than I ever could as a king.

As for you, my dove, I release you from whatever obligation you feel toward me. My love for you will never fade, but you should get to experience happiness with a man whose presence won't remind you of your greatest sorrows and regrets. You deserve a fresh start. And so I leave my wreath with you as my pledge to never interfere with your life again. May Millam bless you and keep you all the days of your life.

Kadoc

Seren's tears blurred the dried ink before she even reached the king's signature, but neither relief nor gladness inspired her tears—only sorrow. Kadoc had been by her side for the worst moments of her life, but he'd also been instrumental in the best ones… the day they met at the Festival of Lights and couldn't take their eyes off one another… the evening they shared their first kiss under a trellis draped with thalsach vines while butterflies fluttered and glowed around them… the moment he vowed to protect her and love her until his dying breath.

Yes, the presence of those memories was evidence of Kadoc's final sin against her, but they were more than that. They were evidence of a love that survived the greatest evil in the land and death itself. And the only thing keeping Seren from truly embracing the man she loved was the self-protective resentment in her heart.

I have to forgive him, she resolved fingering the three-stranded cord around her neck. *I can't accept Millam's forgiveness for everything I've done but hold Kadoc's deeds over his head when he is clearly so remorseful about them.*

Humbled yet convicted by her hypocrisy, Seren re-rolled the scroll and placed it in her satchel along with the laurel wreath and the rest of her belongings. After dressing herself with impressive efficiency and leaving hastily written epistles for Tierna, Doran, and Fedhlim, she hunted down Eidin. She soon found the scribe taking a stroll in the gardens and watching as a few elves who were especially talented with greenery repaired the damage from the previous day's battle.

"Eidin!" she called.

"Good morning, Your Majesty," he greeted with a bow. "I'm surprised to see you out so early. Is there something I can help you with?"

"Yes, there is. You wrote the letters to the first villages that Kadoc planned to make restitution to, correct?"

"Yes, I did."

"Do you remember the first village he was going to visit?"

"He was planning to visit Iacha first."

"And after that?"

"Telna and Kian."

"Thank you," she breathed, kissing the scribe's hands before flitting away as suddenly as she'd arrived.

Without delay, she donned her armor, hurried to the stables, mounted the same mare she rode on the journey from Brigh, and set off for Iacha, a small village two hours away on the shores of Lake Abbon. Many of the townspeople were fishermen who enjoyed the gold and silver their catches brought in at the nearby markets almost as much as their time on the sea. Their talent for fishing went beyond simply catching the slippery animals. The gods had also blessed some of them with the ability to keep their fish fresh without salting it, so elves in landlocked towns could enjoy fresh fish just like the elves in seaside and lakeside villages could... for a slightly higher price. During her time as queen, she and Kadoc had feasted on the fresh almost buttery fish more times than she could count, and a ghost of the familiar taste teased her taste buds and growling stomach as the village came into view.

Unlike Seren's hometown, Iacha had no walls to protect it, so she could see the more primitive wooden and stone houses with their thatched roofs long before she reached it. Upon dismounting her horse, Seren led her steed through the village, scanning her surroundings for Kadoc or at least a friendly elf she could approach with questions. As she passed through the streets and saw thalsach vines crisscrossing each street, draped from one roof to the next, Seren remembered that the Festival of Lights began at dusk.

The elven holy day was typically marked by mirth and celebration starting when the elves awakened in the morning and culminating at the lamp lighting, but joy was far from the people's hearts. Some combination of grief, anger, guilt, and a dark satisfaction haunted every elf Seren passed, and her pulse climbed with worry each time she surreptitiously peeked inside a villager's heart. Though no one accosted her, most elves avoided looking her in the eye, and disgust swirled in the hearts of the few who did.

Something was terribly wrong.

Suppressing her fear and double checking that her dagger still hung at her waist, Seren decided against going to the market and instead sought out the temple. There, she found three heavy-hearted men preparing for the night's festivities—sorting incense and polishing lamps with troubled spirits.

"E-Excuse me," Seren called. "I'm sorry to interrupt your festival preparations, but may I speak with a priest please? It's urgent."

The elves looked to one another for a moment, one shaking his head in silent protest as the priest, a man with deep chestnut tresses and sad gray eyes came forward. Scratches and bruises marred the priest's skin, but the grief and regret in his soul pricked Seren's heart more than his haggard appearance.

"My name is Irdhel, and I'm the priest for this village," he greeted. "I take it you're looking for your husband."

"Yes, I am."

"Come with me."

Seren followed the priest back outside and to the smaller storehouse a stone's throw from the temple. Instead of immediately going inside, Irdhel stopped short of the door and faced his guest again.

"Before we enter, I must prepare you for what you're about to see. Kadoc arrived in Iacha early this morning and asked me to gather the people for him. Once everyone was in the agora, he explained that he'd abdicated the throne and had come to return the powers he'd stolen from three of our people. They came forward and received their gifts anew, but as soon as the third elf left him, a man accused him of killing his son and asked how he planned to right that wrong. One by one, other elves began shouting their grievances until the crowd was drunk with ire. Then, one hooded man threw a stone, striking Kadoc in the leg. When he didn't lash out in return, the crowd acted on their rage and hurled whatever they could find at him. I—"

Seren pushed past the priest, threw the storehouse door open, and stepped inside. There, she saw Kadoc lying unconscious on a lumpy straw mattress. Innumerable bruises and cuts covered his body, and both of his eyes were swollen shut. The pungent aroma of healing balms and poultices stung Seren's eyes, but heartbreak alone inspired the tears that streamed down her cheeks as she fell to her knees at his side. The weeping woman reached forward to touch Kadoc's swollen face, but she stopped short, fearing that even the gentlest touch would cause him pain and rob him of the rest he desperately needed.

"I'm so sorry, my lady. I tried to stop them, but I was knocked unconscious during the attack and didn't awaken until they'd already finished the deed. He's been lying in here for about four hours."

"What powers did he give back to the three elves?"

"I can't remember. I'm sorry."

Seren squinted at the deep violet bruise on Kadoc's left cheek and it lightened just a bit as she studied it. Seeing Kadoc's advanced healing at work eased her anxiety a bit, but anger also flickered within her. Knowing that he'd been closer to death after the stoning than he was in that moment grieved her deeply, but her desire to ensure Kadoc's safety during his convalescence outweighed her mounting wrath. Unsure of what else to say, Irdhel quietly cleared his throat and knelt beside her.

"We've done everything that we came to make him comfortable while he heals, but is there anything I can do for you, my lady?"

"No, I just need some time with my husband."

"Of course. I'll be in the temple if you need me, but I'll come back in an hour to check on you both."

After giving Seren a comforting pat on the back, Irdhel rose and left the storehouse. Finally alone with Kadoc, Seren gently took his seemingly uninjured left hand in hers.

"Whether it takes an hour or a day, I'm not leaving your side until you open your eyes."

With tears still wetting her cheeks, Seren leaned forward and placed the lightest of kisses on an unbruised spot on Kadoc's cheek, praying that her small display of affection wouldn't cause him pain. Then, she drew her dagger and placed it at her side, fearing that the vengeful villagers would come to finish their dastardly deed if they caught wind of his survival.

As the hours crawled by, Irdhel came in periodically to check on the couple. Though Kadoc didn't open his eyes, his bruises gradually faded and his gashes and scrapes mended themselves inch by inch. Despite the former king's healing powers, the priest still changed the bandages and applied fresh poultices to aid the recovery process. He also brought Seren a small meal of bread, fish, and vegetables several hours later. Though the fish, which Irdhel had lightly salted and seasoned with fresh herbs, tasted as delicious as she remembered, it did little to assuage her disquiet as she questioned it they could leave Iacha peacefully.

Even if they slipped away after sunset, the Festival of Lights would just be beginning. Elves would start surrounding the temple just before sundown, and Millam's greatest devotees wouldn't leave until dawn. Kadoc being forced to heal the whole night should have consoled Seren a bit, she found no comfort in knowing how close his attackers would be.

By the time Seren finished her meal, Kadoc's wounds had all closed, and she sensed his heart stirring though he remained conscious. Regret and dread danced in his slumbering mind, and Seren wondered if her husband was reliving that day's events or simply dreaming. Hoping to calm him with her presence, she smoothed his hair off his forehead and some of his distress abated at her touch. Watching Kadoc dream called to mind the Song of Inneh, which the royal musicians performed on their wedding day.

In the lengthy ballad, the Goddess of Love told the story of a young prince and the common maiden he loved—starting with their first meeting and ending with their wedding day. Though the prince fell in love quickly, the woman doubted his affections for her because of her humble beginnings. When the woman finally believed his declarations, she eagerly expressed the warmth bursting in her heart. Finding comfort in the familiar tune, Seren took Kadoc' hand and sang what she could remember, whispering the lyrics to keep from disturbing him but also hoping the song would provide a little consolation if it reached his ears.

> *"The farmer's daughter who once gazed at the skies*
> *Found greater delight drowning in his eyes—*
> *Eyes that shone brighter than Millam's three stars,*
> *Eyes that saw beauty in all of her scars.*
> *For he saw in her what no man had seen.*
> *Beauty and grace that were fit for a queen.*
> *A most precious gem once hidden from his sight,*
> *Until he saw her in the silver moonlight."*

As the ballad's lyrics passed through her lips, Seren reflected on how much their fortunes had changed. Though she was raised in a wealthy household in her previous life, she'd still seen Kadoc's affections as too wonderful for her. He was a prince who would one day be a king, and she saw herself as one of the many flowers blooming in the kingdom—overshadowed and outshone by the blossoms with brighter petals and sweeter perfumes.

Yet in her second life, the man she once esteemed as too good for her saw himself as too lowly to remain by her side while she desired nothing more than his continued companionship despite the challenges it would bring. In that moment, she finally understood why Aire had chosen the now shattered pendant necklace as the vehicle for her powers.

> *"'Prince of the realm and most handsome of men,*
> *Forgive all my doubts and embrace me again.*
> *Your love delights me more than the king's wine,*
> *And for your tenderness I ceaselessly pine.*
> *Praying each day that you won't forsake me.*
> *Waiting and hoping for the day you'll take me*
> *To be your beloved and most treasured wife*

Knitted together 'til the end of life.'"

As Seren transitioned to the next verse, Kadoc's hand squeezed hers, and she turned her eyes from the storehouse door back to her stirring husband. Kadoc finally awakened, and his gaze immediately settled on the woman who hadn't left his side for nearly half a day and had inwardly promised to remain there for every day that followed.

"You shouldn't be here," he weakly scolded.

"I'm your wife, which means I'm exactly where I belong. Where you go, I go."

"How long have you been here?" Kadoc asked as he sat up with a wince, yet he neither condoned nor refuted her declaration.

"Since mid-morning."

"So you saw how badly I was hurt."

"You'd already healed a bit before I arrived, but yes."

"Then you know how much the Iachans hate me. What I've done to you and our people is indefensible at best and unforgiveable at worst, so I will no doubt have many more violent encounters like today's before my life is through. I can't ask you to endure such a perilous, miserable existence."

"You don't have to ask me because I've already vowed to stay with you. I'd rather live a difficult life by your side trying to right out wrongs together than have a life of ease whether alone or with someone who will always be a second choice to me. The gods have made it frighteningly clear that we are still bound to the covenant we made all those years ago, and I don't want to go against them again."

"You've already done your duty by bringing me back from the darkness. *That* is why you were brought back."

"If I was reborn solely to remove the darkness from you, then why did they choose love as the key to unlocking my power and the necklace you gave me on the happiest day of my lives to give me a direct path to you?" she argued, her voice quavering as her tight grip on her emotions loosened. "Inneh has been shaping our story since the moment I awakened, but the feelings in my heart now are truly mine—not just unwanted echoes of love from a former life. I'm choosing to stay with you, and I *want* to stay with you because I love you."

"Even after everything I've done to our people *and* to you?"

Seren nodded, wiping away a tear and fighting the others that threatened to spring free.

"You may have placed us on this dark journey, but I committed too many atrocities of my own volition in the years that followed to lay the blame solely at your feet. If I accept Millam's forgiveness for my transgressions and hold onto bitterness toward you, I'd be the most shameful hypocrite in Eaiven. How can I deny you forgiveness for your few offenses against me after Millam has forgiven me of so many more?"

"Are you sure?"

"I will love you and remain by your side every day of my life and beyond."

Recognizing Seren's wedding vows, Kadoc's heart softened, prompting him to hesitantly take her other hand and reply in kind.

"And I will love and protect you until my dying breath and beyond."

Though Kadoc didn't move to punctuate those sacred words with a kiss as he had on their wedding day, Seren leaned in and pressed her lips against his in an act that refreshed his spirit more than any healing power or potion ever could. Pushing his pain aside, he drew her closer and she melted into his embrace, savoring in the familiarity of his touch and thanking the gods that it no longer inspired guilt and dread. Despite its brevity and innocence, their deep, heartfelt kiss inextricably knitted their souls together and unraveled the unrest that had haunted Seren's soul since the day of her awakening. When the kiss ended, Seren rested her head on his shoulder, closing her eyes and smiling as she savored the sensation of Kadoc's heart beating in time with hers and his hands gently smoothing her hair.

"Are you hungry at all? Irdhel offered to make a plate for you whenever you awakened."

"I'm not ravenous, but I should eat something."

"I'll let him know you're awake and help him prepare something."

"Don't hurry off so quickly. I want to cherish this moment for a bit longer before we join the world again."

A soft growl from Kadoc's stomach punctuated his request, but the serenity radiating from his cheerful heart overshadowed his hunger and lingering pain. So Seren indulged him with a smile, marveling at the fact that his touch once again brought her comfort instead of fear. That contentment and comfort lulled the couple to sleep before they could search for nourishment, but the soft creak of the door roused them from their impromptu slumber minutes before dusk.

The kind priest, who'd changed into the golden robes he only worse for the Festival of Lights, returned with another meal and warned them that the villagers would soon be gathering for the celebration. After giving Irdhel heartfelt thanks for his hospitality and mercy, they devoured the aromatic fish stew and warm bread he left behind.

"If you're feeling well enough, we should leave as soon as we're done eating," Seren suggested. "Between the number cities you want to visit and our desire to find Aled, we have a lot of traveling ahead of us."

"I'd actually like to stay for the festival. One power I returned today was my enhanced healing, and I doubt that Millam spared and healed me today only to have me slink into the night without facing the Iachans again. I can't give in to cowardice, Seren."

Fear flickered in Seren's heart, but she took a deep breath and nodded.

"If that's what you want to do, I'll be right by your side, but I can't just stand aside if they try to hurt you again."

"Well, your presence will certainly force me to be more cautious, my dove," he chuckled.

Once they finished their meals, Seren helped Kadoc wash up and exchange his ripped, bloody garments for a fresh set of the simple garments he'd packed for his journey. At her request, the astonished priest also gave them oil for their lamps, refusing to accept the gold she offered as a donation. Then, the pair lit their lamps in the small storehouse and walked to the door. Memories of her battered beloved still fresh in her mind inspired Seren to take one final pause before they exited the storehouse.

"And you're *sure* you want to do this?" she asked.

Kadoc leaned in and kissed her forehead, giving her the same confident grin that she'd fallen in love with so many years before. In their youth, that particular smile had been indicative of his assurance that his magical and political power would protect him from whatever peril he would soon ride into whether ogres, faeries, or other creatures were his opponents. But that evening, his assurance rested in the gods—not himself.

"I'm positive."

With that affirmation, Seren took a moment to brace herself with a deep breath and a brief, silent prayer before Kadoc opened the door and led the way to the celebration. As expected, elves approached the temple from every direction, carrying the modest clay lamps that their humble wages could afford. Though Irdhel hadn't begun the song they traditionally commenced the Festival of Lights with, enough elves hummed the tune that its melody rang through the village, joining the scents of burning oil and incense to create a comforting atmosphere that would have set Seren at ease had she not been wary of her fellow worshippers.

Instead of remaining by the storehouse, Kadoc took Seren's hand and walked toward the temple. Since the crowd was still gathering, they were able to stand near the rounded temple steps—far more visible than Seren would have liked. When a burly man in a blacksmith's apron caught sight of them across the stairs, his eyes widened as his emotions shifted from shock to indignation to guilt. Sensing Seren's narrowed eyes on him, he averted his gaze and stared down at his lamp instead.

"Was he one of your attackers?"

Kadoc flicked his eyes in the blacksmith's direction before scanning the crowd for more familiar faces. Though he recognized many of his assailants, the former king's heart was untroubled by the man's presence.

"Yes, he threw the first stone, but I took his son's life after Aled's prophecy. A faded bruise is the least he owes me. I stole my healing power from the man two elves to his right. He nearly died in combat with the ogres because he couldn't heal himself as the gods intended. And the woman at the very edge of the crowd hadn't been able to enjoy archery for years because I stole her talent for it," he explained. "They didn't realize it, but I took all of their charges to heart today, and I'm more grieved by what I did to them than I am the pain they inflicted upon me."

Reaching out with her power again, Seren learned that every attacker Kadoc quietly revealed to her shared the same inner turmoil and contrition that the blacksmith carried in his soul. A handful of the elves even bore the three-stranded necklace that she and her husband received in Gridein, a sign that Millam had seen their remorse and forgiven them.

As tempted as Seren was to despise the elves who'd risen up against Kadoc, seeing the braided necklaces reminded her of their own recent absolution. So she turned her eyes to the temple and watched as Irdhel emerged in his golden robes, which glowed in the increasingly radiant lamplight. When the priest raised his hands, the humming and whispered conversations ceased, and he promptly ended that silence by opening the night of song that elves looked forward to every springtime.

> *"Mountains tremble and valleys groan*
> *Wishing the king would claim his throne*
> *Like watchmen waiting for the dawn,*
> *Like watchmen waiting for the dawn.*
>
> *"We ever wait for the true light*

His radiance is our delight
Eyes turned to the east waiting for dawn
When darkness is forever gone.

"Maidens faint in anguish and fright
Yearning for day to cast out night
Like watchmen waiting for the dawn,
Like watchmen waiting for the dawn.

"We long for the night to end
And every elven heart to mend
Eyes turned to the east waiting for dawn
When darkness is forever gone.

"With every dusk our hopes abate
As night creeps over every home,
But patiently we ever wait
For in the dark we're not alone.

"With every dawn our hearts renew
As your radiance drowns the night.
We ever hope and trust in you
To give us rest by your great might
Like watchmen dreaming in their homes,
Like watchmen dreaming in their homes.

"We ever wait for the true light
His radiance is our delight
Eyes turned to the east waiting for dawn
When darkness is forever gone."

The elven singers raised their voices in song, eyes closed and hearts lifted in joyful yet anguished anticipation of Millam's final victory. Kadoc's arrival that morning and presence that evening reminded every elf of the pain they'd endured, the wrongs they'd committed, and the hope they had for a world where Malok's influence no longer crept in the shadows—eager to taint their happiest moments and deepen their most painful sorrows. When the sun finally illuminated the eastern sky, the last of Millam's devotees retired to their homes. No one spoke a word to Seren or Kadoc, but the few furtive, apologetic glances they received were acknowledgement enough for the couple.

After helping Irdhel and the other temple workers cleans up after the festival attendees, Kadoc and Seren bid their unexpected hosts adieu, secretly leaving a small sack of gold by the altar before mounting their horses and cantering away from Iacha. Their eyes were heavy with exhaustion thanks to the sleepless night under the stars, but new-found hope and rekindled love strengthened their weary bones as they traveled to Telna.

Whether hostility or forgiveness awaited them in the next town, neither elf could foresee, but they pressed on—hoping to give the people of Eaiven more peace as common, contrite citizens than they ever did as their spiteful sovereigns by pushing back the insidious darkness that once blighted their lives and embracing the dawn of a new era.

$$\star \qquad \star \qquad \star$$

ABOUT THE AUTHOR

Kristen Belveal, who writes under her maiden name Kristen Reed, is a
Christian author best known for writing *The Heart of a Harlot,* The
Fairetellings Series, and the Bible study *A Look At Luke.* Her faith heavily
influences her writing and is the driving force in her life. She and her
husband Noah reside in the Dallas, Texas area with their son Judah and co-
host the Being the Belveals podcast.

BOOKS BY KRISTEN REED

Second Awakening

The Fairetellings Series
The Jilted Bride
Eirwen's Dream
Ingrid's Engagement
Salvation by the Sea
The Countess of Vakrevet

The Unwritten Testament Series
Out of the Garden
Five Nights With Pharaoh
The Heart of a Harlot

The Way of Escape

A Look At Luke

Visit kristenreedauthor.com and beingthebelveals.com for more information.

www.ingramcontent.com/pod-product-compliance
Lightning Source LLC
Chambersburg PA
CBHW021654110726
47902CB00007B/1930